BONE HOOK

A LEI CRIME NOVEL

TOBY NEAL

BONE HOOK

A LEI CRIME NOVEL

TOBY NEAL

Chapter 1

B ody retrieval in ninety feet of open water wasn't for sissies. Sergeant Leilani Texeira hoped she was up to the task as she stood with her longtime partner, Pono Kaihale, on the deck of the heavy Coast Guard Zodiac while it sliced its way across the ocean toward Molokini, a tiny half-moon-shaped atoll off the coast of Maui. A Maui Police Department ball cap pulled low and tight kept the hair out of her eyes, and in spite of their urgent task, Lei enjoyed the smack of the gusty breeze on her cheeks.

"Got to keep an eye out for whales." Pono scanned the horizon through his trademark Oakleys, worn so constantly they'd made grooves in the brown flesh above his ears. The water around them was the deep blue of lapis, streaked with whitecaps. Both of them watched for whale spouts, scanning the horizon. "We could run into one at this speed."

Pono's `aumakua, or ancestral guardian, was the humpback whale. Lei knew he worried about the many boats crisscrossing Maui's warm waters between November and May, where the whales were calving and breeding.

They soon reached the shallow, sheltered bay of the atoll, a popular snorkeling and diving destination for the tourist industry.

The Zodiac drew abreast of a snorkeling charter vessel that had called in the discovery of a body.

It took only moments for the snorkel boat, a big catamaran, to throw a line to the Zodiac so they could side tie the two boats together. The Coast Guard officers went aboard the catamaran first, Lei and Pono following. Tourists, various degrees of sunburned, clustered in anxious knots, watching as the captain, a deeply tanned young man in a blue polo shirt that read Hokua on the pocket, approached them.

"Hey. Pretty great response time."

"Thanks to the Coast Guard. Took us longer to get through the Kahului traffic than it did to get out here," Pono said.

"We need to totally clear the bay here to secure the scene." Lei spoke to the Coast Guardsman standing beside her, whose name she'd heard but missed. She introduced herself and Pono to the *Hokua*'s captain. "Got somewhere private where you can tell us about the discovery?"

"Yes." The captain led them up a metal ladder to his bridge above the main cabin. "So we took out some snorkelers, and a smaller group of scuba divers. The scuba divers found the body wedged between some rocks at about ninety feet. We could tell it was a homicide."

"How did you know?" Lei asked.

"Had a spear sticking out of her back," the captain said flatly.

"What did you do next?" Lei worried they might have disturbed the underwater crime scene.

"We marked it with a buoy, returned to the boat, and made the calls."

"Perfect." She looked at Pono. "You got ahold of Dr. Gregory already, right?"

"I did. Asked him if he could scuba. He said no, just to do our own investigation of the underwater area and bring the body up."

The portly medical examiner didn't like heights, and apparently, not depths either.

"I should warn you," the captain said. "The body's a little—mutilated. Sharks have been snacking on it."

"Great," Lei muttered. She had discovered a cache of bones underwater during a case on Kaua`i, and couldn't participate in a key part of the investigation involving that underwater crime scene due to being unable to scuba. In the years since then, she'd rectified that by getting certified in scuba in case it ever came up again—but dealing with sharks in a deep open ocean dive was a little unnerving as her first underwater body retrieval.

"We'll go down with you," said a voice beside her shoulder. "We'll bring bang sticks in case any sharks are still interested in the body." She turned, really noticing the Coast Guard officer next to her for the first time. Crisp in his uniform, he had the tilted dark eyes of Japanese heritage paired with the olive-brown skin of part-Hawaiian blood. He didn't have the freckles she suffered across her nose and cheeks, but other than that, he looked familiar, as if meeting a brother for the first time.

"I'm sorry, I didn't catch your name," Lei said.

"Petty Officer Aina Thomas. We met on the boat."

"You're right; we did." She smiled, turning to the catamaran's captain. "Well, thanks, Captain. We'll take it from here. If you could keep all your people on board and wait for us to take some statements, we'd appreciate it."

They climbed back down the ladder and headed for the Coast Guard Zodiac.

"At that depth we won't be able to stay down long," Thomas told her. "I've taken the liberty of calling for some additional personnel support to search the area around the body. Our team is trained in evidence collection and scene preservation underwater."

"Perfect," Lei said. "We can go down, do an initial assessment, and retrieve the body, and your divers can follow up and search a grid. We need to completely clear the boats and tourists out of this whole bay."

"I'll make sure that happens while you're down," Pono said. "And I'll take the statements from the passengers. I don't scuba."

"On purpose you don't scuba," Lei grumbled. "So you can leave me all the dirty work, like chasing sharks away from bodies in ninety feet of water."

"You got me there." Pono grinned. "I'll be the one on deck having a beer until you get back."

* * *

Back on the Coast Guard craft, Sergeant Thomas handed Lei a wetsuit. "We'll deal with the scuba gear when you get this on. I guesstimated. Women's small?"

"Ha. I hope I fit into that." Lei eyed the length of rubber dangling from his hand.

"Oh, I'm sure you will." Lei couldn't mistake the admiring glint in Thomas's eye. She reached out and took the suit with her left hand, hoping he'd spot the wedding ring on her finger.

"I'll yell for a bigger size if I need it." She turned and went into the boat's tiny head. She'd grabbed her bikini out of her truck when they'd gotten the call that the body was submerged, so she got into that first. Sure enough, with some hopping, pulling, and cramped gymnastics in the small space, Lei was able to get the rubber suit on.

She'd put on a little weight in the five years since she and Michael Stevens were married, an eventful five years filled with the joy of her stepson, Kiet, growing up and going to kindergarten, interesting cases, and some heartbreak, too—the death of her beloved Auntie Rosario and the loss of her first pregnancy at four months. That pregnancy had turned out to be a one-time event, in spite of their decision to try again some years ago.

Now, with all that was going on with their marriage, it seemed just as well that they hadn't been able to have another child. She just wished that wound would stop aching. Maybe if they'd had that baby, Michael wouldn't be where he was, doing what he was doing, and she wouldn't be sleeping in the back bedroom for the last few months. She shoved the negative thoughts away with an effort and opened the door of the head, startled to find Aina Thomas right outside.

"The suit fits, I see."

"Barely." Lei brushed past him, flattered by his frank appraisal of her and annoyed that she noticed how well he fit into his wetsuit, too. "Which way to the gear?"

He pointed out to the deck, and she was conscious of his gaze on her body as she walked.

She and Stevens needed to work things out, and soon.

A junior officer handed her a bright yellow buoyancy compensator device, setting a weight belt, a mask, a snorkel, and fins on the deck for her.

"Scuba would be great if it weren't for all the gear." Lei tried to joke. Her stomach was a little hollow at the thought of this deep of a dive when she hadn't been out at all in a couple of years. Was she going to remember everything? She slung on the weight belt, making sure the square lead weights were to the back, and hauled the slide buckle tight.

"I'll help." Thomas strapped the air tank onto the vest with a few efficient gestures. He lifted the BCD, tank and all, and held it open for her. Feeling reassured but highly aware of his proximity, Lei put one arm in and then the other, hopping a little once the vest was zipped on to settle the weight of the belt and tank at her hips.

The sun felt scorching on the top of her head, superheating her body in the layers of rubber and gear even though it was late afternoon. Glancing over the gunwale, she found the turquoise water of the atoll's sheltered interior bay irresistible. In spite of the grim errand they were on and her uncertainty about what they'd find, Lei couldn't wait to get into the water.

"Here's your shark knife. For emergency use only." Thomas handed her a short, thick-hafted knife in a strap-on scabbard.

"I imagine a shark attacking is an emergency." Lei hefted the knife on her open palm. "Seems kind of small."

"There's a compressed air charge in the handle that injects into the shark when and if you have to use it. Highly unlikely, but since we're handling a corpse that's already been bitten, a good idea to be on the safe side."

"Okay." Lei slid the knife onto her right leg and tightened the rubber strap around her thigh, anxious and excited. Having the knife on did make her feel a little more confident.

"We have some coordinates for the body and we'll go down in twenty-foot depth segments, to adjust. Coming back up we'll do that as well." Thomas ran through a quick review of underwater hand signals and pointed out where Lei had a plastic tablet with an attached wax crayon for writing in the pocket of her BCD, as well as a flashlight and waterproof camera for photographing the scene.

Lei took the mask, snorkel, and fins from the officer and stood up at the rubber side of the boat, fighting the sense that she was going to sink instantly with all the weight on her back. She climbed up and stepped off after Thomas, splashing down into the refreshing water.

As she'd known she would, Lei bounced immediately to the

surface, the inflated BCD and full tank doing their job. Floating comfortably, she slid on her fins, mask, and snorkel, looking up at Pono's worried expression as he watched her from the deck. She sent him a thumbs-up and turned to Thomas.

"Follow my lead," Thomas said. They'd been joined in the water by another Coast Guard diver. "This is Officer Kenny Rice. He's trained in body retrieval, and he's in charge of the carrier." Rice gave a nod and held up a tightly woven bright yellow mesh body bag, demonstrating with a tug on his belt how it was attached to him for towing.

They all put in their regulators and at Thomas's signal released the air from the BCD vests by depressing a valve on the front. Lei watched Pono's anxious brown face, buzz-cut head backlit by blue sky, disappear in a cloud of bubbles as she sank.

She felt wonderfully weightless and yet sank steadily toward the bottom at the speed set by Thomas. At intervals they paused, letting their bodies adjust to the depth. Lei felt her heart rate slowing as she turned, taking in the wonders of the reef.

At this moment it didn't matter that they were headed for some grisly body retrieval when all around her the ocean seemed to sing, vivid and crackling with life. The reef below her was a tapestry of colorful darting fish and the graceful shapes of corals. Off in the distant blue deep, Lei could see the sinuous shadows of slow-moving sharks. Her heart jumped a little, even as she recognized them as harmless blacktips and gray reef sharks.

Lei fought a disorienting sense of falling, of dizziness, an illusion brought on by the vast space even as awe filled her at the cathedral-like feel of blue depths pierced by columns of shifting light. Hanging at a pause level in the busy stillness, her breath a stream of silver bubbles marking their descent, Lei felt herself shrink to a dot in the scope of things.

She was so small here, just a little human in a rubber suit trespassing on majesty.

Finally they reached the bottom. Lei adjusted her BCD so that she hovered four feet above the teeming, lively reef. Parallel to her, Thomas took a reading on a compass dive watch on his wrist and pointed.

Lei followed with Rice and his floating yellow bag. She couldn't help looking out at the depths again, at the lazily moving silhouetted sharks. They seemed closer. It was probably just a trick of the eye brought on by the water.

She refastened her gaze on Thomas's well-built form kicking along in front of her.

Yes, it had been way too long since she and Michael had slept together. There'd been an erosion between them over five years of marriage, work, balancing the needs of their child with ridiculously busy schedules and trying to manage even deeper problems.

Michael Stevens had post-traumatic stress disorder. Nothing else explained the night terrors, when her husband woke screaming and lashing out, even hitting her by accident. PTSD explained the haunted look in his eyes, his increasingly withdrawn behavior, and the constant checking that the gate to the property was locked and the alarms armed.

And then there was the drinking.

Thomas paused, hovering and checking his coordinates. Lei scanned around, unable to see anything but the bright, darting yellow and purple wrasse and red squirrelfish, their jewel tones rendered black by the leaching of color at this depth. A nearby school of fish caught her attention, forming a defensive, spinning ball as a big ulua jack circled.

And the sharks were definitely closer, though they didn't seem to be moving any differently.

A whistle, sharp and high, penetrated the loud rustle of the streaming bubbles forming a column to the surface far above her. Thomas had swum off while she was distracted, and she spotted him twenty yards away, gesturing to something on the bottom. Lei kicked off and joined the other divers. She spotted the buoy, a small inflatable yellow balloon, weaving in the slight current as she approached the body.

The woman was facedown, one of her legs wedged between two coral heads. Her hair, brown and long, drifted like seaweed. She bobbed ever so gently, as if she were examining something on the bottom—except for the steel haft of a spear that protruded from her back and the fact that one of her arms was gone at the shoulder.

The amputation wound was bloodless, and so was the chunk of flesh the size of a dinner plate ripped out of her hip. The mutilations had the look of sample bites that hadn't been enjoyed, but even as Lei watched, a small dappled moray undulated out from under the body.

Lei fumbled the waterproof camera out of her vest pouch, gesturing the two Coast Guardsmen back. She moved in, photographing the body first, then the area all around it. She let a little more air out of her BCD so that she sank to just a foot or so above the bottom. From there, she shot photo after photo of the corpse, the coral reef bottom, the body from above, from the side, and even underneath as she placed the camera below the floating body.

She didn't see any unusual objects or disturbances near or around the body, which she guesstimated was that of a five-foot-six female, a hundred and thirty pounds or so, with dark brown hair. Other features were hidden by the woman's mask and scuba gear.

Finally Lei gestured to Rice, who moved in with his bag.

Her O2 meter beeped on her chest, and she frowned, gesturing to Thomas and then to herself, tapping the meter. Its reading was in the yellow zone.

He flashed five fingers three times, telling her they had fifteen minutes of air left. Rice reached into his BCD for a plastic bag, slipping it over the woman's bloodless white hand and tightening strings that ran through the plastic rim of the bag, protecting any trace that might remain under her nails.

Lei moved off to swim a search grid around the body as Thomas helped pull the victim out from between the coral heads. Rice detached the air tank from the victim's BCD, and freed from the clamp, the metal tank arrowed for the surface.

Watching its trajectory, Lei saw a shark pass above, a graceful black shape. Her heart rate spiked, but she tried not to breathe any faster and use up precious air. She waved to get Thomas's attention, pointing to the shark and its several compatriots.

He gave a slight negative headshake, indicating not to be concerned. He fumbled his tablet out and wrote on it. *Just curious. Blacktips. No prob.*

She nodded and continued back and forth over the reef, her camera at the ready, looking for anything unusual. She let out a burst of excited bubbles at the sight of a small, plastic-encased GoPro camera on an extension rod, wedged between some rocks. She photographed it in situ, then swam down and picked it up, retracting the rod to shorten it and tucking it inside her BCD. She turned her gaze back to Rice, who was having some trouble getting the woman's stiff, unwieldy appendages into the bag.

Lei kicked over to help. She pushed the floating arm into the yellow mesh bag. It was stiff with rigor, so the woman had died in the last day. Working together, they removed the woman's fins and maneuvered the body into the mesh bag, pulling the zipper up.

Rice attached the bag to his dive belt and they inflated their BCDs, rising from the bottom at the speed of their bubbles until Thomas signaled for a stop to allow the buildup of gases to expend from their bodies so that they didn't get the bends. Lei still had her eyes on the sharks, alarmed to see that the school of blacktips and gray reef sharks had been joined by a tiger. The tiger shark was at least twelve feet long and much wider, a greenish-gray with barred markings on its back that served as camouflage. It circled their little group in wide, lazy arcs, its powerful tail barely moving, but still faster than the others. The other sharks withdrew, disappearing back into the deep. Clearly this fish was the king of its kind.

Lei pointed, looking at Thomas. She knew her eyes were wide behind her mask. She was breathing too quickly as she fought the urge to bolt for the surface, a move that she knew would be deadlier than a shark attack. Thomas nodded and indicated the metallic rod he held at the ready—a bang stick, a one-time underwater single-shot firearm with an explosive round in the head.

Rice gestured that he had one, too, and Lei felt a little better as the Coast Guardsmen drew closer to her, their backs to each other, facing outward. They were armed and ready, even though they were holding a tasty-smelling shark meal between them.

Rice and Thomas seemed to be communicating somehow. Rice drew a flattened yellow buoy out of his vest just as Lei's monitor began beeping a red alarm, showing five minutes of air. She concentrated on slowing her breathing and watched as Rice attached the buoy to the body bag and filled it with the valve from his BCD, inflating it almost instantly. Thomas touched Lei's arm and they swam away from the body bag, which began rising. It gathered speed as the buoy dragged it rapidly to the surface.

This made good sense. The Coast Guard Zodiac would see the buoy and retrieve the body, and they wouldn't be endangered by being near it.

Continuing their slow ascension, Lei watched the tiger shark follow the body, circling it in a gradually tightening pattern. The mesh container must be emitting smells that flavored the water like a tea bag.

Lei heard the thrum of the Zodiac's engine, saw the movement of the propellers. She couldn't wait to break the surface and get out, but Thomas had stopped them for one last decompression pause twenty feet below the surface. Hovering there, she tried to calm herself. She watched as the crew hauled the yellow bag aboard.

The shark, deprived of its treat, moved away and headed in their direction. Lei felt her whole body flush with primal terror.

Chapter 2

Once again the two Coast Guardsmen drew close against her, feet toward the bottom, heads pointed to the surface. The three of them kept watch on the big fish as it began its circling again.

Lei was drawing her last, thin breath of air as Thomas gave the signal to surface. She kicked up, ignoring his hand on her arm, unable to slow down in her panic. She reached the surface, spat out her regulator, and yelled for the boat, her voice raspy.

"Over here! Hurry. There's a shark!"

Beside her, Rice and Thomas broke the surface, keeping their faces below the water, watching the shark calmly.

The Zodiac fired up and drove the fifty yards to their location. The tiger shark's fin had broken the surface of the water as it passed closer and closer by the time Lei was stroking for the boat's hastily lowered ladder, with Rice and Thomas right behind.

Lei ripped off her fins, handing them up to waiting hands, and grabbed the chain-and-metal ladder. She hauled herself up clumsily, body suddenly heavy with the extra weight of the gear, her muscle resources exhausted. She was grateful as Pono and another guardsman grabbed her under the arms and hauled her up, then helped Rice and, finally, Thomas.

The shark swam by one more time, then sank out of view.

Lei sprawled on the deck for a moment, all her gear still on. Finally she mustered the energy to roll to the side and unzip the BCD. To her surprise, Thomas was already up and out of his gear. He lifted the tank and BCD off of her. She loosened the weight belt, finally rolling to her knees as she shed her mask.

"Thought you were going to lose it there at the last minute, Sergeant." Thomas steadied her with a hand on her arm, his touch kind and reassuring. "Take your time before you stand. Scuba has a way of using up your energy that you don't realize."

"That shark spooked me." Lei stood up the minute she was sure her knees weren't going to fold. "I thought I was going to lose it, too. But you and Rice didn't freak out. Thank God you were there."

"That shark wasn't really hungry. He might have taken a sample bite to see if anything was tasty, but he wasn't that interested." Thomas's bright brown eyes were bracketed by creases from squinting into the sun; he looked a little older than her, probably mid-thirties. She liked his calm confidence and obvious competency, but he didn't rub it in like some men would.

"I saw that mother!" Pono exclaimed, joining Lei from where he'd been occupied with moving the body, still in the mesh bag, to a more traditional black zip-up body bag. "He was huge. I'm glad you're safe aboard. I'd have been shitting myself."

"I just about did." Lei tapped her O2 gauge. "Sucked all my air like a rookie. Sorry about the panic mode," she told Thomas.

"You did well. It was a deep dive, and if you don't go out all the time, you won't be used to how it's affecting your body," Thomas said. "You should go out more. In fact, you could come out with me this weekend. Just going for a pleasure dive around a wreck off Lahaina."

"That sounds nice. I'll check if my husband wants to. We both got certified a couple years ago, but it's the kind of thing that takes a big time commitment, and we're both detectives, so we're always working." She smiled and shrugged, watching to see how he reacted to her mention of Stevens.

"Great." Lei couldn't see any difference in Thomas's friendly demeanor at her frank mention of her husband. "Give me your number and I'll check back with you."

Lei rattled it off and he nodded, memorizing it. "Now what?" She indicated the bagged body.

"We get under way." They were already doing that. Lei felt the engines thrum into life and the bow of the boat lift. This time they were heading downwind. The Zodiac seemed to ride the rolling surge.

"Dr. Gregory is meeting us with the transport vehicle at Ma'alaea Harbor," Pono said. "They're ready to take the body back to the morgue. Any clues about the victim's ID?"

Lei suddenly remembered the GoPro camera, stuck in the pocket of the BCD. She hurried over and retrieved it, handing it to Pono. "Got this on the bottom. Can't wait to see what's on it. And I thought of something. The victim had to have got to Molokini on a boat. Can we do a lap around the back wall, see if there are any more craft there?" Lei asked Thomas.

"Good idea. I'll ask the captain." Thomas went into the bridge to speak to the commanding officer.

"I'd like to change. Do you have a shower?" Lei asked Rice, who was rinsing the gear with a hose attached to a freshwater tank.

"Sure." Rice handed her the makeshift shower. She peeled her wetsuit down and rinsed off as best she could. Lei left Pono sitting beside the black-bagged body, on the phone with someone—probably updating Captain Omura, their commanding officer—and went to the tiny bathroom to change.

In the cramped space, drying her body with a thin hank of towel, she thought of Stevens again, memory sparked by how showers had always been one of their favorite places to play— and get dirty, it turned out.

Those times were nothing but hazy memories.

She could continue to handle their situation if it weren't for the drinking. She knew why Stevens drank—to numb the flashbacks, to sleep—but that didn't make it easier to tolerate his alcohol-reeking body falling into bed beside her at night, the repellent smell clinging to his hair, his skin. The irritability of daily hangovers was followed by withdrawal to his workshop in the evenings, where he kept the bottle.

She'd begged him to get help, to talk to Dr. Wilson, their friend the police psychologist, but after one or two visits, he'd refused. "It only makes it worse to dredge it up," he'd told her.

A year ago Stevens had mentioned that he'd been approached to be a civilian contracted trainer for military police stationed somewhere overseas. She'd blown it off, but two months ago he'd told her he'd accepted a job offer and signed a contract with them. Lei had been so upset that she'd moved out of their bedroom into the guest room/office. "How can you leave me to carry the load? Take care of our child?" she'd ranted. "I'm not the only one you're being selfish to!"

"I need something else to do, while I still physically can." Stevens's crystal-blue eyes were remote, as if seeing something in the distance, even when they were fixed on her face. "I need to do something active, and I can beat this thing."

"This thing." That was always what he called his problem, undiagnosed, unspoken, and all-consuming.

She hadn't realized he was that unhappy in his work as a Maui Police Department lieutenant. Five years ago he'd been reassigned as the main trainer and coordinator for Maui's detectives, a position he'd excelled at. She suspected job dissatisfaction wasn't really it. He wanted to go back to a hot zone, as if somehow he could heal himself by returning to a combat situation. He'd done a tour as a marine in the Middle East right out of high school, but she hadn't thought it affected him.

At least, early in their relationship, it hadn't.

Lei thought it was the attacks they'd lived through here on Maui that had damaged him. Two house fires, a stabbing, and the brutal murder of his pregnant ex-wife along with a steady stream of murder cases had combined to take a toll. Still, it didn't matter what she thought. Her husband had made that abundantly clear, and he was waiting for deployment orders any day now. Their captain had been forced to grant his request for military duty leave when he'd obtained consent from the Hawaii police superintendent, going over Omura's head.

And still she just didn't really believe he'd leave her and his son for some dangerous mission overseas. She was hunkered down in her corner of the house, waiting for the fit of insanity to pass. It was bound to. It had to.

Lei didn't think she had what it took to be a parent alone and do her demanding job, too.

She dressed in the clothes she'd worn before. She wished she had some gel to tame her hair, which was going to dry into a wild tangle, but there was no help for it. She shoved the MPD ball cap on and went back onto the deck.

The Zodiac was moving at a decent clip out of the sheltered harbor. The wind hit Lei, almost ripping the cap off her head. She moved into the shelter of the wheelhouse and stood beside Pono as they hit water so deep off the back side of the atoll that it looked black in the shadows.

"A whale!" Pono exclaimed.

A humpback blew nearby, its sleek gray bulk rising to exhale a blast of fishy-smelling vapor. It was remarkably close to the steep black lava cliff of the atoll, topped with the bright green of a few hardy native plants. The Zodiac shut down its engines, abiding by the law that watercraft keep a hundred yards of distance from the gentle giants.

"All these years and I still can't get enough of these guys," Lei said. The whale lifted its T-shaped tail in a leisurely fashion and submerged. "Whew, did you smell its breath?"

"I know. What's amazing is that they eat enough fish and krill in six months in Alaska, then fast for six months over here," Pono said. "But their breath is still intense. It's good luck to see my `aumakua today. I'll tell Tiare our trip to Vegas is bound to be good."

"You guys going again?" Lei frowned a little. She didn't want to be without her friend and partner with things so difficult at home.

"Every six months, baby." Pono and Tiare had relatives in the seemingly alternate universe of the big Hawaiian community that had sprung up in Vegas, giving it the nickname "the ninth island." Lei sometimes worried that her partner enjoyed his blackjack a little too much when the Kaihales went on their biannual trips, but she restrained herself from anything other than a teasing comment now and then.

The Zodiac rounded a protrusion of the steep cliff, near the curve that marked the beginning of the sheltered interior bay. A sturdy inflatable bobbed, attached to a rock protruding from the atoll's cliff-like wall. The captain cut the engine and the big craft drew abreast.

"We'll have to keep our position by using the engines," Thomas told Lei. "We can't anchor here. It's four hundred feet straight down."

The thought of that depth beneath them gave Lei a shiver. "How can we tell if that Zodiac belongs to the victim? If we take it in, there could be divers stranded."

"We're running the registration. We can make some calls, too. In the meantime we'll board it and search for ID," Thomas said.

"Okay."

Lei and Pono gloved up and followed Thomas down the ladder to the little craft. There wasn't much aboard: a gallon jug of water, spare gas can for the motor, some extra scuba gear.

Lei picked up the only item that looked personal, a backpack. She took out a change of athletic-style women's clothing and a wallet. With Pono looking on, she flipped it open. A Hawaii driver's license with its distinctive rainbow looked up at them from the clear plastic insert.

"Danielle Phillips. Age thirty-five. Five foot six, one hundred thirty-eight pounds, brown hair and eyes." Lei gazed at the woman's photo, feeling a pang as she looked at the pretty, smiling face. "That physical description matches our vic. Couldn't tell much about her looks without taking the gear off the body."

"Registration comes back to the University of Hawaii," a guardsman called down from the bigger craft. "That's a staff research vessel."

Thomas finished speaking into a small handheld radio. "Captain says we tag the vessel to contact us. Until we have confirmation that this is the victim's watercraft, we're going to leave it here. Wouldn't want to strand someone who was just out for a dive."

He took out a pad, wrote a brightly colored citation, and attached it to the motor with a loop of twine.

Lei copied the license information and called it in to Dispatch to run, but returned the wallet to the backpack, feeling sure this was their victim.

"We'll get these personal effects after we've verified that this is hers," she told Pono. She climbed back on board the Coast Guard boat, Pono and Thomas close behind, surprised at the exhaustion pulling at her muscles. "Mind if I take a little nap on the way back?" she asked Thomas.

"Make yourself comfortable." He gestured to a padded storage seat against the wheelhouse. "Surprised you made it this long."

Lei felt herself soften and relax at the warm kindness in Thomas's words. He found a padded life jacket and set it on the bench for her as a pillow.

I'm so empty inside, anyone being nice to me feels like more than it should.

"Thanks," Lei said, and Thomas moved off to speak to Rice. She lay down on her side, her folded hands pillowed under her cheek. Her eyes fell shut on the sun lowering toward the horizon, gilding the small nearby island of Kahoolawe with gold, as the Zodiac sped back across the ocean toward Ma'alaea Harbor.

* * *

It was dark by the time Lei pulled up to the automatic gate of her home in Haiku. They'd turned the body over to the medical examiner, Dr. Gregory, at the dock. She'd dropped off the retrieved GoPro with Jessup Murioka, their tech support staff member. They'd checked in with Captain Omura, their commanding officer, and started the case's files. Now she and Pono had taken a break to go home, eat, and change before going back into the station to work on confirming the victim's identity.

The first twenty-four hours on a murder case were crucial. She and Pono had to keep the momentum going as long as they could.

Lei hit the gate's remote. A ten-foot cedar section of wall retracted with a rumble. She pulled her silver Tacoma into the open garage attached to the side of their house, a single-level cement-block ranch finished tastefully with stucco and roofed in terra-cotta for a slightly Mediterranean look.

Aesthetics had been the last thing on their minds, though, when choosing the materials for the house. Their priority had been a building that was both fireproof and secure, and as it always did, arriving at the house brought a sense of safety and peace to Lei as she opened the door of her truck to the dogs' ecstatic greetings.

Keiki, her old Rottweiler, gray around the muzzle and creaky in the knees but still excited to see her, wagged her cropped hind end. Her old girl was nudged aside by younger, more energetic Conan, the male Rottie they'd adopted five years ago.

"I know. You guys thought I went off-island. Nah, just another homicide case." She took a moment to rub the dogs' big square heads and scratch their chests, then went toward the house, flanked by their strong, glossy bodies.

The dogs made her feel safe and secure, too.

Kiet met her on the porch. "Mama!" The little boy threw his arms around her waist, pressing his face into her midsection. "Where were you?"

Lei dropped her backpack and squatted to embrace him at his level, treasuring the feel of the boy's slender, sturdy body in her arms. As she often did, she sent a quick, silent thank-you to his birth mother in heaven for the gift of her son to raise.

"Mama had a case. You know I can't come home at the usual time when I have a case. Sorry, honey. Did Daddy pick you up?"

She'd left a message on Stevens's voice mail not to expect her until later, but today was Stevens's turn to pick Kiet up from elementary school and take him to his mother Ellen's house for afternoon babysitting, a daily ritual they treasured as an opportunity to see their son during the workday. Wayne, Lei's father, who lived with them on the property and had provided childcare in Kiet's early years, had his own business now, a small breakfast and lunch restaurant at the Haiku Cannery. He was still able to help out some afternoons, but they'd roped Michael's mother, Ellen, into doing much of the after-school care. Now clean and sober, Ellen worked from home as a paralegal and enjoyed afternoons with her grandson.

Lei tipped Kiet's chin up to look into his eyes. His mother Anchara's Thai heritage had mixed beautifully with Stevens's gene pool, resulting in thick black hair, jade-green eyes, and caramel skin.

"Yeah, Daddy came. But I missed you." Instead of letting go, Kiet tightened his arms around Lei's waist, burrowing his head against her side. "Daddy's packing."

"What?" Lei felt her stomach drop. "Where's he going?"

"Daddy said he had to tell you first."

"Okay. Thanks, little man." Lei straightened up, keeping a hand on the boy's shoulder as they went into the house. The living room was modestly furnished with a big coffee table, currently littered with Kiet's Legos. A flat-screen TV, a lounger, a couch, and two big dog beds, where the Rottweilers immediately went to lie down, completed the decor. Stevens was nowhere to be seen. "Daddy leave any leftovers for me?"

"We had Costco lasagna. It's in the oven," Stevens called from their bedroom.

"Thanks. I'm starved," Lei called back, injecting cheerfulness into her tone, suppressing the apprehension that was already curbing her appetite. Packing wasn't good, but whatever was happening, Lei couldn't stay long. She took out the casserole and served herself a piece, putting it on a plate. "Kiet, did you do your homework?"

"With Nana." The little boy knelt at the coffee table to continue building the Lego construction he'd been working on.

"Do you want to watch a cartoon?" They limited his TV time, so Lei wasn't surprised when Kiet jumped up with enthusiasm and turned on Cartoon Network. That would give her a chance to talk to Michael in privacy.

The microwave was still ticking as she headed down the hall to their bedroom at the back of the house. A king-sized bed dominated the small room, and Lei paused in the doorway at the sight of her husband rolling a garment into a tight bundle and stowing it in a duffel bag.

Gazing at his bent head with the ruffled dark hair, broad shoulders, and the lamplight falling on his deft, long-fingered hands, she felt the quickening of emotion that seeing him always brought, in spite of everything.

"Where are you going?" Her voice was soft. Maybe this wasn't the deployment she'd been dreading.

Stevens looked up. His crystal-blue eyes were ringed in shadows, as they so often were these days, and his dark brows were drawn together. His jaw was tight, a resoluteness there that told her what she didn't want to hear.

"I've got orders. Leaving tomorrow morning for the assignment."

"Where to?" She felt anger blaze up her spine to light up her eyes.

"I'm sorry. It's classified."

"That's frickin' insulting," she hissed, modifying her

language in case of listening ears. "You haven't told Kiet. Were you going to leave that to me, like everything else?"

He looked down. Turned away, went to the dresser, took out a pair of socks and rolled them in a tight ball. "I wanted to talk to you first."

"Like that will make a difference. You're still going, no matter what I say." Her throat closed. She wanted to cry, but a wave of anger energized her. He wasn't the only one who battled demons. He didn't have the corner on PTSD, or grief, for that matter—and yet he was going away, indulging himself, while she stayed here, being a mother, doing her job.

"I have to go, Lei. I'm sorry I can't make you understand why." He tucked the socks into the rest of the clothing. "I'll be back in six months."

"Six months." She echoed it. "Six months you're going to leave me here to carry the load. Six months away from us, so you can drink all you want without hearing shit about it."

"I knew you were going to go off." He turned, went to the dresser, took out more socks. "So say what you gotta say. Get it off your chest."

"I've said it all before. This isn't necessary. You got a problem? We have help available. Dr. Wilson. There are programs..."

"Not for me. Not for this. I'll beat this in my own way, and whether or not it makes any sense to you, this is the way I need to go. I'm not going to be drinking. I had to sign a contract agreeing to that. I'm going to be working, in a place where I can't even get my hands on any booze."

"It's too extreme. It's so unnecessary." Lei could barely speak past the tightness in her chest.

"Part of what I need to get off the sauce is to put myself in a situation where I don't have the same old ruts to deal with."

"So now...we're a rut. Your family is what's dragging you down." Lei's eyes prickled with tears and she tightened her hands into fists.

He brushed past her and shut the door so Kiet wouldn't hear them fighting. He grabbed her wrist to pull her up against him. His gaze was hot and intense on her face. "Don't do this. Don't start this now. We only have tonight."

Lei was up against his chest, her wrist in his hand, his big body against hers. It had been months since they'd slept together. She felt the proximity weaken her knees, just as looking into his blazing blue eyes did. He wanted her—it vibrated in the chemistry between them, in the hardness she felt pressed against her waist. And she wanted him, just as much. But it wasn't enough. Anger stiffened her spine.

She pulled back. "Let go of me."

He let go, and she stepped back. "You think I'm going to just—let you kiss me and make it better? Send you off with my blessing? Not going to happen."

Stevens turned away, went back to his duffel. "Then we don't have anything to say to each other. Because this is happening."

"When does your plane leave?"

"Ten a.m. tomorrow."

"So you get to take Kiet to school. And tell him you'll be gone for six months. Because hell if I'm going to do that for you." Lei grabbed the door handle and cranked it open. She stomped down the hall and into the kitchen, where her reheated dinner was cooling in the microwave. She took her plate and sat down at the small, round dining room table, eating the tasteless food with quick, hard bites, just trying to get it down.

Stevens joined her, bringing her a Longboard Lager from the fridge. She pushed it back toward him. "I pulled a fresh homicide. Got to get back to the office."

He sat beside her anyway, leaning into her space. "I'm sorry. I know this is hard."

"You have no idea." She stood up, whirled to walk to the sink, dumped the remaining lasagna, and ran the plate under the water. She scooped up her small backpack and, ignoring Stevens, went into the living room to drop a kiss on Kiet's head.

"See you later, little man. Mama has to go back to work."

"Bye, Mama." Kiet's gaze was still on the cartoon. Stevens came in and sat on the couch beside his son, looping a long arm over his shoulder and pulling the boy close to his side.

Lei shut the door on the tender scene, feeling sick. Sick at heart and sick to her stomach, the lasagna she'd hastily wolfed down both not enough and too much. The Rottweilers pressed against her, one on each side, as she walked back to the truck. She reached for the door of her vehicle, but Keiki, in a rare display of defiance, pressed against it, looking up at Lei with worried, intelligent brown eyes.

"Oh, girl. You don't want me to go. I don't want to go either, but I have a case." She squatted to embrace the dog quickly as she looked back at the house, wishing she could sit with Stevens and Kiet for the few hours Michael had left, wishing he wasn't going tomorrow, wishing that instead they were going back to the bedroom to make love until dawn.

But she knew she wouldn't do that. Couldn't. Because then he'd think this crazy plan was okay with her, and hell if it was.

They'd been through so much together. At first he'd been the strong one, pursuing her past her fears, healing her brokenness. They'd built a life together, just as they'd built this ugly, sturdy home, literally on the ashes of all that enemies had stolen from them.

She knew exactly when the tide had turned, when she'd become the stronger one—the day Anchara, Kiet's mother, had been brutally murdered and Stevens had been set up to find her in her last moments and be accused of her murder. Stevens had gone on, but in spite of his love for Lei and his son, he'd never been the same. It was one horror too many in a series of horrors. He had flashbacks and nightmares ever since, and it sickened her to see him go down the same alcoholic road as his mother, his eyes wide open about it, knowing better but unable to stop.

Lei nudged the big dog aside with her knee, patting Keiki's head. "I'll be back later." She hopped into the truck, fired it up, and got back on the road to the station. *Forward motion.* It wasn't an answer, but it was something.

Chapter 3

D riving down the narrow, two-lane road leading from her house to Hana Highway and back into Kahului, Lei put in her Bluetooth and called her best friend, Marcella Scott, on Oahu. She pictured her beautiful friend as the agent answered on the first ring.

"No, I haven't popped yet," Marcella said.

Lei had been calling often for updates on Marcella's late-stage pregnancy. Now Lei was so upset by her own news that her friend's upbeat greeting felt jarring. She adjusted her tone to Marcella's. "Aren't you already due?"

"Two days ago. But Baby Kamuela apparently wants to spend a few more days kicking me in the bladder." Marcella had married a mutual friend, Detective Marcus Kamuela with the Honolulu Police Department, and they'd opted not to know the sex of the child now distending Marcella's formerly tiny waist to an alarming degree. "I've been having some Braxton Hicks contractions when we take walks. Frankly, I can't wait to get this part over with, so I'm dragging Marcus out for a pep-step every chance I get."

A mental picture of her friends walking together on the beach, handsome Marcus with a brawny arm around Marcella, her giant belly leading the way, was an emotional twist of the knife for Lei.

She'd so enjoyed being pregnant. The tiny fluttering of their child had felt like butterflies in her belly, the emotional attachment already strong. Losing the baby had been a terrible physical and emotional ordeal. She hadn't wanted to live for a few days, and it was baby Kiet who'd brought her back, given her purpose, and healed her as much as anything could.

Lei forced a smile into her voice. "Well, if it's on your to-do list, Marcella, I know it's gonna get done."

"What's wrong?" Marcella's voice had gone concerned. "I can tell you're not happy about something."

Lei paused the truck, making a left turn. Her headlights cut twin bars of golden light into the velvety darkness, scented with the night-blooming jasmine that grew in that area. "Michael's going overseas. For six months. Starting tomorrow."

"Oh no!" Her friend's immediate, heartfelt cry brought tears prickling to Lei's eyes. "I didn't think he was really going to do it!"

"I didn't either. But he ships out tomorrow morning."

"Do you know where?"

"No. He said it's classified. He's going to be working with military police for this private-contract company. Supposedly they recruited him because of his training background and the diversity of Hawaii. All that's going to make him better at teaching the MPs overseas to work with their native populations. Not that I wanted them to pick him. I've been freaking out about this every step of the way, but he's not listening." Lei swallowed. "He doesn't care what I think. What I need."

"Lei. You know that's not true. That man adores you. But I get the sense that he's fighting for his life. I don't agree with how he's decided to deal with his problems, but it's obvious he thinks there's no other way. Maybe it's a little bit of a midlife crisis, too?"

"Yeah, it could be. I'm in my thirties now, and the clock is ticking. He's seven years older."

"You guys got checked out, right? And there was no reason you couldn't get pregnant again after the miscarriage."

"That's what they say. But three years, Marcella." Lei's eyes overflowed. She pulled over onto the grassy verge of the road, putting the vehicle in park. She leaned her forehead on the steering wheel. "Three years we've been trying to get pregnant. Trying to move on from all that happened with the Changs. It just makes me so mad that they ended up beating us in the end!"

"Oh, honey." Marcella was quiet as Lei sobbed until she was done, finally reaching for a beach towel on the passenger seat and mopping her face and eyes. "They didn't beat you. You're still alive, right?"

Lei snorted a laugh. "Guess I need to remember how deadly that game really was. Yeah, we're alive, but we're not together."

"You can be mad at him, Lei. Be mad, go ahead. But don't let him leave without showing him you love him. If something happens..." Marcella's voice caught, and then she went on. "If something happens, you'll never forgive yourself. And even if it doesn't—six months is a long period of abstinence, especially after the, what, couple of months since you moved out of the bedroom?"

Marcella knew everything about their problems, and her friend's perspective was bracing. Lei turned the truck back on, put on the signal, and pulled back onto the road. "You're right. I can't let him go tomorrow the way I left things tonight. I may cave and give him a hug."

"Send him off with more than a hug, damn it. Make him regret all he's leaving behind."

"Well, I'm on my way back into the station, so I can think that over. Got an interesting case. Went on my first deep-water body retrieval today." Lei described the case so far.

"Well, have fun with that. As for me, I'm kind of enjoying maternity leave." Her friend had worked her last day the week before. "Other than being extremely, uncomfortably pregnant, of course. Anyway, promise me you won't go all stiff-necked on this. Marriage is for the long haul. For richer, for poorer, in sickness and in health, for better or worse, right?"

"I just didn't expect so much of the last couple of years to be for the worse." Lei sighed. "What I wouldn't give to be where you and Marcus are right now."

"I know. I wish we were having babies together, too."

A long pause. The phone connection buzzed faintly with the distance between Maui and Oahu, and the different stages of a woman's life.

Finally Lei said, "Call me the minute Baby Kamuela gets started on his or her grand entrance, okay? You know I'll be on the next flight out."

"What about Kiet? He's going to miss his mama now that Daddy's going."

"I'll bring him. He can stay at my grandpa Soga's while I visit you. I've been wanting to take him to the zoo, anyway."

"Sounds like a plan. Let's hope it's sooner rather than later."

Lei ended the call with her spirits lifted a bit as she pulled into the parking lot at Kahului Police Station, a rectangular cube of utilitarian architecture. Inside, things were quiet with only graveyard-shift personnel on the job, but Pono was already back in their cubicle.

He looked up at her entry, frowned, rubbing a finger across his bristling mustache. "Who died?"

"Never ask a homicide detective that. She'll have too many

answers." Lei flung herself into her office chair. It emitted a squeak of protest. "Stevens is being deployed. That training gig he took on for Security Solutions."

"Aw, no. I didn't think he was really going to follow through with that bad idea." Pono scowled. "When does he leave?"

"Tomorrow."

"Holy crap. All the military deployments I've heard of get a lot more notice than that!"

"Yeah, well. That's all he's seen fit to tell me." Would Michael have sat on his deployment date and not told her? Just sprung it on her like this? No. That would be too horrible. She refocused with an effort. "Let's get to that GoPro footage and confirm identity of the victim so I can get home for the few hours that he's still gonna be here." Lei blinked away more threatening tears as Pono reached over to squeeze her shoulder.

"You'll be okay. Tiare and I will help with the boy. Whatever we can do."

"Thanks. I'm going to need it." She blew her nose on a handy tissue. "Now, where are we?"

"The Coast Guard didn't find any more evidence in their dive after we were there. And Jessup has extracted the GoPro footage. I'll see if he can come up and help us get it user-friendly." Jessup Murioka was MPD's computer specialist. Though all Maui detectives were trained to do the basics, Jessup came in for anything requiring extra skills. The Kamehameha student, only seventeen, reveled in his role as MPD boy genius. Pono called the boy down to his lab.

"You rang, O Great Ones?" Jessup said in an exaggerated accent.

"Bring us that GoPro footage on a tablet, will you? And we need physical prints of the photos for the file," Pono said.

"Let's take a look at the photos together," Jessup's tinny voice said. "That's a lot of colored ink. I'm sure you don't need all the photos."

Pono hung up.

A few minutes later, Jessup arrived, a little out of breath from jogging up from the basement, where he'd taken over a whole storage room for his "projects." Gawky and pale from his indoor pursuits, Jessup was still wearing his blue Kamehameha polo shirt and shorts. He pushed his glasses up his nose as he woke up a tablet to show them. "I've got them here. Just pick the ones you want printed."

Grainy and a little out of focus, the photos showed the black bottom of a Zodiac from deep underwater. Another photo showed two divers in scuba gear, apparently wrestling with a branchlike coral. Another shot showed the same divers, rendered anonymous by their gear, using a net to capture small decorative reef fish.

"I can't tell anything about these divers." Lei frowned in frustration, studying the photos. "Except that they appear to be male."

"I can. In that first photo, they're harvesting coral. Probably illegal. And the aquarium-reef-fish catching is illegal, too. Interesting situation out at Molokini. The front side, with the bay, is all protected, but fishing is allowed two hundred yards from the atoll on the back side. My guess is that these photos are an attempt to document illegal fishing," Pono said.

Lei pointed to the speargun carried by one of the divers. "Looks like it could be the murder weapon."

"Let's do a quick check." Pono scrolled to the photos he'd added to the newly opened case file on the homicide. They found a photo of the spear, still embedded in the body. Lei had shot it at the body-retrieval site and again at the dock when the body was handed over to Dr. Gregory. "We'll have to wait until Dr. Gregory removes it from the body. But it looks like it could be." The short metal shaft was the type shot from a compressed-air speargun, such as the one carried by one of the divers.

"So your murder was out at Molokini? The person who took these photos was the murder victim?" Jessup's eyes gleamed behind his thick glasses, and he pushed them up again.

"You aren't supposed to see these crime scene photos." Lei frowned. She liked the young tech, and she especially liked his wide-eyed innocence and didn't want to see it tarnished.

"I can totally handle it," Jessup said. "I'm seventeen, for God's sake." He leaned in to get a closer look at the mutilated body. "Not much blood from those wounds."

"I'm guessing she bled out internally, but she definitely lost some fluid to those shark wounds," Pono said.

"I took prints off the hand she had left at the dock," Lei said. "Let me run those as soon as we get done looking at these pictures."

"Sounds good." They continued to scroll. Many of the photos were blurry or hard to make out, but as they went on, Lei noticed changes in the depth and water color, as well as subject. Lei noticed that, preceding each series of photos, there were at least three of land locations before underwater shots.

"Look at this. Totally different location." She pointed. "You can see how shallow it is here. Look at the black lava cliffs. Looks like La Perouse area."

"Yeah. These must be over a period of time. It looks like our vic might have been trying to catch illegal fishing in the act." Pono frowned. "Looks like some more reef fish being captured for aquariums. See this net?" He pointed to an almost invisible filament in the water, covering the area of several coral heads. "The divers are driving the tiny fish into it."

"But I can't tell where these are taken," Lei grumbled. "At least there's a date and time stamp."

"If you knew where the reference photos at the beginning were taken, you'd be able to say. We have to talk to the Department of Land and Natural Resources right away. They might know something about these photos. What I know is that when they ticket someone for illegal fishing, there has to be proof the fish were taken from a protected area, which makes it tough to bust people," Pono said.

"Adding DLNR to the to-do list." Lei found her eyes growing heavy. "It's nine p.m. already. I want to process the prints and hit the ground running tomorrow morning with an identity for our vic." She took the card with the victim's prints on it out of the case file and scanned it into the computer, then set the matching program to working, which usually took an hour or more. "Jessup, get home. You have school tomorrow. Just e-mail and print us the photos we marked, please."

"You got it, Sergeant." Jessup gave a mock salute. Lei could swear the boy skipped as he went down the hall toward his basement domain.

"Oh, to have that kind of energy again."

"Go home." Pono squeezed her shoulder. "You look beat, and you don't have long to make Stevens sorry for leaving."

"Ha-ha, that's what Marcella said." Lei stood up. "You okay with running the prints?"

"I'll text you if they come back to anyone we have to follow up on immediately."

"Thanks, partner. I'll be back in right away in the morning. So far we have to track that ID from the Zodiac, contact UH about it, follow up on the prints, and network with the DLNR."

"Go," Pono said. "And don't be back so early that you don't see your man off properly in the morning."

"I'm not sure he deserves it."

"C'mon. He deserves it for putting up with you for so long, if nothing else." Pono pushed her toward the door so hard she staggered. "I'll keep things moving until you get in."

Chapter 4

The dogs got up to greet Lei, coming around from the dog door in the kitchen, but they didn't bark, used to her late-night comings and goings. She let herself in with her key and sent them back to their beds. Heading down the hall, she felt her heart aching, a dense and sorrowful feeling.

How was she going to get the motivation to go to Michael, when she'd left in such anger and still felt that way? And yet she knew Marcella was right. She couldn't let Stevens go overseas for six months the way they'd left things.

Lei peeked her head in to check on Kiet. He was sleeping peacefully, his arms flung wide, the night-light bathing his sleeping face in soft golden glow. She smiled at the sight. Her son needed her, and that felt good. She went into the bathroom next, stripping out of her clothes and dropping them into the hamper, soaping up quickly in the shower and checking in with herself. Was she up for this, after so long and so much anger?

The flow of water over her skin reminded her of the early days of their marriage, when passion had seemed unquenchable, when they never seemed to get enough of each other. She knew that passion still burned, only a touch away.

Silence is key. Words were like bricks forming a wall

between them, and if all they had was tonight—then let it be a bubble of peace, a respite from all that was wrong between them. Touch had always been the place where, no matter what else was happening, their two bodies told the truth of what lay between them.

Lei turned off the water, dried off, and wrapped up in a towel. She tiptoed to the bedroom. She hadn't entered the space, except to grab clothing, for two months.

The curtains were open. Milky silver moonlight fell across Stevens, lying on his back as was his habit, one hand tucked under the pillow, the other resting alongside his body. A pattern of lacy tree shadow fell across the bed.

She clung to the doorjamb, hesitating, and he sat up. He hadn't been asleep, and she remembered that was one of his problems. He didn't sleep much at all.

Stevens tossed the covers aside and stood up. He was naked, and the sight of him, all looming dark angles and light-touched muscle, made her suck in a breath as he came to the doorway. He stood close but didn't touch her. The heat of his body made her heart pound, but neither of them spoke.

She didn't pull away. Instead, she stepped a tiny bit closer. She couldn't see his face, dark and backlit as he bent to hers, but there was hesitation in the way he touched her upturned mouth with his. A cautious hope in his tentative touch increased as she opened to him, dropping the towel to puddle at their feet.

He took her in his arms at last, squeezing her hard as he had always done, as if to enfold her into himself. A soft groan rumbled in his wide chest, and her eyes filled with fresh tears even as her body caught fire touching his.

She was never sure, later, who led who to the big, moonlit bed.

* * *

The first mynahs were chattering in the trees outside and dawn brightened the sky to gray-pearl. The morning was unkind to Lei's hair, and she scraped the unruly thickets into a ball and anchored it on the top of her head with a rubber band. Stevens, up on an elbow, watched her as she dressed.

"Do you have to go in so early?" His voice was hoarse. They'd hardly slept, instead alternating bouts of lovemaking with drowsing as they bridged with touch the chasm that had grown up between them. It had been that bubble of peace and ecstasy Lei had hoped for, but words could still destroy it.

She glanced over. He was sitting up, pulling on a pair of boxers. They'd taken this long to make up, and in spite of the intimacy last night, he was still leaving. She felt achy and heartsick, as if coming down with a flu, her muscles heavy as lead.

"Got a fresh case, I told you. It's not fair to Pono to leave him holding the bag." She couldn't feel worse, but she wanted to get to work. Needed to. As if on cue, both of their phones, plugged in on the nightstand, beeped. She glanced over and saw a message from Pono to both of them.

Got it covered. Don't come in until 9 a.m. at least.

Damn her partner, taking away her excuses.

Stevens picked up his phone and read the message there, too. He set the phone down and gave her hand a tug.

"Come here." She let herself fall over, and he pulled her fully clothed body into his arms. "You needed a shower anyway. We both do."

"Yeah." She turned her face to lean her ear against his bare chest, listening to the slow thud of his heart. "I have something for you." She rolled out of his arms, going to the jewelry box he had given her five years ago. She took out a small velvet jewelry pouch. "I bought this for your birthday, but I'd like you to have it now."

Stevens's eyes were hooded, hiding his emotions, as she sat cross-legged on the bed in front of him. He opened the pouch, taking out a beautifully carved bone hook pendant on a handmade coconut-husk thong.

"I bought it at our favorite gallery, Native Intelligence in Wailuku. There's a *kahu* craftsman who carves them. It represents the legend of the magic hook the demigod Maui used to pull the Hawaiian Islands up out of the sea."

Stevens held the pendant on his palm, looking at her. She could see the feelings in his eyes now: sorrow, determination, regret. "I'm sorry it has to be this way. You know I love you. I'll wear it if you put it on me. And I won't take it off until I get back."

Lei covered his palm with hers, closing her eyes in a brief prayer. "Bless this hook and may it remind my husband how much he's loved. May it remind him of Maui, our home. Keep him safe for us, please, dear God." She leaned forward to kiss the bone pendant, and then fastened it around Stevens's neck with the simple bone clasp.

Stevens pulled her close again. She laid her cheek against his chest, stretched out alongside him, his heart beating against hers.

She must have fallen asleep, because the next thing she knew, the door was flying open and Kiet ran in to throw himself onto them. As Lei opened her bleary eyes, she could see happiness in the little boy's smile that they were together in bed. Kiet had asked Lei why she slept in the office, and she'd made excuses about a bad back. She knew the situation worried him.

It crushed Lei to think what Stevens's news would do to their son's smile, but she knew better than to interfere. Stevens had his own relationship with his son, and though Lei was the only mother Kiet had ever known, she was respectful of Stevens's role and of Kiet's birth mother's memory. She had tried to keep Anchara's heritage and culture a part of their lives, and she honored the sweet ghost she sometimes sensed watching over the boy.

It wasn't her job to make this goodbye easy for Stevens. She'd have her hands full picking up the pieces after he left. The thought gave her enough energy to crawl out of bed.

"I have to get that shower."

She left Kiet gleefully pelting his father with a pillow as Stevens tried to preserve some dignity, the sheet around his waist. The clock in the bathroom read 7:15 a.m. as she stripped off the work clothes she'd prematurely donned and took the rubber band out of her matted hair, getting under the shower and working the tangles out with conditioner.

Lei wished they'd had time for the shower. She knew Stevens had meant that, too, but they'd fallen asleep. She was just finishing shaving her legs when he slipped into the steam-fogged stall with her. She widened her eyes.

"Where's Kiet?"

"Cartoons. Thank God for TV." He slid under the water, gently moving her out of the stream. "Now, where were we? I was imagining this, earlier." And he put his hand there, and then his mouth. Soon all was a kaleidoscope of slippery movement and muffled sighs and heated pressure building to ecstasy, and Lei wondered how the hell she'd go for six months without him.

Chapter 5

L ei headed her truck out through the automatic gate, waving at Stevens, who held Kiet in his arms on the porch. Wayne had volunteered to take Stevens to the airport and bring Kiet in to school late after they saw him off. This was going to be her last glimpse of her husband, and she kept her eyes on him in the rearview mirror until the gate rumbled shut and he disappeared.

Lei felt a lot better than she had on her way into work last night, but worse in a different way. Why hadn't she been able to accept her husband's decision sooner? At least then they wouldn't have lost the last few months to chilly silence and cold shoulders—though, on second thought, he hadn't been drinking last night, and that was at least in part why it had been so incredible with him.

She would never understand why he was doing this—but he was as stubborn as she was, and she should have known that.

"It is what it is," she said aloud, her favorite therapy saying. She rolled down her window. The breeze off the ocean at Ho`okipa blew softly on her face as she drove down the coastal highway past the surf break on her commute into Kahului.

Morning came to Maui dramatically, and today was no

different. Sunlight broke over Haleakala, House of the Sun, and struck the West Maui mountain range across the waist of the island in a sharp line. Alongside the highway, the slate-dark ocean transformed to turquoise as the light hit, and beyond, mounds of creamy clouds caught fire with golden light.

Lei spotted surfers in the water at the popular break and wished she had time for a quick paddle out. That would loosen her tired muscles and wash away the hangover-like feeling of too much emotion better than the coffee she sipped from a travel mug.

But she was late enough. The day was wasting, and there was nothing to be done but to get through it—the first day of six months without her husband.

Pono was in the cubicle as if he'd never left when Lei arrived, but she could tell he'd gone home by the fresh smell of the lemony aftershave he favored and his clean polo shirt.

"No match on the prints," he greeted her. "And you look— like crap."

"At least I took a shower. You should have seen my hair before." Lei looked at his monitor as he swiveled it toward her. "What are we doing about the driver's license on the anchored Zodiac?"

"I thought of going out to her house because I've got a strong feeling our vic is Danielle Phillips. I hope we're wrong, but I think we should get eyes on the husband ASAP." Pono stood. "Your car or mine?" Pono flipped a coin, catching it on the back of his meaty hand as if it were any other day of their work together. Lei smiled, grateful for that.

"Tails."

"Heads. Purple truck today."

"You have a weighted coin for these, I swear," Lei complained, following him out of the station building.

Pono's jacked-up purple truck, whose color he blamed on his dash of Filipino blood, sported a tiny war helmet dangling from the mirror and Keep It Hawaiian stickers. It was already over-the-top, but the chrome shifter ball in the shape of a skull was her favorite feature in the tricked-out cab. Lei hopped up on the metal step and got in. She gave the skull a pat. "Hey, Stanley."

"Stanley. You kidding? Dat guy one Hawaiian. Goes by Makana."

"Thought Makana was a musician, and he's alive last time I checked." The banter kept the soreness of her heart at bay, even as she glanced at her phone. From the time, she knew Wayne was driving Kiet and Stevens to the airport.

Nothing to be done. It was what it was.

Her phone chimed with a text from Stevens. *Left a satellite phone from Security Solutions for you. Will call when I can and text every day. I love you.*

Okay. Glad we had that shower. I'm still mad you're leaving.

I know you are. The little man took it okay.

I don't think he knows what it means. But okay. Travel safe.

Will do. More later.

Lei slid the phone into her pocket and deliberately focused on the scenery as they drove through town. They wound up into Wailuku Heights, a newer residential area near green, jungled Iao Valley. They pulled into the neat driveway of a nicer ranch-style home near where Stevens had lived with his first wife. Lei preferred to forget that particular chapter, a time when she'd been trying out a career in the FBI.

Pono leaned on the doorbell, and they both showed ID to a six-foot Caucasian man with dark hair and a bodybuilder's physique who Lei guessed was Frank Phillips, Danielle's husband. He was wearing workout clothing and carried a hand towel, as if they'd surprised him lifting weights.

"Sergeant Lei Texeira of Maui Police Department, and this is my partner, Pono Kaihale. We are following up on an ID we found in a Zodiac anchored off Molokini yesterday."

"You found my wife?" The man's complexion paled and he mopped his sweating face with the towel. "She didn't come back last night. I was getting ready to call you."

"Can we come inside? We're trying to figure out whose boat we found," Lei said.

Frank stood aside. "Please. Come in." He shut the door behind them and led them to a living room with a vaulted ceiling and a view of nearby Iao Valley, clouds beginning to catch on the lush, steep slopes. "So what is going on?"

"Why don't you tell us why you're concerned about your wife? Then we can determine what might be going on here." Lei kept her gaze on his face.

The man was breathing rapidly. Red spots had appeared on his cheekbones. His hand shook as he pushed it through thinning black hair. Through an open door, Lei glimpsed the home gym he must have come from. Air conditioning and eighties rock music drifted out of the doorway. He went over and shut the door with a *thump*, then returned to sit on the couch across from them.

"I don't know where she is. She works for the University of Hawaii—a marine biologist. She often goes out on the ocean for one of her research projects, or doing something for Save Our Reefs. Have you heard of it?" He looked up at Lei with bloodshot eyes, the picture of a stressed, worried husband.

Lei nodded. "So did she take out a Zodiac belonging to the university?"

"She did."

Pono had risen to his feet, and with an aimless air, was circulating around the room, looking at assorted photos clustered on the sideboard. "Your wife is lovely." He held up a photo of the couple, arms entwined. Danielle's long brown hair framed a smiling face that Lei had last seen, puffy and discolored, on a dead woman lying on the dock at Ma'alaea Harbor.

"Thanks. Well, I thought a person was supposed to be missing twenty-four hours before I called anyone, so..." Phillips's voice trailed off.

"If you thought she was doing something dangerous like scuba diving alone, a call much sooner would be fine." Lei tried not to snap. "So where did you think your wife had gone?"

"I didn't know. I was at work." Suddenly he stood, slapped his thighs, and glared at Lei and Pono. "What is this about? You never told me."

"We found the body of an unidentified woman in scuba gear off Molokini. In searching for an identity, we found a Zodiac anchored off the atoll. Your wife's ID was on the vessel, and that led us here."

"Oh God." Phillips's knees collapsed, and he folded onto the couch. "I thought that might be it when I first opened the door."

"Why is that?" Lei was on him like a mynah on a grasshopper.

"Because. She was out all night, and she did damn fool things like go scuba diving alone!" he exclaimed, and broke into a sob, covering his face with his hands. Pono fetched a box of tissues and patted the man's back. Lei got up to roam the room, looking for clues.

All the pictures clustered on the sideboard appeared to be roughly from the same period, early in the marriage, to judge by the wedding, honeymoon, and carrying-across-the-threshold theme. The rest of the decor, arty nature shots, yielded nothing personal.

The house was almost antiseptically clean, with white carpet and a collection of expensive-looking shepherdess figurines that looked out of place, as if inherited from a relative and too valuable to get rid of. No children or pets.

"Let me make a quick call," Lei said. "Be right back."

"Tell me about your wife's daily routine," Pono said as she stepped outside to call Dr. Gregory at the morgue.

"Howzit, Lei!" exclaimed the ever-cheerful ME, a Mainland transplant who sometimes overdid his enthusiasm for all things Hawaii. Dr. Gregory even tried pidgin and Hawaiian phrases on her sometimes, and Lei wondered which bright aloha shirt he was wearing under his rubber apron today.

"Hey, Dr. G. We have a witness to come down and do an ID on that Jane Doe diver we brought in yesterday. Can you get her ready for us?"

"Sure. Haven't done the post yet, but I did get the spear out of her. You can take that back and log it in."

"See anything else of interest?"

"The injuries to the body, aside from the spear wound, were postmortem, as you suspected, Sergeant. Consistent with shark bites. She had no defensive wounds that I could see in an initial exterior exam. No trace under the nails on her remaining hand. I'll know more when we do the full workup."

"Okay, thanks. We'll be there in half an hour or so." Lei hung up and put her head into the garage for a quick look. Against the back wall, she saw a row of wetsuits and dive gear. Beneath the gear rested a sleek kayak with a paddle stowed in it and a small electric trolling motor on the back.

* * *

Maui Memorial's morgue was below the ground floor. With Lei on one side and Pono on the other, Frank Phillips stared stoically at the changing lights of the elevator, then followed them into a hall shining with waxed linoleum. Pono hit the automatic door button outside the sally port, set up to open for gurneys. The twin doors swung into an anteroom used for viewing, an area Lei usually passed through to go into the bigger workroom beyond.

This time, a draped body on a gurney awaited them. Dr. Gregory, looking official in a white lab coat and holding a clipboard, looked up with a smile. A foot with a toe tag protruded from beyond the sheet, and Frank Phillips gave a little cry.

"It's her! It's my wife!"

"You can tell from a foot?" Lei asked, already knowing the answer. She'd know her husband's foot anywhere, the long narrow shape of it, the high arch, and the middle toe longer than the rest. God, she never wanted to have to identify his body.

"Lani has a dolphin tattoo on her ankle." Phillips pointed. Lei leaned closer, and sure enough, a tiny blue dolphin leaped over the victim's ankle bone.

"Still, for a formal identification we need you to take a look at her face," Dr. Gregory said. Lei spotted an aloha shirt covered with bright pineapples peeking out of the lab coat as the medical examiner lifted the drape off the woman's face.

Frank Phillips looked at the bloodless features, still a little distorted from immersion and scuba gear, for a long moment. "It's Lani. It looks like her, but it doesn't."

"Death does that to people." Dr. Gregory had a kindly tilt to his head. He wrote something on the papers attached to the clipboard and handed it to Phillips to sign.

"I thought her name was Danielle?" Lei asked.

"Lani is her middle name. She's part Hawaiian, and she often went by that." Suddenly Phillips's shoulders hunched and he turned away, covering his face.

Pono patted him on the back as Dr. Gregory wheeled the body back into the morgue, gesturing to Lei. Out of view of Phillips, he handed her a longish packet, closed with an evidence seal.

The murder weapon, he mouthed. She took it and rejoined Pono and Phillips.

"Can you come down to the station with us?" Lei asked Phillips. "We need to take a statement."

"What? Why?" The man appeared blinded by grief, stumbling a little toward the door.

"Because her death wasn't accidental," Lei said gently. "It's just a formality."

Phillips made it through the automatic doors and blundered to the elevator, stabbing the up button repeatedly. "Not accidental? What happened?" He turned to them, his eyes wide and bloodshot.

"I can't say more at this time." Lei wanted to offer to call someone for him, but they needed to interview him when the news was fresh.

In Kahului Station's cleanest interview room, Lei Mirandized Phillips and settled into the seat across from him after turning on the recording equipment. Pono brought Phillips a Styrofoam cup of the station's coffee, black, as he'd asked for it. The man sipped, staring into the middle distance as Lei recited the date, time, and persons present for the record.

"So, Frank. Take us back to yesterday. Tell us about the day."

"Well, we got up as usual to go to work. She has a class to teach at UH early some mornings and keeps office hours. I have my business in Wailuku. I'm a CPA. Phillips Accounting, LLC."

"Was there anything...different about Danielle's behavior yesterday morning? Did you know she was going out to Molokini?"

"No. She seemed...as usual." He rubbed a hand over his pallid, sweaty face. "Just as usual."

"So...help us understand your wife. What does that mean?" Lei asked, probing.

Phillips looked up, suddenly alert. "You don't think I had anything to do with it, do you?"

"Did you? Have anything to do with it?"

"What? How could I? She was out there, going alone like she was always doing, trying to gather evidence for the DLNR on fish poaching. It was her passion, and it got her killed, just like I told her it would a hundred times!" Phillips was so emphatic that spit flew from his mouth. "She never listened to me. So that's what 'as usual' meant in our house, damn it!"

Lei felt the hurt behind the words, the betrayal. She couldn't help but identify—with her own marriage and how so often she had ignored Stevens's more cautious approach and attempts to protect her. Now his departure went against her needs in the same way.

Pono, leaning against the wall, stepped forward. "What she was doing sounds kind of reckless. You must have been worried sick."

Lei restrained herself from an eye roll as Pono laid on the "good cop" role a little thick, but Phillips nodded. "Yeah, I was. All the time. She was so involved with Save Our Reefs, and she was doing this fish-population study of Maui. She'd tell anyone who would listen about the declining fish populations, both from human impact and use and the runoff problem."

"Runoff problem?" This was new information, and Lei perked up.

"From the development on the south side of the island. We've had a wet winter, and the soil is washing and blowing into the ocean. Loaded with phosphates, the soil covers the reef, changes the chemistry. Then we've had global warming temperature increases, leading to algae blooms and coral bleaching. All of that impacts the health of the reefs. The healthiest reefs are in the La Perouse Bay area and farther out, because it's protected and there's nothing but lava fields inland, so there's nothing to run off into the ocean." Phillips rubbed a hand across his face.

"I heard even sunscreen can harm coral," Lei said.

"That's right. But we're not here to talk about that. I imagine you're working up to asking me where I was when she died. I was at work all day yesterday. You can check with my assistant."

"Thank you for volunteering that information," Pono said. "Like Sergeant Texeira mentioned, it's just a formality."

"Can I go, then?" Phillips started to rise.

"Well, we need a DNA sample, to rule you out of any trace we find." Lei held up a swab. "This won't hurt a bit." She ran it around the inside of his cheek, deposited it in the holder. "And your prints." Using a card, she rolled each of his fingers and got the prints as he sat in stony silence. When done, she set the collection materials aside and made herself smile at him reassuringly. As usual, her smile didn't seem to work. He glared at her, angry and defensive.

"So tell me why you didn't call anyone about Lani being missing last night," Lei said.

"I didn't think anyone would listen to me or take it seriously. And I suppose..." Phillips stopped, his throat working. "I suppose I was a little angry with her. For blowing me off yet again. We'd had a few words that morning. So I thought maybe she went to a friend's. To, you know, cool off."

Lei knew all about cooling off. In the end, it wasn't a good strategy, from what she could tell. Cooling off could lead to permanent distance.

"So, would you say you had a happy marriage?"

"I don't see that asking me that is relevant," Phillips growled. He was pissed now. She could see high color in his neck.

"She's dead. It's a homicide. Everything is relevant," Lei snapped back.

"Well, then, I want a lawyer." Phillips smacked a fist on the table, making them both jump. Lei's hand settled on her weapon as she locked eyes with the surly man.

Pono leaned in. "I don't think that's necessary at this time, Mr. Phillips. We're done for today, anyway. We'll be in touch if there's anything else we need to ask you. For instance, we may need to search your home for items belonging to your wife."

"Then bring a warrant." Phillips was not appeased and stood to his full bulky height. Lei tried to imagine the petite Danielle with this block of a man and failed. They must have started out differently.

"We'll be in touch. Thanks for your cooperation." Pono backed up and opened the door for Phillips, who brushed past. Her partner turned to narrow his eyes at Lei. "Barking up the wrong tree this time, partner." Pono shut the door behind the CPA. "We always say the husband did it, but there's not a shred of anything so far to indicate he's involved. The logistics alone rule it out."

"I know." Lei sighed, stood up. "I'm off my game. Sorry I set him off."

"Well, we've still got a full day to chase leads. Which next, DLNR or the University of Hawaii? Heads, we call DLNR; tails it's UH." He took out his trusty coin, flipped it, and covered it on the back of his arm.

"Tails."

"Heads wins. DLNR it is, then. I'll get an interview lined up with some agents. Get them down here to look at the GoPro footage."

"Sounds good. I'll meet you at the evidence room." Lei held up the short, sharp steel spear, still sealed in brown paper sacking, that had been used to kill Danielle Phillips. "I still have to log this in after we compare it to the one in the photos. And get some coffee."

Lei headed for the break room. A yawn rocked her body, and her jaw cracked. Yes, she was definitely paying the price for their night of wedded bliss. Still, her mouth quirked up in a smile. It had been worth it.

Lei got a text from Stevens while she was in the break room. *Between planes. Thinking of you.*

Where are you going, exactly? Lei texted back.

Sorry, still classified. I would have told you. But I'll check in every day via text with the satellite phone I left you.

I wish I'd asked you more, she wrote back, leaning against the wall by the coffee machine. *I'm just sick that it took this for us to make up. I'm sorry I was such a bitch.*

A long pause. Then, *I can't believe what I'm reading here. Something happening at work to make you all mushy?*

Yeah. My case. Unhappy marriage. A stubborn person on a mission. Now that person's dead.

Another long pause. Then, *That won't be us. We're both stubborn and on a mission.*

She laughed, a snort that had tears behind it, looking around and grateful the break room was empty. She texted again. *I love you so much.*

I know. And you know how to make me sorry I'm gone already, damn it. Six months. It'll be over in no time, and things will be better when I get back. I promise.

She sure as hell hoped so.

Lei poured herself a cup of the tepid coffee and, the bagged spear tucked under her arm, headed for the evidence room.

Chapter 6

The DLNR agent for the area, Mark Nunes, was on his way to meet with them, so Lei took the time to call the University of Hawaii. She was connected with Dr. Rebecca Farnsworth.

"How can I help you, Sergeant?" The woman's voice sounded older, deep and confident.

"I'm calling regarding one of your staff. Dr. Danielle Phillips." Lei had the case file open. She felt a twinge of sorrow seeing the bright, fresh smile on Danielle's face in the driver's license photo.

"Lani? What's going on?" Dr. Farnsworth's voice quickened with alarm.

"We're calling to inform you she's deceased and that there was foul play involved."

"Oh no!" A gasp. "What happened?"

"We can't discuss an open homicide investigation, but anything you could tell us regarding her responsibilities for you would help. And if you could assemble a list of people for us to interview, that would be great. Also, keep this confidential for now. MPD is working on a statement for the press."

Pono looked up from the notes he was jotting with a nod.

Pono was in charge of their PR, never Lei's strong suit.

"Okay. Wow, I'm in shock. But I guess, on second thought, I'm not that shocked. I knew what Lani was doing was dangerous." Lei could tell the woman was working hard to regroup. "She answered to me and she was the senior marine biology staffer here on Maui. As you know, we're a smaller satellite college in the University of Hawaii system. She was our only full-time marine biologist."

"What can you tell me about her?"

"She was working on several research projects, most notably a longitudinal fish-populations study for Maui, which was going to be coordinated with projects on the other islands. Oh, dear, what's going to happen to her research?" The woman was still trying to assimilate the news.

"Did Danielle have a private office? We're going to need to search that."

"Yes, she does."

"I'll send an officer over to seal it. Please don't allow anyone in or out until we've had a chance to go through it."

"All right. It's kept locked anyway, but I'll make sure."

Lei turned aside to tell Pono about the office. "Seal the home, too," Lei said. "And get us the search warrants." Pono got on the phone to Dispatch.

Dr. Farnsworth went on. "Anyway, Danielle was such a hard worker. She was never too busy to help a student or another staffer. She loved what she did and she will be greatly missed."

"I'm sure. What can you tell me about her use of the University's Zodiac?"

"Was that involved?"

"Yes, it was. It's still anchored out at Molokini. I might as well tell you, she died scuba diving off Molokini." Lei made a note on a paper and passed it over to Pono. *Call Coast Guard about retrieving the Zodiac and impounding it for our search for trace.* He was still on the phone about the warrants, but he nodded.

"Oh no! I bet this was something to do with her illegal-fishing documentation. When she was out doing her fish counts, she kept seeing fishing violations. So she started documenting it for the DLNR, to get it stopped."

That had to be Danielle's GoPro footage they'd retrieved. Pono had been right in his guess about the fishing documentation, and it looked like it might have gotten her killed.

"Thanks for this information. After we search the vessel, we'll return it to the University of Hawaii. In the meantime, if you could work on a list of other useful interviewees for us, that would be great."

"She had a stalker, you know," Dr. Farnsworth said.

"She did?" Lei's pen was poised over the notes she was making. "Tell me more."

"He was a grad student whose work she was supervising. She complained to me about it. I had the kid in for a lecture. We were actually processing paperwork to get him expelled from the campus and dropped from the PhD program because he hadn't stopped his activity toward her."

"What did he do?"

"He would follow her around on campus. Take pictures of her all the time. Texted and called her constantly. She asked him to stop, then told security. After that he would wait by the parking lot for her. I advised her to take out a temporary restraining order on him. Did she do it?"

Lei had already punched up Danielle's police record, which was clean. "Nothing on file."

"I think she thought it was getting better."

"What's this man's name?"

"Ben. Ben Miller. He lives somewhere in Kahului. She told me she was going to cut him from the program if he didn't stop bugging her."

"Do you think he would be angry about that?"

"Oh, yes. He was several years into his PhD. To continue, he would have to move and start all over, if he could even get a university to accept him. She told me she was documenting his behavior in his student file."

"Hmm. I will probably want to re-interview you, Dr. Farnsworth, later down the line." Lei got the contact information for Ben Miller and Dr. Farnsworth's personal cell and hung up.

She turned to Pono with a tight grin. "Got a hot suspect here."

"I'd say let's go get him, but here's Mark Nunes now, here from the DLNR to answer our inquiries." Pono gestured to a man standing in the doorway of their cubicle.

Nunes was dark-haired, around five foot ten, deeply tanned, with the tilted eyes and lean but muscular build of a local. He was dressed in the DLNR uniform of navy pants and shirt with identification patches, boots, and a duty belt much like a police officer's. Lei stood and shook his hand.

"Sergeant Texeira. Did you know the victim, Danielle Phillips?"

"I did." The man nodded, his eyes on the floor.

"Yeah, I talked with him while you were on the phone," Pono said. "They were friends."

"I'm sorry for your loss. Okay, we should do a more formal interview, then." Lei cut a glance over to Pono. "Why don't you get him set up in an interview room and I'll get the photos we want him to look at on a tablet so we can go through them there?"

"Sounds good." The two men exited. Lei sat down, routing the GoPro pictures to a tablet device for them to review and finishing her notes from the phone call to Dr. Farnsworth. While she was at it, she called in a Be On Lookout for Ben Miller. The last thing they needed was for Danielle's stalker to slip off the island. Lei hoped they were in time to bring him in, even now.

She picked up the tablet and headed for the interview room.

The two men were already seated, and Pono had the recording equipment on. He added Lei's name and rank for the record as she took the third chair.

Nunes sat quietly, but there was an air of coiled distress about him. His dark eyes were red-rimmed and he blinked repeatedly. "I was shocked to hear Danielle is dead."

"Yes, it's a real shame. So how long have you worked for the Department of Land and Natural Resources?"

"Ten years."

"Then you've been through some lean times." Pono rubbed his mustache briskly. "I heard the furloughs were really tough a few years ago, when the state cut way back on resources."

"Yeah. The economic crash of 2009 hit the state really hard. Teachers and all state employees were furloughed. We were cut back to just four days a week and lost all personnel who weren't permanent state employees. It was really hard to keep up back then. Still is. I've come to realize we can only do what we can do." Nunes held his hands open philosophically, and Lei spotted a carved hook pendant in the neck of his shirt.

"I just gave my husband a bone hook like that." She pointed to the necklace.

"Symbol of fishermen and providers." Nunes touched the pendant, a gesture that had a feeling of superstition about it, and Lei smiled.

"So you do some fishing yourself?"

"Of course. I love the ocean and all that's in it. I fish to feed my family, like so many do here on Maui. I'm proud to be with

DLNR so we can make sure the reefs are healthy and there's food for generations to come."

"So tell me about Danielle Phillips and her relationship with DLNR."

"Lani. She loved the ocean, too. She helped us with our investigations." Suddenly Nunes's clear brown eyes clouded, and he pressed the thumb and forefinger of one hand over his eyes. "I can't believe she's gone," he whispered.

"Tell us about your relationship with her," Lei said. Nunes seemed to be reacting personally to this. Could there be something more between the two?

"Relationship?" Nunes removed his hand, blinked his eyes, and sat up straight. "We were friends. I was her main contact when she handed over evidence. To issue a citation, we have to have hard evidence that a rule or regulation has been broken, such as ocean biologics taken from a protected area. She was in the ocean so much for her research that she was able to boost a lot of photos to us that helped us win cases."

"So not only do you have to bust people with the fish in hand, but you have to have evidence the fish were caught illegally?" Lei frowned. "That seems challenging."

"It is. But it's kind of like being a detective." Now Nunes's eyes gleamed a little. "I do a lot of stealth photography with a long lens or underwater, with a GoPro like Lani used."

"So did she do assignments for you? Like, follow so-and-so; we suspect them?" Lei asked.

"No. She wasn't an agent. She would just spot things, document them, and boost them to me when they came across her path."

"Okay. We need to know that you'll keep this whole conversation confidential, because this is a homicide investigation."

Nunes reared back a little in his chair. "Someone killed Lani? I just thought she drowned. Accidentally."

"No. It was a homicide."

"Oh God." He covered his mouth with a hand, eyes wide. "Whatever I can do to help."

"Yes, that's why we called you in. We found a GoPro on the bottom of Molokini's bay with a lot of photos on it. We're having trouble interpreting them." Lei woke up the tablet, moved her chair around the table to show Nunes. The agent and Pono both leaned in to look. "We can't tell where these locations are, but I think the opening shots are to establish location."

"Yes. This is the way I told her to do it. Put the location in context, then date and time-stamp the photos." They scanned through. Nunes pointed to the ones with the net. "That's illegal aquarium capture happening."

"Can you see anything identifying in the photos?" Pono asked. Several divers in snorkel, not scuba, gear were chasing fish into an underwater net. Nearby was a submerged white plastic drum, a ring of buoy around the top keeping it upright at the water's surface. Nunes pointed to it.

"They'll put the fish in that and ship them off-island in the same water they were captured in. Helps keep the fish from dying of shock." A few photos further on, Danielle had snapped a shot of the three divers rolling the white barrel up out of the water onto black volcanic rocks. "Looks like La Perouse Bay. And those are the Micronesians we've been busting."

"Micronesians?" Lei squinted at the grainy photo. All three men, wearing baggy trunks, had bushy black hair and darker skin than most Hawaiians.

"Yeah. They've been immigrating to Maui for years now under our agreement with their government. Because we nuked Bikini Atoll and it caused a lot of unforeseen damage, the native people can come live in the United States and get free health care. Every year there are more and more of them, and some of them fish like they do in their islands—no size or count limits. They don't respect our conservation laws."

"Oh, man," Lei said. "Talk about integration problems."

"Right. So this is an entirely different kind of fishing." Nunes tapped the screen, expanding a photo where two black-suited divers appeared to be retrieving an ahi tuna. "It's legal to fish or dive on the back side of Molokini, the part they call 'Ono Alley,' because there are so many pelagic fish over there. But not on the inside. Usually fishermen are using line gear for those fish, but maybe what happened was that these divers were chasing a fish and he came in shallower, to the protected area. They weren't willing to let him go. A fish like that is worth thousands."

They scrolled on.

"What can you see from these pictures?" Lei indicated the black hull of the boat overhead from the final photos on Danielle's GoPro.

"It's a Zodiac hard bottom, twenty footer or so. Quick and easy way out to Molokini on a calm day. Zoom in." They did. Nunes went on as he studied the photo. "Can't see anything. That's the difficulty. Lani had to find something we could track later that tied people to the photos and establish date, time, and location. She knew that, so she'd have tried to find something."

"I don't see any identifying marks on the Zodiac," Lei said as they all scanned the underside of the black boat.

"The motor in the water looks like about a sixty-horse outboard, but I can't see anything either. I know she'd have tried to get a shot of the registration number on the hull," Nunes said.

"This is the last photo on the GoPro. Maybe they killed her before she could get that identifying shot," Pono said. Lei gave him a sharp look. It wasn't a good idea to speculate in front of a witness.

"We try not to jump to conclusions," Lei said, addressing Nunes. "You can't talk about what you saw here. We'll turn these photos over to the DLNR after the investigation."

"Where's that list of people cited for illegal fishing I asked you for?" Pono said.

Nunes produced a typed list from his pocket. "Here. These are poachers and fishermen cited for various infractions in the last six months."

"Thanks for pulling that together so quickly."

Nunes shrugged. "All in the database. Is that all for now?"

"For now." Pono let him out of the room as Lei switched off the recording equipment. She walked to join her partner as he held the door ajar. "Let's do a quick comparison of the murder weapon with the spear these divers had in the last photos on the GoPro."

"Don't you want to go pick up the stalker?"

"I called in a BOLO to get things started. I want to follow up on a slew of search warrants next, but if we know what kind of speargun we're looking for, so much the better."

They were headed down the hall toward the evidence room as they talked, Lei carrying the tablet. "So I'll get on the horn and get a search warrant for Ben Miller's place, too," Pono said. "Already got the ones for home and office."

He thumbed his phone open as Lei stopped at the half door to the evidence room. "Sergeant Lei Texeira checking an item I dropped off earlier."

Officer Clarice Dagdag was a short, plump woman whose legs made a *whisk*ing sound in her crisp uniform as she bustled off to retrieve the spear for Lei. Lei gave the spear, still in its paper wrapping, to Pono as she signed the logbook. "Thanks."

Clarice inclined her head, her glittering rhinestone cat's eye glasses already aimed back toward a tiny television monitor on her desk, where a soap opera played out a muted drama.

They carried the spear to one of the workrooms with a computer and an evidence processing table. Pono unwrapped the spear shaft as Lei pulled up the photos on the tablet and scrolled to the ones of the divers at Molokini.

When Lei had the right photo, one that showed a diver holding a trigger speargun, she looked at the shaft Pono had taken out.

The shaft looked like hardened steel. Pono picked it up and looked at the flat end. "Eight-millimeter diameter by sixteen-point-five length." There was a hole in the end of the shaft and a double-barbed head. The metal flanges of the barbs slid open or closed easily. "I can make out 'Mares' here on the shaft. Almost worn off. But this is definitely a pneumatic gun."

"A what?"

"A compressed-air speargun that fires the shaft using air pressure and a trigger. Someone removed the nylon cord that connects to the speargun body." He tapped the empty hole in the shaft. "Mares is a popular brand. We just need to look through their catalog to find the types of guns that fire this shaft to know what was used."

"Okay. I'll pull that up." Lei didn't bother turning on the ancient computer in the corner, instead opening a search window and punching in the Mares brand on the tablet. She keyed in the shaft specs.

"Looks like the smaller model of the Sten Pneumatic Pro." She pulled up a window with the photo from the catalog, dragged the GoPro shot of the diver holding the gun, and positioned the photos side by side. Pono leaned in close as they eyeballed the photos.

"Just visually comparing, it does look like it could be this size." Pono pointed to the Mares catalog. "This little Mares gun would have to be pretty close to the victim to drive the spear as deep into the body as the shaft went into Danielle. I can't see clearly enough to check if there's a rubber band on the diver's gun in the photo. Can you zoom in?"

"Why would there be a rubber band on it?" Lei used her fingertips to open the photo further, and though the resolution got fuzzy and grainy, they could see a faint line at the top of the speargun in the diver's hands.

"Different type of weapon. That's definitely a rubber band gun. I was going to tell you I didn't think a pneumatic had the juice for big fish. Deep-sea spear fishermen tend to use longer guns with multiple rubber bands to get more torque."

"So that's not the murder weapon in the photo."

"Correct."

"But it could be one of the other divers, or someone not pictured."

"I guess. Still, diving at that depth—they wouldn't have brought only a small gun like that Mares pneumatic."

"Okay. But at least we know what we're looking for when we go out with the search warrants." Lei rewrapped the spear shaft, trying not to remember how it had looked protruding from Danielle's body. "Since it was a smaller gun and it had penetrated her deeply, wouldn't the diver who shot her have to be pretty close?"

"Probably. That sounds like some fun research." Pono grinned, rubbing his hands together in anticipation. "I'll see if my buddy who owns a dive shop can loan us a Mares gun and we'll figure out exactly how close we'd have to be and in what position to get the shaft into a body like what was done to our vic. Dr. G will love helping us reconstruct the scene."

"Yuck." Lei shook her head. She found her imagination was sometimes her enemy on projects like those. "It's enough for right now that we know the other diver had to get pretty close to Lani. That could mean she knew the shooter."

Chapter 7

L ei and Pono logged the spear back into Evidence and
headed down the hall.

"Just need to check the fax machine for the warrants.
Judge said I'd have them by noon."

"It's noon already?" Lei looked at the clock in alarm. "I have
to go to Kiet's school at two. Don't let me forget. He's going to
be upset about Stevens leaving, and I want to check in on him."

"We should have time to get started with one of the easier
searches," Pono said as they arrived at the big fax/copier
machine off the break room. He picked up three sheets of paper,
nodded. "Let's do her University of Hawaii office first. That
should be relatively quick, and you can pick the boy up
whenever you need to."

* * *

Lei cruised to a stop in the line of cars in the turnaround
pickup area at Haiku School, Kiet's elementary school. The
kindergarteners, in their bright school tees with their backpacks
on, were the cutest gaggle of adorable kids waiting for parents.
Lei's heart sank, though, when she saw Kiet, standing close to

his teacher, holding her hand. His face was turned into the fabric of the woman's jeans skirt.

Mrs. Hayashi, a veteran kindergarten teacher, walked Kiet over to the cab of the truck as Lei put it in park and jumped out, hurrying around to the sidewalk. Kiet detached from his teacher and jumped into Lei's arms. She hefted him up, feeling his hot, wet face pressed into her neck as his little arms clung to her.

"It might have been better to keep him home today." Mrs. Hayashi had a crease of worry between her tattooed-on brows. "He cried a lot. Very upset his daddy was going away to the military?" Those expressive brows rose in question.

"Yes. Michael will be gone six months." It wasn't worth trying to explain Stevens's role. "I was worried he'd be upset. Thanks for understanding."

"It was no problem. Kiet's just usually such a happy boy." Mrs. Hayashi patted Kiet's back. "You come back tomorrow with that smiling face I know and love, okay?"

Kiet nodded but didn't lift his face from Lei's neck. She had to pry him off to put him in his booster seat in the extended cab as the other cars waited behind them.

She pulled back onto the highway for the drive to his grandma's house, feeling the stab of her own loss as she glanced in her rearview mirror at her son's woebegone face. He leaned his head on the window, looking out at the passing landscape.

"I'm sorry you had a bad day, little man. I had a bad day, too, missing Daddy."

"Why did he have to go?"

"He has an important job to do. Wants to help people overseas." Stevens had put Lei in the position of having to defend a decision she didn't agree with. One more reason to be pissed.

"I think he should stay here at home and help people." Kiet's lip trembled.

"Do you want to call and leave him a message on his voice mail? He might not answer, because he's taking planes today, but you can tell him how you feel." That would serve Stevens right. She picked up her phone and voice-dialed Stevens, then handed it to Kiet.

"Daddy, I miss you. I had a bad day," Kiet said when the Record button beeped. "I want you to come home. Love you, Daddy." The little boy pressed the Off button and handed Lei back the phone. She put it away.

"So what did you do today?"

"We made a piñata. For art." Leaving the phone message seemed to have helped Kiet. In the rearview mirror, she saw the boy rub his puffy eyes with his hands. "We sang the alphabet song and Auntie Sherry played the ukulele." Auntie Sherry was the aide, and Lei smiled at the thought of the big Hawaiian lady in her bright muumuu accompanying the kids with the small guitarlike instrument.

"I hope someone recorded it."

"Mrs. Hayashi did with her phone."

"Did you sing?"

Kiet shrugged and didn't answer, and Lei felt her heart squeeze.

They'd reached Ellen's house, and Lei turned into the driveway. A small ohana cottage, Ellen Rockford Stevens's place was set off the driveway of a bigger home, nestled under a spreading lychee tree. Her dog, Charlie, a medium-sized stray of unknown breed that she'd adopted from one of her homeless friends, barked a greeting from the porch, his plumy black-and-white tail wagging. Ellen came to the door.

"How's my favorite grandson?" she exclaimed. Kiet fumbled

his seat belt off and opened the truck's door himself, hopping down and running to give his grandma a hug.

Lei followed more slowly, carrying Kiet's backpack. Her mother-in-law was a few inches taller than Lei, with a slender build and Stevens's crystal-blue eyes. Ellen had been painfully thin when Lei met her, physically ravaged by alcoholism. Five years of healthy living in Hawaii had brightened her eyes, cleared up her complexion, and put healthy, toned flesh on her frame. She now worked from home as a paralegal, a profession she'd had when Michael and his brother, Jared, were young, and taught yoga three times a week at the senior center.

Her eyes met Lei's as Kiet embraced her. "I was sad to hear of Michael's plans," Ellen said to Lei over the little boy's head.

"Me too. Our boy here had a hard day at school."

"Did you, now?" Ellen dropped to her knees in front of Kiet. "You know, Daddy is my little boy and I miss him, too. Thank God I have you. Today's a day for ice cream and cartoons, don't you think?"

"Yes!" Kiet exclaimed, glum face brightening. He clapped his hands and ran into the house, Charlie following him with an excited yap.

"Oh, Lei." Ellen opened her arms, and Lei leaned in for a hug, squeezing the older woman tightly. They'd been through a lot of slow, steady healing in the five years since Ellen had moved to Maui, landing on Lei and Stevens's doorstep. "I'm so sorry he decided to go through with deployment. But we know alcoholism, however it gets started, is a cunning, baffling, and powerful disease. It makes people do crazy things."

They'd never come right out and talked about her husband's drinking. Lei had never wanted to go there even though Ellen had left openings to talk about it before. Even now she felt defensiveness rise up but die again as she gazed into Stevens's mother's steady eyes, so like his.

Ellen would know alcoholism when she saw it, even in her own son.

"He says part of why he's going is to get sober."

Ellen shrugged. "He wouldn't listen to me when I told him pulling a geographical wasn't going to work. But I told him anyway."

"Well." Lei gave a deliberate shrug. "Let go and let God, right?" One of the twelve-step sayings her dad, Wayne, sometimes used.

"Let go or go nuts, is what I say."

Lei snorted a reluctant laugh. "Thanks for taking Kiet. I wanted to pick him up today because I suspected he'd be upset, and I'm glad I did. But without Michael doing half the pickup, I need help. Can you get him on days I can't? I've got a fresh case right now that's taking every extra minute."

"Sure. Of course. In fact, I'd be able to pick him up the rest of the week."

"Nana! Come watch cartoons!" Kiet called from inside.

"Thanks again." Lei walked back to the truck, raising a hand to her mother-in-law. Ellen would bring Kiet home and Wayne would watch him until Lei got home, whenever that was.

Back on the road to the station, she thought over the search they'd done of Danielle Phillips's University of Hawaii office.

Dr. Farnsworth, the UH department head, was an imposing woman with iron-gray hair in a tousled shag and a mass of handmade bead jewelry decorating a substantial chest.

"I can't tell you how saddened I am to hear about Lani." Farnsworth's eyes were red-rimmed. "I put together this list of friends and colleagues of hers, but everyone's reaction has been the same: We're all shocked and grieved."

"I'm sure. Thanks so much." Lei took the list. "Do you know if there was a computer password?" She indicated the desktop and laptop computers on the victim's cluttered desk.

"I'm sure she had her own passwords."

"We'll have to take them in, then. Temporarily," Lei said, even as Pono went around unplugging. Gloved up, they had done a thorough search of the small space, and by the time Lei had to leave to get Kiet, they had a small pile of files that looked potentially interesting, most notably Danielle's file on Ben Miller.

Now she was on the way to a brief meeting with Captain Omura before she and Pono left to search the victim's primary residence. She pulled into the station and hurried inside, meeting Pono, already seated, in front of Omura's desk.

Her commanding officer for years now, Captain C. J. Omura was aging gracefully. Omura's sparkling dark eyes had a few creases beside them, and she'd succumbed to wearing heels of a slightly lower height. Otherwise, the elegant captain was unchanged.

"Glad you could join us, Texeira." Omura cocked a finger at Lei. "I didn't want to grant Stevens's military leave, for what it's worth. I denied it, and he went over my head. Felt like busting him down a rank for that alone." Omura's diamond-hard eyes glinted. "So you'll pardon me if I wish him a little bout of diarrhea or fleas over there in the Middle East, or wherever he ended up."

"You aren't the only one he left short-handed." Lei brushed down her black jeans briskly. "Thanks for understanding. I'm going to be covering parenting for both of us for the next six months, and I know it's going to play hell with my schedule."

"That's why I'll let you go home after the searches. I'll put a couple more crime techs on processing the evidence you two bring in."

"Thank you, Captain. What has Pono brought you up to speed on?"

"What's been done so far on the case?" Omura tapped her manicured nails together, a castanet-like clicking.

"Well, we're following up in several directions at once. We're headed out to search the house now. We have some interesting files from her office to comb through. We have her stalker, Ben Miller, to bring in. We have the list of illegal fish poachers."

"What do you think is most urgent?" Omura asked.

"The home search," Lei said promptly.

"Why? Bringing in Ben Miller seems like a priority. And following up with these cited fishermen from the list the DLNR gave us." Omura touched the document in question.

"I've got a feeling about the husband," Lei said. "And I want to search Danielle's things. Get to know her better."

"I told you, I think you're off about the husband this time." Pono fiddled with his Oakleys, spinning them by one of the stems. "The doer was most likely one of the fishermen, realizing she was photographing. Or maybe the stalker, following her out there. The husband has an alibi, and the logistics alone are near impossible."

"I know. But we need to probe everything. Something was strange about his worry about Danielle, and then the lack of follow-through—to not report her missing when he knew she was doing something dangerous like scuba diving alone," Lei said.

"All right. Here's how I want you to tackle this list of leads. Have a couple of uniforms go out and scoop up Ben Miller and bring him in for an interview. Meanwhile, go to the victim's house and do the search. We want to see if Danielle had any secrets of her own besides the DLNR reporting. Then search the

Zodiac. That ought to take you through dinnertime." Omura already had her eyes on her computer screen. "Dismissed."

Pono wanted to call home before they left, and that reminded Lei that she wanted to pick up the extra set of keys to their house and cars that Stevens kept in his office desk, in case anyone got into it while he was gone.

She jogged up a floor to the administrative level, where the background functions of the Maui Police Department took place—the bookkeeping department, administrative support, regular tech department. It was also the floor where Stevens's office was located. Lei hurried to the door with LT. M. STEVENS on it—and noticed it was ajar.

She pushed it lightly with a finger, looking inside. A young woman, shapely in a tight-fitting uniform, was sitting at her husband's desk. "Help you?"

Lei frowned at the sight. "Saw the door was open. This is my husband's office. He's on military leave."

"Oh. I share his office." The woman stood up, straightening her shirt, and came around the desk with her hand extended. "My desk is right here." She indicated the similar setup across from Stevens's area. "I was just on his computer doing some reports. You must be Sergeant Texeira. I'm Sergeant Kathy Fraser. Michael's partner." Fraser had deep blue eyes under dark brows, neatly braided long brown hair, and a firm handshake. "We worked closely together training the new recruits. I'm covering his duties for him."

Lei kept her expression neutral with an effort, the back of her neck prickling with heat. She didn't like finding this attractive female in her husband's space. "Funny. He never mentioned you."

Fraser had a strained tightness around her mouth, but she flapped a hand dismissively. "Oh, well. It was boring stuff.

Presentations, PowerPoints, training exercises. I'm sure you're too busy with cases to keep up with each other's activities. Though I told him months ago I thought it was a bad idea for him to go overseas."

"Months ago?" Had her husband told Fraser his deployment date and kept it secret from Lei? The betrayal stole her breath. There must be some mistake. "It was a sudden deployment."

"I guess, relatively, but he had to have immunizations and such, and we had to plan coverage for him." Fraser must have seen the savage expression on Lei's face, because she retreated hastily behind the desk. "I told him he was crazy. Seriously, I tried to talk him out of it, and not just because I have to cover his duties. But if you have any questions about my use of his desk, I'm sure Captain Omura can answer them." Fraser sat down and looked pointedly at her computer, clicking the mouse as if too busy to talk.

Lei stood there for another moment. Her mouth was dry, stomach roiling, fists balled. He'd known his departure date for months and he hadn't told her. But she couldn't let it on to this woman. It was too humiliating. "Well, I came up for his spare keys. In the desk."

"Oh. Of course." Fraser pulled out the middle drawer, grabbed the keys, and set them on the edge of the desk closest to Lei.

She knew right where they were.

Lei scooped the heavy handful of metal into her hand. "It was nice to meet you," she managed.

"Likewise." Fraser looked up with a bright, fake smile.

Lei shut the office door behind her a little harder than necessary. She really, really needed to talk to Stevens, and she needed a moment to compose herself. She went to the women's room. After using the stall, she eyed herself in the mirror over the sink as she washed her hands.

"You look like hell," she muttered. Her hair roiled around her freckle-spattered face in a mass of frizz, most of it twisted back harshly in a ponytail. Her tank top and jeans had dog hair on them, and as usual, she wore no makeup.

Why would Stevens have been talking about his plans to beautiful, well-put-together Kathy Fraser? He'd been so secretive with Lei—she hadn't even known he was going at all until after the contract was signed.

Fraser was his partner. The woman probably had to know because she had to cover Michael's duties. He probably hadn't told Lei because he knew how pissed she was going to be. He'd waited until the last minute to tell her when he was leaving, hoping to avoid more drama.

Lei did some relaxation breaths and splashed water on her face. *It's probably nothing.*

But she didn't really believe that. She wanted to scream at Stevens, rip the hair right out of his head, and kick his ass for good measure. She couldn't help remembering the complicated loyalties they'd dealt with during his marriage to Anchara—they hadn't slept together until after his divorce, but their love for each other had been a betrayal of another kind.

Could that be happening again?

Lei paced and breathed, not leaving the bathroom until she had her face and demeanor back under control. This was simply going to have to wait until she could talk to Stevens about it.

Back at her cubicle, Lei won the coin toss this time, and they took her silver Tacoma back out to the pretty house in Wailuku Heights.

Lei frowned as they turned into the driveway. The garage door was down, but there was a car parked in front, a cream-colored Mercedes coupe. "Someone's visiting."

They parked behind the Mercedes. Lei snapped on latex

gloves at the doorstep, setting down her crime kit, as Pono rang the bell.

No answer.

"They must be distracted." Pono leaned on the bell this time.

The door finally opened. Frank Phillips faced them, pushing thinning black hair back with a hand. His shirt was unbuttoned, exposing hairy six-pack abs over a pair of jeans.

"We're here to search the premises." Pono handed Phillips the warrant. Lei averted her eyes from the man's disheveled appearance, brushing past Phillips and walking into the house. She had a target for her rage, and it was whatever lay at the back of the house.

"I'll begin in the bedroom," Lei said over her shoulder. She strode down the carpeted hall.

"Hey!" Phillips exclaimed, grabbing Lei's arm.

Lei stopped, eyes narrowed. "Remove your hand. Or I'll remove it for you."

Phillips took his hand off her arm. "I demand to know what this is about."

"Standard operating procedure in any homicide," Pono said. "Remember what we told you at the station? We always search the home of the victim. Haven't you watched *CSI*?"

"Hey!" Phillips yelled after Lei. "I'm calling my lawyer!"

Lei pushed open the bedroom door. She came to an abrupt halt as a blond woman in the king-sized bed drew black satin sheets up to her chin with a squeal.

Chapter 8

Frank Phillips, Pono in pursuit, came to a halt beside Lei. "I can't believe it's legal for you to barge into my home like this!"

"It's legal, all right." Lei felt a righteous anger boil up through her from someplace deep inside. "I'm looking at some nice motive right here. Not sure your wife is cold in the morgue yet, Frank, and yet here you are, banging a bottled blonde."

"I'm naturally blond, thank you very much. And I'd appreciate a moment to change." The woman tried to gather some dignity.

"I don't believe we got your name," Lei said.

"Barbara Selzmann. Can I get a moment of privacy?"

"This is outrageous!" Frank blustered. "Harassment!"

"We'll give you a moment. But only a moment. Feel free to call your attorney, Frank. You're going to need one." Lei gave him a ferocious smile.

She hated Frank Phillips at this moment. Married to a dedicated, passionate, beautiful woman like Danielle and screwing some country-club matron on the side? That's what Barbara Selzmann looked like, from her expensively touched-up hair to the diamond tennis bracelet that winked from her wrist.

Lei couldn't help thinking of Kathy Fraser, sitting at her husband's desk. Touching his keys. Knowing important business that he hadn't told Lei, his wife.

Lei stomped through the house, hearing the murmur of Pono's voice in the background. She looked for where Danielle had been sleeping—because she was almost sure it wasn't in the king-sized sleigh bed with those tacky black satin sheets in the master bedroom.

Lei turned into a guest bedroom done in shades of turquoise and gold, evoking a beach feel. She pulled a drawer out of the night table beside the bed and looked inside: a vibrator; a dog-eared copy of Darwin's *Origin of Species*; a thin, leatherette journal filled with small, precise block printing; and a black Beretta semiautomatic.

Pay dirt.

Lei slid the journal, vibrator, and weapon into evidence bags. Who had Danielle been so afraid of that she needed a handgun? Was it Ben Miller, or was it Frank Phillips? Maybe the journal would hold the answer. She continued on, rifling through the lower drawer, which held nothing but a series of marine biology tomes. A phone charger cord coiled around the nightstand, and Lei realized Danielle's phone must be in the backpack she'd seen so briefly on the Zodiac.

It was important to get that phone. Lei took out her own phone and made a voice memo of that loose end just as Pono came in, shutting the door behind him.

"Awkward," he said, encompassing the scene with Frank Phillips. "I got the blonde's information, in case you're interested. Both of them are coming in for a formal interview tomorrow morning. Frank said they'll both be bringing representation."

"They'll need it." Lei held up the evidence bag with the gun in it. "Danielle was afraid of someone. Who was it? My vote is Frank."

"I'm still not seeing it." Pono shook his head. "The guy's a sleazebag, no doubt, but he's got an alibi."

"We haven't checked it yet, and with this other woman in the picture, I want to probe it extra hard."

"You go right ahead. I just got a call on the radio that they picked up Ben Miller, so let's wrap this up and get back to the station."

The two of them went into speed mode, tossing the blankets and furniture, opening cupboards and pulling out anything that looked of interest. Lei bagged all of Danielle's medications.

"I see an antidepressant here with a psychiatrist's name on it." Lei held up a bottle. "What I don't see is any birth control."

"He could have had a vasectomy or something. He seems older than her, and obviously they weren't sleeping together."

"Obviously." They were looking at a troubled marriage, and Lei felt a twinge of identification again. They had problems, all right—but she sure hoped infidelity wasn't one of them.

They swept through the house, making no effort to clean up or replace the items dislodged or overturned, which they would have done if they weren't in such a hurry. They ended the search in the garage, where Lei pointed out the scuba gear and kayak she'd spotted earlier to Pono.

"This is way too big to be Lani's." She held up a large-sized BCD. "I see gear here for two people. He could have gone with her and come back to shore in the kayak."

"That's a lot to bring in, and I'm not sure what it will tell us," Pono said.

"I'll just photograph everything." Lei took off a glove and felt the gear. "It's dry." She swiped a finger over the larger-sized gear and tank, held up a finger. She showed Pono the dust. "It hasn't been used in a while."

"More evidence he didn't do it."

"I'm going to get a warrant for his work office and financials." One of the things she'd taken from Frank's desk was the card from their Rolodex labeled Financial Adviser with a number on it.

"I still think we should be focusing on the poachers," Pono said, as Lei took the camera out of her crime kit and photographed the scuba equipment and kayak. "I'm willing to lay money on it."

"Getting ready for Vegas?" Lei swiveled to shoot the whole interior of the garage in case there was something they missed. "Okay, I'll spot you lunch if I'm wrong. I think we're done here."

* * *

Lei suppressed surprise at finding that Ben Miller was a six-foot, good-looking athletic man in his late twenties. Somehow she'd expected someone less attractive. The grad student's eyes were bloodshot, and he moved with the exquisite care of the severely hungover, resting his elbows on the steel table and combing tousled, ocean-bleached hair with his fingers.

"I can't believe she's gone," he said, when they'd Mirandized him and started the recorder. "Lani was an incredible person."

"Tell us about your relationship with her." Lei looked down at the phone records for Miller she'd pulled up. They showed multiple, daily phone calls from his number to Danielle's personal cell, and to her surprise, calls from Lani's number back to his in the last week.

"We were having an affair. I loved her. I was trying to get her to leave that piece-of-shit husband of hers."

Lei kept her expression neutral. "When did this begin?"

"Six months ago. I fell in love with her right away. When I first started working with her."

"You mean when she was supervising your PhD," Lei said dryly.

"Yeah. It was against the rules and all that, but we're adults. She tried to get me to give up on her at first, but I wouldn't let her." He looked up. The blue of his eyes seemed to burn against the swollen redness around them. "Are you sure there's no mistake? She's really gone?"

"Yes. She's really gone," Pono said. "And not by accident. We had it from another party that this 'affair' wasn't mutual. That you stalked her."

Miller made a flicking gesture. "She was married. She felt bad. She needed time to see it how it was."

Lei felt a chill blow across her skin, raising the fine hairs on her arms. He seemed normal, but what he was saying was downright creepy, and the conviction in his voice and gaze was a little unnerving. "Tell me more about how she felt bad about your alleged affair."

"She tried to tell me it was wrong, that I was her student. That she still wanted to make her marriage work with Frank. That son of a bitch was screwing around."

Lei made notes about her impressions of Miller and added an item to follow up on Barbara Selzmann's background and how she'd connected with Frank.

"So when did you finally wear down her resistance?" Pono had a harsh note in his voice. He was playing "bad cop," and not doing too poorly at it either. Miller shot him a glare and then fixed his woebegone gaze on Lei.

"We slept together for the first time a week ago."

"That sounds kind of recent for a six-month love affair," Pono said.

"Oh, come on, now," Lei moderated. "She had a lot at stake, didn't she, Ben?"

"Yes, and she was always so conscientious. Always putting others above herself, including that bastard Frank."

"So when you finally...you know...got together..." Lei flashed Miller her dimple, sympathetic and supportive. She should start acting for the community theater; she was getting so good at faking. "Where did that happen? I'm sure it was really romantic."

"We went night diving. Checked a fish-population-count device. And then—in the boat. Under the stars." He covered his face with his hands.

"What day was this?" Pono asked.

"A week ago, I said."

"We can check when the Zodiac was taken out," Lei said gently. "In fact, we're going to search it right after this. She died off Molokini. Where were you yesterday? Tell us a step-by-step rundown."

Miller looked down, picking at a thread on his sleeve. For the first time he seemed uncomfortable. "I was on campus yesterday morning. I have a job at the tutoring center. It doesn't pay much, but it helps keep me going."

Pono made a note and dug in. "I'm having a hard time seeing Dr. Phillips peeling out of her wetsuit and doing the nasty in a rubber boat with her grad student when she'd been treating you like a stalker up until then." He opened one of the files they'd taken from Danielle's office. "She kept a log of your harassment. The phone calls, the times she had to call security to walk her to her car after dark on campus. This affair was all in your sick imagination."

"No!" Miller shot to his feet, then groaned and clutched his head, sinking back into the chair. "It might have been that way at first, but she just needed me to show I was sincere, that I wasn't going to give up. That my love was real. So I respected when she told me to back off, and we worked it out. Then she found out about Frank's affair."

"Oh, how upsetting," Lei said. "That must have been devastating to her."

"Not really. She didn't love him. They were separated pretty much. But it was embarrassing for her."

"So she screwed you to get back at her husband and you took what you could get?" Pono said.

"She was finally ready to accept my love!" Miller had a fanatical glint in his eyes that raised the hair on Lei's arms for a second time.

"So how many times did you sleep with her?" Pono said. "Dates, times?"

Lei could see this dose of reality was jarring to Miller as he groped for a way to make it seem like they'd been together. "She was working on her divorce, so we—we were waiting. She had to be free for us to be together for real."

"So you didn't actually have sex." Pono squinted.

"We might as well have!" Miller's eyes were wild. "I mean— we almost did. In the boat that night."

A pause as Pono rolled his eyes. Lei reached over to pat Miller's hand. "So you were at the tutoring center all day yesterday?" Lei prompted.

"Do I need to get a lawyer?" Miller seemed to finally realize he wasn't looking good in their estimation.

"Of course not. Just ruling out everyone close to Lani. Totally routine." Lei took out the fingerprint kit and DNA swab. Miller opened his mouth and let her collect it and cooperated with the fingerprinting.

"Anything else you can tell me about Danielle, her friends,

her work?" Lei smiled encouragingly as she put away the evidence collection.

"Well, she was determined to help protect the reefs," Miller said. "When we went out together, she was always looking for poachers, trying to gather evidence for the DLNR."

"Did she have any enemies that you know of?"

"She had one fisherman she'd turned in for illegal aquarium-fish harvesting. I saw them get into it. He came up to her at the docks, and they had words. He threatened her if she ever messed with him. I had to go over, lend backup."

"Who was this guy?" Pono asked.

"I didn't get a last name, but his first name was T.J."

"What did he look like?" Lei was taking notes to crosscheck the list they'd received from Mark Nunes of fishermen who'd been cited.

Miller shrugged. "Five ten or thereabouts, bald-headed and tan, looked like a local. Lots of tats."

"Did you see what he drove?"

"A white Ford pickup. He used a Zodiac, too. They're easy in and out of the water, fast for getting into and out of places like La Perouse Bay or Honolua Bay, where there are a lot of fish in protected water."

"Anything else?"

"I would never, ever hurt Lani." Lei had given Miller a wipe to get the ink off his fingers, and he was still rubbing his hands with it as he stood.

"Don't leave town." Pono opened the door for the young man.

"Screw you. I'd have given my life for her." Miller brushed past Pono and out into the hall. They waited until he was out of earshot.

"I like him for it." A wolfish grin showed all Pono's teeth.

"He's creepy, I'll grant you that. I'm looking forward to reading her journal."

They took the recording equipment and left the interview room. Evening was casting long shadows outside the windows as Pono patted her shoulder.

"I'll make sure the techs are working on all the stuff we've collected. Why don't you get home to that boy? I'll call if anything new breaks, and we have a full day tomorrow."

"Thanks, partner." Lei couldn't wait to get home to Kiet and see how he was doing after his rough day at school. She also wanted to talk to her husband on the satellite phone he'd left.

Chapter 9

Kiet ran out to meet her as he usually did, his face much happier than when she'd picked him up earlier. "Hey, little man. Mama's going to grab the phone Daddy left and check it; then I'll throw the ball with you for a while." Kiet was already wrestling Conan's favorite ball away from the big Rottie as Lei ran into the house.

"Hey, Dad!"

"Hey, Sweets. Dinner's ready in a few." Wayne was in the kitchen, running some water. Lei's father turned to her with a smile, light from the rustic overhead sconce falling on his salt-and-pepper curls.

"Thanks. I'm throwing a ball for the kids outside." Lei looked around for the phone.

Stevens had left the satellite phone, a slightly larger and heavier button-type model than her usual one, on the sideboard on top of a boldly printed Post-it note: *I LOVE YOU*, with his signature smiley face. It made her heart squeeze.

Kathy Fraser was just his work partner. Hell, she told Pono things she didn't tell Stevens, and it didn't mean anything.

But some part of her still didn't believe it.

She checked the phone's screen. No calls. No texts, either.

And now wasn't the time to try to get ahold of him and text him about Fraser—their son was waiting for her. She slid the phone into her pocket and went outside.

"Do a little windup," she told Kiet, backing up onto one leg and cranking the old softball that was Conan's favorite toy. The younger Rottweiler bolted after the ball, his shiny, muscular hindquarters propelling him in great leaps across the length of grassy lawn. He pounced on the ball, his powerful jaws engulfing it, and trotted back, head high and proud. Keiki looked on with dignity, such silliness beneath her in her golden years.

Kiet grabbed the ball out of the big Rottweiler's mouth and imitated Lei's windup, but let go of the ball too soon. It hit the ground early, causing Conan to fishtail to a halt and look at the little boy reproachfully.

"I can do it better." Kiet did his windup, pink tongue showing a little in the corner of his mouth in earnest effort.

Lei felt a pang of love for the boy. The tension unwound from her body as the little boy threw the ball, and the dog ran, and her beloved old girl Keiki leaned her considerable weight on Lei's legs. The last of the salmon-pink sunset light bled out of the sky and rendered the yard in shades of deep blue, black, and gray.

"Dinner's ready!" Wayne called from inside the house, and they went inside to eat. Sitting down at the mango-wood table Stevens had built out in his workshop, Lei touched the wood he'd planed and sanded by hand. It felt satiny and warm under her fingers, almost as alive as skin, and it reminded her painfully of him. She picked up her spoon and dug into the Portuguese bean soup and cornbread her father had made.

"Delicious, Dad."

"Just a little extra I had left over from the restaurant." Her father's craggy face split in a smile. Wayne's Hawaiian Grinds, his breakfast and lunch restaurant in the old Haiku Cannery building, had been turning a nice profit since the day it had opened.

"I'm surprised you had anything left. This is so *ono!*" Lei dipped a chunk of the cornbread, speckled with bits of jalapeño, into the soup.

"The cornbread is too spicy, Papa," Kiet complained.

"That's why I made you toast." Wayne pushed a slice of toast on a plate toward the little boy, who dipped it in the soup. "So where did Stevens go, exactly?"

"I'm not entirely sure. He said it's classified."

"What's 'classified'?" Kiet asked.

"It's a secret. To make sure everyone is safe." Lei gave her father a meaningful glance, conveying that he shouldn't ask any more questions in front of Kiet.

"He told me he was going to one of three places and he didn't know which one." Kiet spooned up another bite.

"Is that so, little man?" Lei's eyebrows went up.

"Malaysia, Afghanistan, or Korea," Kiet said in his clear little voice, reciting the words as though he'd memorized them.

Lei and Wayne exchanged a glance. This was a lot more than Stevens had told Lei, and each of the names sent a pang of apprehension through her.

"Well, I'm sure Daddy misses us already." Her hand stole down to touch the satellite phone in her cargo pocket. So far no new message had come in.

They finished the meal, and Lei washed up the dishes while Kiet enjoyed his evening half-hour ration of TV. Wayne joined her in the kitchen. He took a clean, wet plate out of her hand and dried it.

"I don't like where Kiet said he went. What is this outfit he's working for called?"

Lei sighed. "I feel bad now, Dad, because I didn't ask enough questions. I was so mad at him that I just kind of stuck my head in the sand about it all. I know the company is called Security Solutions, and according to Michael, the gig is to train military police in investigation and security techniques. He told me he wasn't sure where he was going, and he couldn't tell me even if he knew. The sat phone was all he could do to make sure we had some line of communication. I keep checking it, but so far, nothing."

Wayne took another washed plate from her, dried it. "I'm keeping him in prayer with our group." Active as a lay minister in his church and a sponsor in AA, Wayne was consistent in his approach to every kind of life stress, and Lei had come to find comfort in the certainty of his faith, and to share it. Lei and Stevens now attended the same church he did, but Lei was still too busy with work to get very involved.

"Thanks for that, Dad." They finished the dishes in companionable silence, and Wayne dropped a kiss on Lei's head.

"I'll pick the little man up from school tomorrow. Ellen and I worked it out for the rest of the week."

"You two. I don't know if I could keep all this going without you!" Lei dried her hands on a dishtowel and turned to hug her father. "Thanks so much. For being there for me."

"I like to think it helps make up for all the times I wasn't there for you. When you were younger." Wayne's arms tightened around her. "So much happened to you I couldn't do a thing about."

"Water under the bridge. It was what it was, and I love what we have now." That comment covered his lengthy stretch in prison and the abuse Lei had suffered as a child in his absence. She followed him through the house to the front door. "Thanks for picking Kiet up. He loves his time with Papa."

"Papa's picking me up tomorrow?" Kiet asked from the living room couch.

"That's right, buddy. See you after school." In the doorway, Wayne pulled one of Lei's ringlets playfully. "And I'll fix dinner tomorrow, too. It'll be like old times."

"Seriously. Thanks, Dad. This homicide is taking all I've got."

"And you should have Jared over, too. Kiet loves spending time with him."

"Definitely." Lei's spirits lifted at the thought of seeing Stevens's firefighter brother. He was always full of energy, good humor, and interesting stories.

Later, after she'd supervised Kiet's shower, read him his stories, and tucked him into bed, she changed into her favorite tank top and boxers. Turning to face the big king-sized bed, she felt the emptiness too much to settle there. Carrying Danielle's journal, she went back to the guest room, where she'd slept for the last two months.

In the little twin bed, Lei curled up with the slim leatherette volume. Made for taking science notes in the field, it had a water-resistant cover and thin, lined pages. Danielle had clear, concise writing. Most of the journal was impersonal: a list of fish counts in certain areas, tidal and ocean conditions, and reef descriptions, until the last couple of entries.

I'm not sure how long Frank and I can continue to keep up this farce. I found a bill for a credit card I didn't know he had, and on it were charges for dinners out on days he said he had work meetings and for hotel rooms here on Maui when he told me he had CPA trainings off-island.

He's having an affair. Some part of me can't believe it, when he's the one who pursued me until I married him. I wonder if we'd been able to have a child, whether it would have changed anything. If we would still have ended up in this place. But that wasn't meant to be. That's all I've been able to figure out from all the miscarriages.

I realize that the strong feeling I had when I knew for sure about his affair wasn't grief at knowing that he betrayed me, but relief.

He doesn't love me. I don't love him. Nothing remains but to formalize it. He's not going to make the divorce difficult.

So now I've had a consultation with a lawyer I've heard is good, Meg Slaughter. I hope she "slaughters" him, ha-ha! In the meantime, I'm still dealing with so much. The DLNR really needs the photos I've been giving them; there's so much to do...

Another entry:

I slept with someone...I still don't know if I should have. It had been too long since I'd been with anyone, and there he was in the moonlight, looking hot with his wetsuit off, saying he loved me. It felt so good to hear, and I feel something for him, too. Something new and full of possibilities. I was going to wait with him until Frank and I divorce, but what the hell. If Frank can screw someone and still look me in the eye in the morning, I can do it, too.

Lei frowned. The personal entries weren't dated, and there were only two of them. It looked like Ben Miller might have been telling the truth when he implied they'd slept together.

Lei had been hoping for so much more information from the journal, but at least she knew now that Danielle had been in the process of getting a divorce. Not having a child was an element of the marriage's breakdown. Lei had seen no evidence that having a child improved a troubled marriage, but not getting pregnant when you wanted to definitely didn't help.

She knew that from first-hand experience. Her hand slid down to touch her flat belly in a familiar gesture.

Lei shut the book after using her phone to photograph the relevant pages and e-mailing them to her work computer. Meg Slaughter, Esq., was one more name to add to the long list of follow-ups.

Chapter 10

L ei and Pono stood on either side of the drawer as Dr. Gregory popped the clasp and pulled out Danielle's body. A waft of chemicals and the faint scent of decomp made Lei's fingers curl, but she held her ground as Dr. Gregory lifted back the sheet to expose the body.

Danielle had been covered in her black rubber suit until her autopsy, so Lei hadn't had a good look at her body before. As always, she was struck by the stark contrast between a live and a dead body. Danielle's once-tan skin, now sallow, was marked by the pale lines of a bikini. Triangles of lighter skin over her breasts sharply contrasted the crude stitches of the Y incision left by the autopsy. The woman's face looked like a plastic mask, faintly purplish with lividity from floating facedown. She'd had a nice figure, slim and shapely—but all the definition was lost as the muscles degenerated.

"She died of exsanguination and drowning, almost simultaneously," Dr. Gregory said. "It's kind of hard to tell which came first. The spear hit a major artery, and she essentially bled out internally." He used a ballpoint pen to illustrate the dark coloration around the abdomen. "Lividity was less extreme than usual due to the body floating in the water, but she was facedown when you found her, right?"

"Right," Lei confirmed, feeling a little queasy as she imagined the moment of Danielle's death. "One of her legs was trapped between some coral and held her in place."

"That was no accident," Dr. Gregory said. "She was likely put there after she drowned. The lungs were full of water. What I think happened was this: she was shot, at close range, I believe, judging by the small size of the spear shaft."

"We were just wondering about doing a reconstruction," Pono said. "I was thinking it would be fun to shoot some spearguns into a pig underwater, or something."

"Fun idea!" Dr. Gregory grinned, but shook his head. "Not necessary. I can tell the range was close to drive the shaft that deep into her body. Within six feet, I'd say. She was wounded, but might have had time to get to the surface and get help. The murderer didn't want that. Probably wanted time to get away. So he pulled her regulator out of her mouth. She sucked water right away, probably too debilitated by the wound to retrieve her regulator. When it was over, he tucked her leg into the coral head to keep her there."

"Sick bastard." Pono's tone was ripe with disgust.

"Doesn't seem like the impulsive crime of opportunity it would have been for one of the fishermen," Lei said.

"Not necessarily. Someone might have shot her, realized she could still make it to the surface, though without enough stops for off-gassing it would be dangerous. So he could have grabbed the regulator to finish the job." Dr. Gregory took off his glasses and polished them on a paper towel, replaced them, flipping the external loupe lenses aside.

"I don't see how it could have been the fishermen," Lei persisted. "There were two of them. Do you really think they would have done that together? On the fly?"

"But one of them could have held her and the other shot her. Would have made it easy. Anyone who knew her habits could have ambushed her," Pono said.

"What if she was out with someone?" Lei asked.

"Hers was the only gear in the Zodiac," Pono argued.

"First of all, we haven't gone over that yet, so we might find some trace in there or something. Second of all, she could have gone out with someone who went down with her, did the deed, surfaced, and got picked up by an accomplice, then went and retrieved their gear from the Zodiac." Lei was scrambling to think of a way Frank Phillips could have done it, but it still wasn't adding up.

Pono shrugged, looking unconvinced. "I guess."

"Well, you two can haggle over that later. I did her blood work myself to speed things up." Dr. Gregory handed Lei a printed report. "Nothing interesting to report—except that she was pregnant."

"What?" Lei felt the blood drain out of her face, and she grasped the pullout shelf for support, inadvertently touching the cold arm of the corpse. The feeling of the chill, stiff flesh took her straight back to the morgue in Hilo many years ago. She'd had to identify the body of a friend, and she'd never forget it. Pono, close to her side, steadied her—as he'd done that long-ago day.

"She wasn't far along. Just eight weeks or so."

Lei's mind churned. Had Danielle gotten pregnant from her night with that unknown lover? Or had it been her husband? According to the journal, they hadn't been sleeping together—but for how long? Lei took the reports from Dr. Gregory, keeping her face neutral.

"Very interesting development, Dr. Gregory. Could be motive."

"Could be. Or could just be part of the tragedy, which it certainly is. I doubt she even knew she was pregnant."

"Why do you say that?" Lei asked, looking down at the body in front of her. The features were swollen, but Danielle Phillips had once been beautiful. The essence of Lani was long gone from the husk before her, and so was the spark of life she'd carried. "She'd been trying to have a child with her husband for years. According to her journal, she'd had a number of miscarriages. So she might have been very aware of the signs."

Dr. Gregory shrugged. "It was early, is all I'm saying. I checked for sexual activity. Swabs came back negative. The body had been in the water long enough that I don't think I could get an accurate read on that, but I'd still guess she hadn't had sex within the last day."

"According to her journal, she slept with someone who told her he loved her. She had feelings, too, apparently, but had been planning to wait until after her divorce," Lei said.

"I like Miller for it," Pono said. "He's a hot guy. You know. If you notice that kind of thing."

"So you noticed that, too, eh, Pono?" Dr. Gregory teased.

"Like my wife says, and I quote: 'I'm married and straight. Not blind.'"

"Do you need Lani anymore?" Dr. Gregory quirked a brow in question as he indicated the body.

"No. I think she's told us all she can tell us." Sorrow squeezed Lei's chest as Dr. Gregory covered the body up and pushed the shelf back into the refrigerator.

"I'll e-mail the full report to your case file."

"Thanks." Lei made an effort to smile. "I like your shirt." Today's atrocity was bright yellow with tiki gods scattered over it, and his rubber apron featured Garfield curled up in a lasagna pan.

"Keeping things interesting." Dr. Gregory pulled on a fresh pair of latex gloves. "This case looked like a straightforward crime of opportunity to me, but it's getting more complex the more we know."

"Too many suspects and not enough evidence is what we have so far," Lei said. "Is it possible to do a DNA profile on an eight-week-old fetus? It would help us to narrow down who the father was."

Dr. Gregory rubbed his hands together in anticipation. "Oh, definitely. I've never dealt with this situation before. Let me consult with some colleagues and get back to you on that. In the meantime, let me know if you need anything else. I'll take good care of her for you." He patted the steel door of the refrigerator unit almost fondly.

Lei restrained herself from shuddering at what she imagined he'd have to do to get the baby's DNA profile. "Okay. Thanks, Dr. G. Let us know what you find."

Chapter 11

The University of Hawaii Zodiac was trailered in the Coast Guard storage lot. "We found the trailer registered to the University of Hawaii in the parking lot," Petty Officer Aina Thomas said. He was crisp in his uniform, a pair of mirrored aviators hiding his eyes in the bright afternoon sun. "We put the backpack in a storage locker inside headquarters."

"Great." Lei blew into a latex glove, inflating it, and snapped it on. "We're going to go over this craft really carefully for trace."

Sweat was already gleaming in Pono's buzz-cut black hair as her partner bared his teeth in a grim smile. "Fine-tooth comb, baby. Where's that Dustbuster?"

"Right here." Lei clambered up into the rubber craft still mounted on its trailer, carrying the handheld device.

"We've got cold soda inside when you're done," Thomas said. "Let me know when you're *pau,* and I'll get the victim's backpack for you."

"Thanks." Lei turned to face the task ahead of them. "Where should we start?"

"Right here." Pono flipped open the padded bench in front of the outboard motor, rustling through several life vests inside.

"Why don't you dust for prints? Then we can rule out the samples we've already collected."

"Oh, my favorite." Lei eyed the expanse of sun-heated black rubber.

"I think he likes you," Pono commented, still rummaging.

"Shut up."

"No, really. Thomas has a thing for you." Pono pushed his Oakleys back up his gleaming nose with a finger. "He was asking me if you were still married. Said he heard some rumors."

"What rumors?" Lei frowned, twirling white fingerprint powder over the hot rubber. Scores of prints, layered and smeared, leaped into relief.

"Rumors that you and Stevens were separated. That your husband had issues."

"Wonder how that got started. We don't talk about our personal business." Lei squinted at her partner.

"Eh, no look at me, sista." Pono held up his hands.

"Well, if anybody asks, I'm happily married. And my husband is a hero doing more than his duty." Lei was in no mood to joke.

"You don't have to tell me. Just thought you should know."

That knowledge didn't improve Lei's mood. She was already conflicted enough about the handsome Coast Guardsman, and meeting Kathy Fraser yesterday hadn't helped her worries about what was going on in her marriage. She pulled the sat phone out of her pocket to check it yet again. Still no message from Stevens. She squelched the stab of worry twisting her gut.

"Stevens does have issues. Anybody would after what he went through with Anchara's murder. Finding her dying like that. Not able to save her. That's when things went sideways for him." Lei dusted the hot rubber, spinning the soft brush. "Dr. Wilson tells me PTSD affects one in three people exposed to a traumatic event, and Stevens—he's had way more than his share, and it can be cumulative. If he could just get over it, he would have."

"Like I said, you don't have to tell me. I've seen a lot of good cops—firefighters, too, military personnel, victims from our cases—get messed up in the head. He is doing what he thinks he has to do. I just hope like hell it works."

"Me too." Lei wiped her hot forehead with her forearm. "It's costing us. Big-time."

It took the two of them well over an hour to vacuum and dust the whole boat down, and by then Lei was more than ready for the cold root beer Aina Thomas handed her when she went into the Coast Guard building.

"Thanks." She put the cool aluminum can against her forehead with a grateful smile. "Man, it's hot out there, and we have way too many prints to go through now. Got that backpack for us?"

"Yeah. Follow me."

Pono was talking story with one of the clerks, so Lei straightened her shoulders and followed Thomas down a gleaming hall. He unlocked a door and held it open. "After you."

Lei brushed by him, feeling that tingle again, and entered a room lined with shelves. One wall was lined with weapons lockers. Thomas went to a shelf, picked up a plastic-bagged bundle the size of the backpack Lei remembered seeing. It was marked with a big yellow ID tag.

"I climbed onto the Zodiac and bagged and tagged this myself," Thomas said. "If anything is missing since we saw it last, someone would have gone aboard and taken it before we went back to retrieve it."

"Good to know." Lei took the bag and headed for the door.

"Lei?"

"Yes?" Lei looked back, surprised by the use of her first name, feeling a prickle of heat on her chest. Thomas had his hands on his hips, his tilted dark eyes, so much like hers, serious and intent. He was closer to her height than Stevens. Once again, she felt a kinship with him, a sense of recognition.

"I just wanted to say—let me know if you need anything. While your husband is gone. Like if your car breaks down or something." Thomas flushed a little, his neck darkening above the collar of his uniform.

"Thanks, but I'm fine. Got a lot of *ohana* around me." Lei smiled, doing her best to dispel the awkwardness. *So sweet, a real gentleman.* "But I appreciate the kind words."

"Well, if you still want to go out and dive that wreck in Lahaina, just say the word."

"I don't think I can. Our son's having some adjustment issues, and I'm just too busy. Thanks, anyway." Lei pushed the door open and fled down the hall, feeling guilty and terrified by how much she wished she could go diving.

* * *

Lei and Pono dropped the backpack off to the new intern, Kevin Parker, who was working on their evidence processing.

"Full process on this?" Kevin asked, blinking owlishly as he took the bagged backpack.

"Yes. Catalog all the contents. Bring photos of whatever you come up with to the team meeting with the captain," Pono said.

Kevin unzipped the backpack and gently dumped the contents onto the counter. "The phone looks important." He thumbed it on. "Still got a little juice, but it's password protected. I'll give that to Murioka."

Pono turned to Lei. "I found a T. J. Costa on the list of cited fishermen. Let's start with him, since that's the name Miller gave us of the aquarium poacher who threatened Danielle."

The coin toss put them back in Pono's truck. "More time with Stanley." Lei climbed up into the cab and patted the chrome skull.

"Keep it up, Sweets, and I'm going to tell everyone your nickname."

"You wouldn't dare. I'll tell the captain you keep fighting cocks."

"Oh, don't go there, sista." Pono's softhearted adoption of broken-down fighting cocks was a secret from everyone but his long-suffering family, who had to put up with the birds' crowing in the mornings.

Pulling up into an overgrown and cluttered driveway in Kahului, a caged pit bull barking at them, Lei felt the hairs rise on the back of her neck. The house hunched among dead, rusting cars, the windows boarded up. A series of rooster hutches with staked-out fighting birds were visible behind a fence in the backyard.

"Steady." Pono glanced at her.

"I've got a feeling." Lei looked at the house. "Did you run this guy?"

"Yeah. Busted for possession to distribute meth, but it was seven years ago."

Lei still didn't get out of the truck. "I'm getting an illegal-activities vibe off this place."

"Doesn't seem to be anyone home," Pono said.

"Let's approach with caution."

Lei got out of the truck on one side, Pono on the other. She used her door, then a rusted refrigerator for cover as she approached the front door, scanning for threats. Nothing moved but the dog, more hysterical by the minute, and the cocks behind the house, prancing and crowing on their tie-outs.

Up on the little weathered porch, Pono knocked. "Maui Police Department. Open up!" Both of them made sure they were out of range of the door.

No answer.

"Maui Police Department!" Pono boomed.

Lei put her hands on her hips and scanned the yard again. Hidden by a stack of wooden pallets and a tarp was a hard-bottomed Zodiac on a trailer. She pointed.

"New. And that shit piled over it is a disguise."

"I see those white plastic drums they use to move the fish, too." Pono pointed to the pile of empty barrels on the side of the house.

"I wouldn't be surprised if they were cooking meth in here, too." Lei indicated a pile of black-bagged refuse. "Let's return with a warrant and backup."

Lei didn't start to relax until they were heading back down the road. She used the radio to call Dispatch, asking for a unit to surveille the house.

"I'm out of those pre-signed search warrants I won from the judge at poker," Pono said. "So it's going to take a little time to show we have probable cause."

"I'll call in the request." Lei got on the radio again. Hanging up, she rubbed her hands on her pants legs. "Hey, we're over by the husband's CPA office. Let's swing by. Probe his alibi."

Pono narrowed his eyes at her. "He's coming in with the girlfriend tomorrow morning."

"I just want to see if it's possible for him to have been elsewhere. Yes, we established he was working, but nothing like going there in person and getting an eyeball on things."

"This is your bird in the ring." Pono pulled the truck up in front of Phillips's neat little plantation cottage in Wailuku made over into an office.

"Think a cockfighting analogy is appropriate, Detective Kaihale?" Lei teased.

"You go in and check it out. I don't like Phillips for this one. I need a snack before the meet with the captain." Pono unwrapped a stick of beef jerky and reached for the extra soda he'd picked up at the Coast Guard station.

"Fine." Lei slammed the truck's door a little hard and ascended the steps of the neatly restored cottage, twisting her windblown curls into a knot. She showed her badge to a sweet-faced receptionist with a big silk hibiscus in her hair. A little brass sign spelled out A. Vargas on the desk.

"Ms. Vargas. I'm Sergeant Lei Texeira. I'm checking on your boss's whereabouts two days ago."

"Oh. Didn't your office call yesterday?" The woman picked up her phone, and her finger hovered over an intercom button. "I told someone what he did on that day."

"We did call. But we have to be thorough. I'd like a step-by-step rundown of Mr. Phillips's day."

"I'd better tell him you're here."

"He seemed pretty upset when we searched his house earlier today. I think it might be best to just give me the information I'm asking for," Lei said sweetly. "He's so stressed out. And of course we don't think he had anything to do with Danielle's death, but the higher-ups always tell us to look at the spouse closely, so I'm just trying to get my captain off my back. We have a meeting this afternoon..."

"Oh, all right." The receptionist put the phone down and scrolled to a scheduler. "I'll make a copy of his day's schedule."

"Would you? Oh, thanks so much." Lei smiled so hard her cheeks hurt as the woman hit Print on something on her computer. A page filled with little boxes spit out from the printer.

Lei took it, scanned down. "So this part from noon to six p.m. that says 'office hours.' What is that, exactly?"

"He's in his office. Working on people's taxes. It's a high-impact time right now."

"Did you see him? During that time?"

"I don't bother him when he puts his signal on. He had it on all afternoon." She indicated a little LED light over the door. "Means he's in there working."

"Does he ever come out when he has the light on?"

"Mr. Phillips has a small lounge and bathroom attached to his office, so he can stay in there all day, take breaks, and keep up his concentration. He's stressed out, as you mentioned."

"So he was in there all that afternoon. But you didn't physically see him."

"Yes, he was here, and no, I didn't see him after he turned his light on. But all his work was logged in." The receptionist pressed a few more buttons and generated another printout. "The accounts he was working on. This is our auto-billing service. It's connected to work product."

"I think I'd like to have a word with him after all." Lei indicated the door with her head. The receptionist thinned her lips, picked up the phone, and hit the button. It toned. Lei could hear it even through the thick door. *Beep-beep-beep.*

"He must be in the restroom," the woman said. Lei brushed past her and twisted the handle.

"It's locked."

The receptionist got up and knocked. "Mr. Phillips? Frank?"

No answer.

She frowned and took out a key. "Perhaps he's napping. That happens sometimes."

She unlocked the door and opened it. Two former bedrooms with a wall knocked out formed a spacious office area. Lei could see a door that led to the bathroom. The "lounge" was an area with a couch, television, and minibar in one corner. In the other, a large L-shaped desk, piled high with files, adding machine, and computer, stood empty.

The receptionist hovered at her shoulder. "He must have stepped out for a minute."

Lei walked across the room to a large fabric wall hanging, lifted it aside. "What a handy exit." The receptionist looked genuinely upset, her eyes wide and a hand over her mouth, as Lei opened the exterior door and looked outside. Two wooden steps led down to a graveled parking space, empty. "Is this where he keeps his vehicle?"

"Yes," the receptionist whispered. "But that day he uploaded work product. So he had to have been here."

There must be some way to do that remotely, but Lei wasn't going to argue with this loyal employee.

"Please let Mr. Phillips know we look forward to our interview with him tomorrow." She walked down the two steps and around the front of the building, surprising Pono by approaching from a different direction.

"Poked a hole in the husband's alibi." Lei hopped into the truck. "Got to get the tech department to have a look at his work computer—come to think of it, I better take it now. Good thing I brought a copy of that search warrant." She took the copy out of the case file, went back into the office, and rattled the receptionist further by leaving the warrant, which included "all data-storage units." She carted the computer back to the truck over the woman's objections.

"Now we just gotta figure out how he did work that went up into a time-stamped data-storage unit that generates an auto-billing," Lei told Pono. "I hope Jessup is ready for a project."

"Jessup is always ready for work." Pono helped Lei put a seat belt and some spare towels around the computer to steady it in the jump seat of the cab.

Back at the station, Lei texted the young tech to come in. Her phone dinged with a message from Murioka. *Will get on it right after class!!!*

She smiled at the young man's enthusiasm.

Leaving his computers for you at your desk. She slid the phone back into her pocket and headed for the elevator, toting the computer console with Phillips's laptop balanced on top of it. She went down a level and squeezed the equipment onto the worktable in a back room. The most junior of MPD's tech staff had created a nest for himself there with yards of electrical cord, blue Internet cable, and computers in various states of disembowelment.

Her cell phone rang with a call from Pono.

"Time for the team meeting review with the captain," Pono said. "Dr. G has his results of the fetal DNA to share, and Omura wants to review where we are."

"Great. Be right there."

Captain Omura had taken over the conference room, whose table was littered, as usual, with an assortment of doughnut and malasada boxes. She swept all the leftover treats into the garbage, and a waft of haupia pudding scent teased the air.

"Aw, man, boss! Did you have to pitch them all?" Pono groaned. Omura flicked a crumb off her chair and sat down.

"Yes. None of our waistlines needed any of that. Let's review."

Lei looked at the team assembled around the table. Kevin Parker, the young crime scene tech doing an internship from the University of Hawaii's new forensics program, cleared his throat. "I've been working on the trace collected from the boat and searches. I haven't met everyone."

"By everyone I assume you mean me," The portly medical examiner stood up from his chair and extended a hand to the college student. "Dr. Phil Gregory, ME. I'm guessing your captain called this meeting because I got back some information pertinent to the case."

"This is an opportunity to review and was already scheduled," Omura said. "But we're glad you've got some information to add. Texeira, will you keep us organized on one of the boards?"

"Yes, sir." Lei got up and uncapped an erasable pen. She appreciated the chance to keep the discussion moving. "I have some new information, too."

"Then let's get started. What do we know about the victim? Just call out the facts as you know them."

"Danielle 'Lani' Phillips, age thirty-five, only University of Hawaii staff marine biologist on Maui," Pono said. "Five six in height, one thirty-eight in weight, brown hair and eyes, Caucasian and Hawaiian ancestry. Eight weeks pregnant at the time of death." Lei jotted as fast as she could.

"Her hobby was catching ocean poachers while she was out on her research projects," Lei added. "She took reference photos used by DLNR to bust violators, thus providing possible motive."

"She also had a stalker, grad student Ben Miller," Pono said. "First he stalked her and she resisted his overtures; but it seems like they might have slept together before she died."

"I read her journal." Lei noted each of the names on the board as they went along. "It was mostly scientific notes, but there were a couple of undated personal notes. She slept with someone who told her he loved her. I'm wondering if it was Ben Miller.

He was kind of creepy—but an attractive guy. It's possible she just gave in to temptation, since her husband was having an affair."

"Since when was sleeping with a stalker a good idea?" Captain Omura twiddled her pen. "Go on."

"Then there's the husband." Pono inclined his head toward Lei. "Lei's favorite candidate. Today she poked a hole in his alibi."

Lei filled them in on the situation at the CPA's office.

"I'm seeing possibility but not motive." Omura frowned. "Why didn't they just get divorced?"

"I don't know. I'm hoping to find something more when I get into the financials." Lei felt a prickle under her arms and folded them, tightening her jaw. Her gut was still insisting on Phillips. "I think there's more going on with him. And I just don't like the guy."

"Maybe my results will shed a little light on the situation," Dr. Gregory said. "I was able to get the fetus's DNA, a fascinating project. I didn't have to mess with the actual fetal tissue—it was available in the cord and also in the amniotic fluid, in case you're interested. I ran it against Ben Miller and the husband, Frank Phillips. The child was neither of theirs."

Lei sat down abruptly in surprise. She shook her head. "There's someone else in her life."

Dr. Gregory pursed his lips thoughtfully. "I wish I could tell more from the DNA profile. Someday we'll be able to tell not only the sex, but the ethnicity, hair color, and more. All I could do in this case was a comparison with the paternal markers."

"So now we know we don't have all the players in the mix," Omura said. "We're still hashing out all theories here. What are some others?"

"We still need to interview and search the suspicious residence of T. J. Costa, a man who is known to have threatened Danielle," Pono said. "We are waiting on a warrant to search his premises. We saw evidence of some suspicious-looking activity."

"That seems like a viable lead. So does the jilted stalker, Ben Miller. Personally, I'm finding the husband a stretch, Texeira. No motive and unlikely to have been able to physically pull it off. I could see one of the poachers nailing her when he noticed she was taking photos, or Miller going with her on her dive and then turning on her. Perhaps she told Miller she was pregnant and that it wasn't his," Omura said.

"That's my favorite scenario," Pono said. "Miller can't have her, so no one can. He was obsessed with her."

"Kaihale and Texeira, wrap up the day by going out to do the search on this Costa character's house, and if you have more time, dig into Miller's alibi further." Omura stood, straightening her immaculate uniform. "There's more going on. Find it. Dismissed."

* * *

Lei and Pono rolled up T. J. Costa's driveway in her silver Tacoma. The house hunkered, dark and unwelcoming, the boarded-up windows like blinded eyes under overgrown mango trees. As before, the staked-out fighting cocks crowed from the backyard, accompanied by the aggressive barking of the pit bull. But this time, a jacked-up truck with heavy off-road tires and a trailer hitch was parked in front of the house.

The drive-by patrol had reported when the truck had arrived and that it hadn't left.

Lei cinched down her tight, hot Kevlar vest. She had a bad

feeling about this place, and as she got out of her truck with the warrant in her hand, she pointed to the nearby metal can filled with bulky black trash bags. "We want to check some of that."

"Let's talk to the guy first." Pono pushed his Oakleys up on his head as they approached the front door.

The dog barked frantically, heaving its heavily muscled brown body against the metal sides of the cage, adding to a sense of danger that made Lei's hands prickle.

They ascended worn wooden steps onto the porch, cluttered with an outboard motor with a broken blade, a stack of chicken cages, and a disorderly pile of old rubber slippers. Standing to the side of the door, Pono reached over and pounded on the hollow wood.

No answer.

He pounded again. "T. J. Costa! Open up! This is Maui Police Department!"

No answer.

"Maui Police Department!" Pono yelled again. Lei, leaning close to the door, thought she heard the sound of running feet inside.

She pulled her weapon and leaped back down the steps, weaving around discarded boxes piled against the house and a hibiscus bush that scratched her with lank, tangled branches. Lei heard the crash of the back door closing as she reached the corner. The rooster fence, a six-foot chain-link pen, interfered with her approach, and she ran along it, scanning for whoever had exited the house. She tripped over a stack of lumber, heart thundering as she caught sight of a fleeing man heading for a metal toolshed deep in overgrown bushes.

"Halt! Maui Police Department!" Lei bellowed as the man reached the shed and threw open the door, revealing a four-wheeled all-terrain bike. She bolted around the chain-link fence toward him, weapon in ready position, as he jumped on the quad. "Stop! Police!"

The man's eyes were narrowed and glittering under a black ball cap in the dimness of the shed. He lifted his hand. The flash of metal in it made her dive for the hard-packed, weedy ground.

The quad started with a roar.

Lei rolled, seeking cover behind the rounded white shape of the house's propane tank. Peeking around it, she spotted Pono's jeans-clad legs running toward her position.

Her heart seemed to stop.

"Gun!" she yelled.

Too late. She heard the weapon discharge from the shed, a boom like a cannon. She saw her partner stumble and go down on one knee.

Her heart thundering, the red dirt of the yard thick in her nose, Lei jumped up and aimed as best she could around the metal cylinder toward the quad, but heard it accelerate, crashing through the bushes.

Lei stood up fully, firing after the fleeing vehicle, discharging the rest of her clip after the shooter in a burst of adrenaline-fueled rage as she ran after it. The quad bounced through the yard and, tires squealing, careened onto the road.

Lei pulled her radio off her belt and called for help, as she turned toward Pono, terrified of what she would see.

"Shots fired! Officer down!" Yelling the emergency codes, Lei ran to her partner, who'd collapsed onto his side on the hard-packed dirt.

Chapter 12

"I'm okay," Pono growled. Blood oozed between the thick brown fingers clutched around his upper arm. "Bastard just winged me."

"You sure? Let me check you out." She pushed Pono to lie down flat. "Keep pressure on it." She ran to get a piece of lumber from the pile, elevating his feet on top of it. "I'll find something to cover the wound."

"Stop fussing, damn it." But Pono was pale under his tan, gritting his teeth as shock set in.

Lei looked around hurriedly. She spotted a roll of paper towels inside the toolshed. She ran over and grabbed it, pulling off a wadded handful. Her quick visual sweep of the shed's interior revealed bags of chicken and dog food and assorted tools. Returning to her downed partner, she pried Pono's fingers off his wound, packing the paper towels against it.

"I'm okay," Pono repeated, but his voice was weak. "Let me up. We need to get that guy."

"I called it in. They'll get him. And I'm not okay. My partner's just been shot." Lei's voice wobbled. Pono's Oakleys had fallen off, and that more than anything brought a wave of tears to her eyes. She tried not to think about what it would be like to have him die—it was too horrible to contemplate. She kept pressure on his arm, reaching out to retrieve the sunglasses and sliding them awkwardly onto his forehead. "Tiare's going to kick my ass for letting something happen to you."

They heard the wail of approaching sirens. "Don't worry about that." Pono gestured with his chin toward the house. "Do the search. Get the guy."

"Not until I know you're going to be okay." Lei knelt beside her best friend, the man she thought of as the brother she'd never had. Her hands pressed on his wound, and she thanked God silently for another lucky escape.

The ambulance arrived, disgorging a team with a gurney as their backup arrived. Lei surrendered her partner to the EMTs' expertise as they shouldered her out of the way, kneeling beside him. She stood, wiping Pono's blood off her hands on another paper towel with a sick feeling.

One of the backup officers approached. "You all right, Sergeant?"

"Yeah, thanks." He handed her a packet of germicidal wipes, and she cleaned up as best she could, turning to look around the nearby toolshed. She gestured to cases of cold remedies behind the chicken feed. "Looks like meth production going on here." She had a phone call to make before she took another officer to search the house. "I'll be right with you. Can you get started searching?" The officer nodded, and Lei held down a speed dial number on her phone.

"Hey, Lei." Tiare's voice was brisk and no-nonsense. Pono's wife was a busy nurse and wedding planner, and Lei must have caught her in the middle of something. "What's up?"

"Tiare, Pono's been shot. Just an arm wound. But they're taking him to the hospital." She glanced over at the EMTs, who were loading the big Hawaiian onto a gurney. "I have to keep working our case, but I wanted you to know right away."

A pause. "How bad?" Tiare asked. Her matter-of-fact tone hadn't changed. "I'm on shift at the hospital, so I can go meet the ambulance."

"Not bad. But it's a gunshot and looks painful." Lei pinched the bridge of her nose with her forefinger and thumb. "He needs to get thoroughly checked out. I'm sorry."

"You better be. You both can tell me how it happened later." Tiare punched off.

Lei exhaled a long breath and accompanied the gurney to the ambulance.

"I don't need all this," Pono was protesting to the medical personnel. "I can walk, for God's sake."

"Protocol," the EMT said.

Lei laid a hand on his good arm. "I called Tiare. She's already at the hospital, working, so she said she'd meet you."

Pono groaned. "I'm going to be in so much trouble." His rich brown complexion was ashy with shock, and beads of sweat shone on his forehead.

"Not you. Me. I let you get shot."

"Hell, no. I shouldn't have just run out like that. Getting sloppy in my old age," Pono grumbled as they slid the gurney into the ambulance. "When do I get some pain meds?" he asked plaintively.

"I'll see you later, bro," Lei called after him as the metal doors shut. She watched the ambulance go, hands on her hips, then sighed out a breath. Her knees trembled with adrenaline overload. She turned toward the back door of the house, raising the radio to her lips as she gestured to the uniformed officers who'd arrived in response to her earlier call for backup.

"Dispatch. Any luck catching the suspect on the four-wheeler?" she said into the mouthpiece.

"Negative, Sergeant," Dispatch replied. "Responders found the vehicle ditched a few blocks over."

Lei paused to swear. "Put out a priority BOLO on T. J. Costa. Circulate his photo everywhere." She rattled off the address, though as she replaced the handheld, she realized she didn't know if the suspect, unrecognizable under a ball cap and in the heat of the moment, really was Costa.

She gestured to the officers. "Follow me. We're looking for evidence related to the scuba homicide."

Chapter 13

The back door of Costa's residence fed directly into the filthy kitchen. Dishes piled in the sink buzzed with flies, and bags of smelly garbage lined a wall. Lei stalked through the room, weapon drawn, tripping a little on the peeling linoleum.

"Maui Police Department!" she called, for the benefit of any remaining inhabitants. She was pretty sure the house was empty, but it never paid to make assumptions. "Step out with your hands on your head."

No answer or reply. Lei peeked around the doorway of the kitchen into the living room, gesturing to one of the officers to check the nearby hallway.

In a few moments they swept through the house, making sure it was clear. Lei then went through each room for a closer look. In one of the bedrooms, large white plastic oil barrels were filled with darting ocean fish. The room was kept cool with a wheezing air conditioner.

The bedroom next to it contained long tables set with Crock-Pots crusted with the remnants of meth cooking.

It took hours to clear the place of all the evidence she wanted collected, and she ended up having to call in their evidence processing tech after handing off the meth-related part of the retrieval to a couple of the narcotics detectives.

"Kevin, how should we deal with these fish?" she asked the pimply-faced intern, standing over one of the open barrels. Inside, bright yellow tangs, darting Moorish idols, and a couple of spiny puffer fish paddled around a central bubbler.

"I'll photograph them. Then we should call the DLNR and have them take the fish back and let them go," Kevin said. "They'll have the right transport vehicles and should be able to make sure the fish don't die of shock getting reintroduced to the ocean."

"Good idea."

Lei got on the phone to Mark Nunes, the agent they'd interviewed about Danielle's involvement with the agency.

"Mark, hi. It's Sergeant Texeira. I've found some barrels of reef fish during our investigation at a private residence. No way to tell at this point where they came from, but they need to be returned to the ocean. Can you deal with them?"

"Absolutely. I'll bring transport. On my way."

Lei hung up after giving him the address, liking the man's prompt response and still a little curious about his relationship with Danielle. This was another chance to see him in action. She continued her search, working her way to the garage, a lean-to stuffed to the brim with Costa's packrat collection of odds and ends. There, under a pile of wetsuits in decent shape, she discovered a Mares speargun of the right size.

She bagged it, along with a wetsuit that was still damp. She found more dive gear out by the small Zodiac with an eight-horse Honda that she was pretty sure could set a speed record out to Molokini. She photographed it thoroughly.

T. J. Costa was shaping up to be her prime suspect. She still flushed with rage thinking of him shooting Pono. Impatient, she picked up her radio and called Dispatch again. "Anything on our suspect?"

"Negative, Sergeant. We'll let you know. It's a top priority."

She had to be content with that for the moment. She busied herself by collecting fingerprints off the door of the storage shed. Hopefully Costa, or whoever the shooter was, already had prints in the system.

Nunes drove up in a heavy duty white county truck with another male agent in the front seat. His jaw was stubbled and his eyes looked heavy, his uniform creased. The two agents lowered a hydraulic gate off the back of the truck loaded with a large dolly, and Nunes wheeled it toward Lei. "Which way to the fish barrels?"

"Follow me." Lei flipped down a wooden ramp that covered the stairs leading into the house. "This must be the way he gets the barrels in and out."

"What a sty." Nunes wrinkled his nose as he followed her to the back bedroom.

"He was cooking meth, too. Didn't leave much time for housekeeping. Here we are." Lei pointed to the row of huge barrels. The room was cool, thanks to the window AC unit, and smelled salty and fresher than the rest of the house. "I know this is a long shot, but we're still looking for some way to connect this with Danielle's murder. Anything you can tell me about these fish or this perp that puts them together?"

Nunes shook his head regretfully, hands on his hips. "I wish. No, these are just typical Maui reef fish. No telling where they were captured. But Barker and I will take them off your hands, get them back into the ocean."

Barker, a hatchet-faced redhead with a sun-blasted freckled complexion, gave her a brief salute with two fingers before wrestling the barrel onto the dolly with Nunes's help. There was controlled fury in Nunes's movements as he heaved the barrel onto a dolly, preparing to follow Barker down the hall, his muscular back straining. His dishevelment and agitation were related to Danielle's death. Lei put an arm on his, stopping him.

"Listen. I need a DNA sample from you."

"Why?" He looked up, bloodshot eyes defensively flaring wide.

"We collected a lot of trace off the UH Zodiac," Lei fudged. "You were out on it a few times with Danielle, right?"

He nodded.

"We need to rule you out."

She helped him with the barrel, steadying it down the ramp, and as he and Barker rode the Tommy lift up onto the back of the county truck, she retrieved a cheek swab from her crime kit.

"Thanks." Lei avoided Barker's interested gaze as she swabbed Nunes's cheek and stowed the sample. She looked at the other man. "Were you ever on the University of Hawaii Zodiac with Danielle Phillips?"

"I never knew her, but I was sorry to hear she's gone." Barker frowned in puzzlement.

"I'll take a sample anyway." Lei did so for form's sake, and patted her kit where she stowed the samples, giving the men a reassuring smile. "Thanks so much."

Nunes ducked his head briefly and headed back into the house with Barker to retrieve the rest of the barrels. Lei left a couple of patrol officers on duty and got into her truck. She had to remember to make a brief stop at the morgue after going to the hospital to check on Pono.

Captain Omura had already heard the news about Pono when Lei reached her by phone.

"Damn sloppy," Omura said. "Am I going to have to put you

two through a remedial course on house approach and suspect apprehension?"

"It went down fast, Captain. In hindsight, we should have assumed Costa was armed. I did find enough possible evidence at the residence to tie him to our vic." She listed the scuba items she'd recovered as well as the confiscated fish. "I'm going to have Kevin go over the scuba items with a fine-tooth comb and check that Mares gun right away."

"Doubtful you will find anything going back to Danielle's body," Omura said. "But if you can match that murder weapon, it would be a good start."

"On it, Captain." Lei hung up.

She didn't mention her stop into Dr. Gregory's lab. Time enough to report on that if anything came of it.

Chapter 14

Pono was sitting on the edge of the emergency room table, his arm wrapped and in a sling, when Lei pulled the curtain on its dangling rings aside. Tiare, statuesque in bright purple scrubs, her thick black hair in a waist-length braid, looked up at Lei's arrival.

"I'll have a word with you later." She narrowed wide brown eyes at Lei, but Lei could tell it was for show. Pono flapped his good hand at his wife's attempt at assisting him off the table.

"Let me get down, woman. I'm fine. It's just a flesh wound. I've always wanted to be able to say that."

"You don't look fine." Lei's partner's color was still off and beads of sweat pearled in his buzz-cut hairline. "You're going home. Omura's orders. And I bet you need to take a couple of days off."

"That's right," Tiare said. "I have the Workers' Comp form started already. You're off for four days minimum."

Pono looked at Lei, an apologetic smile pulling up one side of his mouth. "I'm sorry to leave you holding the bag."

Lei shrugged, striding alongside Pono as he leaned on his wife, walking slowly down the hall. "I'll make do. Omura will just assign me someone else. Of course, no one else will have Stanley and the purple truck."

"Yeah. You just have a thing for my skull." They exchanged a smile. "What did you find inside the house?"

Lei told him the results of the search. "Got Narco involved for the meth cooking, and Mark Nunes with DLNR and his partner took the fish we found back to the ocean. Soon as I get back to the station I'm checking the speargun and all the prints I collected. It occurred to me that we don't know for sure that your shooter was Costa."

"I thought of that already, before the Vicodin addled my brain," Pono said. "Could be a partner or a cousin. Did you get a good look at the guy?"

"No. Five ten or eleven, stocky build, dark hair and eyes, wearing a ball cap," Lei recited. "Could describe half the men on this island, and that's Costa's description, too. But we sealed the house with scene tape and left a couple of uniforms. If Costa comes back, he's going to get a surprise. I figured out how he could have shot Danielle. He might have been out catching fish, spotted her taking pictures of him, killed her, gone back in his Zodiac. Easy peasy."

They'd reached the exit, and Tiare turned aside for a moment to check Pono out at the clerk's desk.

Pono slumped into a chair. "Those pain meds are really making me feel out of it," he murmured.

"I'm sorry, talking your ear off with all of this," Lei said.

"No, it's all good. Keeps my mind off it. But something's bugging me about the poacher motive. Why would Costa commit murder over catching illegal fish, which only carries a fine? He was cooking meth at home, too, and that's a much more serious offense."

"Meth makes you paranoid." Lei shrugged. "He might have

overreacted to seeing Danielle with her camera. Or maybe he didn't want the attention of any authorities for any reason."

"I guess." Pono shook his head with an uncoordinated movement. Tiare left the checkout booth with a sheaf of paperwork.

"Say goodbye to your partner," she said sternly. "No more work for at least a couple of days."

Pono stood, gave Lei a big hug. Lei clung to his sturdy form a little longer than necessary, blinking tears out of her eyes at the thought of losing him.

"Don't worry. I'm fine." He detached gently.

Tiare rolled her eyes and took Pono's good arm. "You're going to be, if I have anything to say about it."

She steered her husband out the door. Lei trailed them, feeling at loose ends. She watched Tiare help Pono into their big family four-door truck, waving as cheerfully as she could as they pulled out.

Watching them go, Lei missed Stevens with a bone-deep ache. *Six months is way too long.* She was in danger of feeling sorry for herself. She unsnapped the deep cargo pocket on the side of her pants and took out the satellite phone, checking it for the hundredth time.

No message.

She was really getting concerned now, a potent cocktail of frustration and worry bubbling under her sternum as she worked the phone with her thumbs.

Michael. I need to know you're okay. Please text me at least. I love you.

She slid the phone back into her pocket, snapped the button shut, and went to her truck, where she retrieved a package from her crime kit. She headed into the hospital, going down a floor to the basement where the morgue was located. Dr. Gregory was just shutting the refrigerator shelf on a body when Lei pushed the main door open.

"Lei! To what do I owe the pleasure?" He peeled off gloves and dropped them into a nearby biohazard bin. "Our conference at the station wasn't too long ago."

She held up Nunes's DNA sample swab, still in its wrapper. "I have another contributor for you to rule out as the father of Danielle Phillips's child."

* * *

Lei called Wayne from the office to make sure Kiet was okay. Her father said brusquely, "You need to come home. Boy's not doing well with both of you gone."

Urgency immediately speeded Lei as she headed home after making sure the evidence collected at Costa's house was being processed by Kevin and that everything had been logged in. Captain Omura had gone for the day, leaving a message on Lei's voice mail: "Debriefing in my office first thing tomorrow morning."

The light was going purple and orange across the ocean on the drive home, but Lei was too anxious to get to Kiet to enjoy the sight of a few surfers still pumping the small waves at Ho'okipa as she passed the well-known sport area.

She had time for one more case-related phone call. She fished the Phillipses' financial planner's number out of her backpack and dialed it, putting in her Bluetooth. Truman Ching had already left the office, but she set up a meeting with him for the following day through the receptionist. There was truly nothing more she could do on the case at the moment, and her son needed her.

Kiet ran down the steps the minute her truck came through

the automatic gate, the dogs flanking him. Lei frowned at the sight of tear tracks on the little boy's cheeks as he ran around to pull her door open.

"Mama! Where were you?"

"Oh my goodness, little man!" She pushed the door open wider and swung her legs out, reaching out her arms. He leaped into them, wrapping his arms and legs around her like a monkey and burying his face in her neck. "What's got you so upset?"

"I thought you weren't coming home. Like Daddy." Kiet squeezed hard, his voice muffled.

"Daddy's coming home," Lei said stoutly. "And so will I. Every day. And you had Nana and Grandpa to take care of you."

"The TV said a police officer got shot," Kiet muttered. "I thought it might be you."

Five years old and he already lived with the fear every law enforcement family dealt with. Her father must have been listening to the news while he was cooking, as he liked to do.

"Oh, honey." Lei smoothed Kiet's thick black hair. "I'll always come home to you."

She somehow had to keep that promise. No matter what. He'd already lost one parent, whom he'd never know. She stood up with Kiet in her arms and carried him into the house. Wayne, light from the kitchen falling on his silver-shot curly head, took a plate out of the microwave. "I reheated something for you."

"Thanks, Dad." She set Kiet on the couch. "Want to watch some cartoons with Mama while she eats?"

"Yeah." The little boy plugged his mouth with his thumb. He hadn't sucked his thumb since he was three.

She wanted to yell at Stevens all over again for what he'd done to them by leaving, what he was continuing to do by being gone. She took the plate from her father, sliding the phone out and checking it again.

This time there was a text.

I'm sorry. We were on communication blackout. I'm in place where I'll be working and I'm okay. Not feeling well at the moment, but I haven't touched a drop since I left. I love you. I'll be back before you know it.

"Liar," she muttered. But her spirits lifted to hear from him. "Dad, Kiet—Daddy says he's where he's going to be working, and he's okay. He sends his love."

"That's good. Hey—can I have a word about today?" Wayne wiggled his brows significantly. Lei followed him into the hall, out of Kiet's earshot.

"It would be great if you could keep him from hearing the news," Lei said. "Please."

"He turned it on himself while I was in the kitchen and saw the report. Is Pono okay? I called down to the station when we heard an officer had been shot."

"Yeah. He's home already. Just a flesh wound. Says he's always wanted to be able to say that." They exchanged a smile.

"I'm sure there's a story there, but now's not a good time with Elephant Ears listening. I'm heading out, then," Wayne said.

"Thanks again, Dad." Lei hugged her father goodbye. "I couldn't do this without you and Ellen helping me with..." She tipped her head to indicate the boy, his gaze intent on the cartoons. "I'll probably have another long day tomorrow. I hope you and Ellen are okay picking up Kiet and keeping him busy?"

"Sure. You know we love spending time with him," Wayne said, as they walked into the living room. "I am getting him tomorrow and planning to take him to the restaurant with me."

Kiet looked up and grinned at his grandfather. "I can help you chop stuff, Grandpa."

"We'll see." Wayne reached over to ruffle the boy's hair.

"Don't give your mama a hard time." He lifted a hand and shut the door behind him.

Lei checked that he'd fed the dogs, who seemed a little needy, too, pressing against her legs. She stroked their broad heads, rubbed their chests, and played with their silky triangle ears, murmuring loving words. Keiki leaned her large, square forehead on Lei's breast.

Lei felt a tightness in her throat at the sight of the many white hairs around the dog's muzzle. She didn't know how much longer she'd still have her old girl, already ancient by Rottweiler standards.

When Lei finally sat down beside Kiet, her plate was cold. She felt herself sink deep into the couch with exhaustion.

It had been a truly long day.

She ate, set the plate on the coffee table, and snuggled Kiet against her side.

Lei woke to the sound of Kiet screaming, the high, thin rabbit-like cry of one of his night terrors. She'd fallen asleep with him on the couch, she realized, and he was tangled in her arms, both of them overheated and uncomfortable. The TV murmured and flashed in the background.

He hadn't had one of these episodes in at least a year.

"Wake up, little man," she soothed, rubbing his arm, a technique the pediatrician had recommended.

"He's asleep when these happen," the doctor had told them. "You have to wake him up slowly, bring him out of it. Sometimes he won't wake up, but you can gradually calm him by giving sensory input." As unnerving as the night terrors were, it was better to soothe him out of them than to wake him abruptly, they'd found, since then he switched to hysterical crying that could go on for hours.

She rubbed Kiet's arm, his back, holding his stiff, screaming body against her, whispering in his ear until gradually the wails trailed off and he relaxed at last. She stood up with him in her arms and carried him back to the big bed. They both needed the comfort of being in it together, for now.

Chapter 15

L
ei was on her way back into the station the next morning, her eyes gritty from broken sleep, when her cell rang. She couldn't help the surge of hope that made her grab the phone up without looking.

Jared, her brother-in-law, greeted her. "Lei! Any news on Michael?"

His voice was deceptively like Stevens's at first, and the twinge she felt at realizing that it wasn't her husband was undeniable. She forced a cheerful note into her voice.

"Hey, bro. Yeah, I finally got a text from him last night. Says he's in the place where he's going to be working, and he's okay. I was getting worried. I don't even know where he's stationed. Classified, you know."

"Well, that's good. I've been meaning to call you, but we've had more of those cane fires and I've been doing twelve-hour shifts." A long pause. Lei put in her Bluetooth so she wasn't violating the Maui cell phone ban.

"Yeah, let's get together when my latest case lightens up." Lei wanted to invite him to dinner, but wasn't sure when she was going to be home for that. "In the meantime, Kiet's having some adjustment problems with Daddy gone. I could really use some help. If you could have him on your day off, give him some of that favorite uncle time?"

"Sure, of course. I'm overdue for taking him out on the ocean." That was Jared's special contribution to Kiet's upbringing—he was systematically teaching the boy ocean sports. They'd been out to fly trainer kites several times already, getting him ready to kiteboard, as well as surfing, fishing, and canoe paddling. "I just wanted to say that I told Mike I thought he was nuts going overseas. He's got you, the kid, a great job." Jared's voice was tight with frustration. "I get it that we inherited alcoholism genes from Mom. But he could deal with his problem here. He didn't need to leave you guys."

Lei blew out a breath. "You don't have to tell me. I'm so mad at him I can hardly see straight, but what am I gonna do? He had it in his head he needed to kick the booze and the PTSD by going somewhere that would 'break him out of the rut,' which doesn't say much for family and married life."

"Stop it right now, Lei. You guys have what everyone wants. What I want." Her brother-in-law's voice was thick with emotion. "I just had to tell you. I tried as hard as I could to talk him out of it. But he's bullheaded like that."

"Thanks." Lei felt those easy tears prickling again. "I appreciate you telling me, and any help I can get with the little man. He's really a mess. So am I, but the job keeps me going. Speaking of, you should know Pono's off a few days. Perp at an ice house we busted winged him in the arm yesterday, so pop by and play some video games with him or something, if you find the time."

"Man! That's all you need, your partner getting shot. I'm sorry, Lei. This is a lot to deal with. Let Mom and Wayne know that day after tomorrow's my day off. I'll plan to pick Kiet up from school and take him surfing at one of the beginner spots."

"Thanks so much." Lei rang off, glad once again Stevens's brother had moved to Maui five years ago. Now that she knew he wasn't enjoying the single life anymore after years of uncommitted dating, she was going to have to give some thought to who she could set him up with.

* * *

Omura gathered the team in the conference room. This time she'd brought a plate of sliced tropical fruit. "My mom sent this for you all." She indicated the spread of sliced pineapple, papaya, peeled lychee, and banana chunks with toothpicks. "I wanted to get everyone together for a quick meeting so we maximize our efforts today. I've asked Gerry to fill in for Pono while he's out on medical leave, so he's going to be helping Lei out until Pono's back."

Lei lifted a hand to the wiry little Filipino detective seated across the table from her. She'd worked with him and his regular partner, Abe Torufu, often in the past.

"How's the evidence processing going, Kevin?" Omura dipped her black, shining bell of hair toward the weedy-looking intern. The young man looked up, blue eyes bloodshot.

"I was here all night, sir," the young man said. "I got a good start on the trace from the UH Zodiac. Want me to start there?"

"No," Lei cut in. "Start with the Mares speargun I dropped off. Could it be the murder weapon?"

"Yes, it could," Kevin said. "Make and model match the spear the victim was shot with."

Lei lifted both hands, making a victory sign. "Yes! Costa, you're going down!"

"Not so fast." Omura held up an admonishing finger. "I admit he looks good for it, but I can hear his defense attorney now—

how many of those spearguns there are in Hawaii, let alone the world, blah, blah, blah. Any prints on the weapon?"

"No, sir. It was clean."

"Too bad. What do you have scheduled for today, Texeira?"

Lei pretended to consult her spiral notebook, but she already knew. "First we have follow-up interviews scheduled with Phillips and his mistress. Then I have a quick stop-by planned with the Phillipses' financial planner, Truman Ching."

"I thought I told you to focus more on the stalker and on the poaching possibilities," Omura said. "I hear a lot of effort still going toward the husband."

"We set these interviews up the day we searched his house and found those two in bed together. It's more for form's sake at this point. They're bringing lawyers. But I don't want to miss the chance to record them explaining their relationship," Lei explained.

"Okay, but don't take too long if you don't see it going anywhere," Omura said. "Kevin, anything else popping that I can have Gerry and Lei follow up on today?"

"Yeah. One of the samples from the UH Zodiac tested positive for sperm." Kevin's fresh young face flushed. "Someone was getting busy out there in that boat, but I haven't had time to run the DNA matches. Also, the fingerprints the fleeing perp who shot Pono left came back to Costa himself. So the shooter was definitely Costa, and he's in the system for meth dealing."

"Wish someone had picked him up last night on the BOLO." Lei's stomach rumbled loudly, and Omura looked at her, pointing wordlessly at the tray of fruit. Lei took a lychee, bit in. The sweet, translucent flesh of the fruit seemed to melt in her mouth, its unique, almost floral taste blooming across her tongue. She closed her eyes in bliss. "Oh my God, so *ono*."

Everyone paused to fill paper plates with fruit from the tray.

"Very nice of your mother." Parker lifted a slice of banana on a toothpick in toast.

Omura nodded. "We both want everyone to eat healthier around here." She wiped her fingers on a paper napkin. "Okay, here's the order of the day. Interviews. Pick up Miller and shake him down again, recheck his alibi. Do some canvassing down at Ma`alaea Harbor. See if anyone can identify Danielle leaving in the UH Zodiac and put anyone else in the craft with her."

Everyone rose, and Bunuelos turned to Lei with his typical quick movement. "I'll dig into Miller's alibi."

"Thanks, Gerry. Needs in-person verification. He says he was working in the tutoring lab."

"Lei, hold on a minute," Omura called.

The hairs on the back of Lei's neck rose in alarm, but she turned to the captain with a tense smile. "Yes, sir."

They both waited until the room had cleared.

"I'm sorry about Pono. Take me through how it happened, step-by-step."

"Should I have my union rep present?" Lei tried to sound joking.

"Oh, come on, now. I just want to know what happened." Omura leaned forward, steepling her fingers.

"I have to say, it was both of our faults." Lei sagged in the chair, knowing she shouldn't be confessing like this, but she trusted Omura after all their years together. "I still need to do my official debrief, but where I went wrong was in not calling out "Gun!" the minute I knew Costa was armed. As for Pono, he just charged without stopping to assess or take cover. We were both focused on keeping Costa from escaping, and because we didn't know about the meth production, we didn't think he was that dangerous."

Omura tapped her nails. Today they were a rosy peach. "So you know you should have taken cover, waited for him to try to get away, and captured him with proper backup."

Lei nodded. "I had a feeling about him, about that house the first time we visited it. I should have listened to my intuition."

"Well, he's our top suspect now. I released his name and mug shot to the media, set up a tip line, and added the info that he's wanted in the shooting of a police officer. Hopefully that gets someone to roll on him." Omura set her hands down on her desk and leaned back, cocking her head in that way she had. "That brings me to the personal. You look like hell, Sergeant."

"Kiet's having some sleep problems since Stevens left. Truth is, so am I." Lei combed her tousled curls with her fingers and twisted them up, stabbing a pencil from Omura's cupholder through the unruly mass. "I heard from Michael finally. He's in the place where he's going to be working and says he's okay."

"Well, that's something, though your husband's still on my shit list for the indefinite future. Keep me posted. I'll set up your post-shoot debrief with Dr. Wilson. She's here on the island for a psychology conference."

"Thanks." Lei really was looking forward to talking with her former therapist, now team colleague, about recent events. They'd known each other so long that Lei trusted the petite blond psychologist with her deepest secrets and most painful wounds. Not every officer doing a post-shoot debrief got that kind of luxury, and it might even be a chance to talk about her worries about Kathy Fraser and Kiet's behavior issues.

"Dismissed," Omura said. "And take that fruit out to the office with you. Mom will be insulted if I bring anything home."

"Wouldn't want you to get in trouble." Lei grinned and

picked up the tray. It did Lei good to see that Omura had to answer to someone, too.

* * *

Lei dropped the fruit tray, covered with a sheet of plastic wrap, in the patrol officers' break room as she went to pick up Gerry Bunuelos at his cubicle.

"Stealing my partner again, I see." Abe Torufu turned his squeaky, overwhelmed office chair to face her. She'd partnered with the burly Tongan giant for a brief, unforgettable stint on the bomb squad, and they'd been close ever since.

"She Who Must Be Obeyed has decreed it," Lei said. "Hopefully we're closing in on this thing and Pono will be back soon."

Torufu smiled his tiki god grin, wiggling the toothpick in the corner of his mouth at her. "Good. I need the little dude to do all the running around."

"You said it. We both know I do all the work." Bunuelos picked up his cell phone and weapon harness off the back of the chair. "How do you want to play this interview?"

"I get bad cop." Lei rubbed her hands together in anticipation. "I eat society blondes for breakfast. And not in the dirty way you guys want to picture," she scolded at the grins that comment instantly elicited. "Let's go."

Chapter 16

B arbara Selzmann was considerably better groomed than the disheveled woman Lei had surprised in Phillips's bed. Immaculate cream linen slacks and a lacy top complemented her golden-blond hair and even, caramel-colored tan. Diamonds glittered on her ears and hands, and very blue eyes gazed calmly at Lei. Her lawyer, Robb "Keoni" Chapman, a *haole* from Wailuku whom Lei had dealt with before, opened the interview.

"I've instructed my client that she's to say nothing to you."

"Oh, come on," Lei said contemptuously. "You've got nothing to hide, Ms. Selzmann. I've seen everything you've got."

There was a short, electrified silence at this opening salvo, and then Selzmann laughed. "You've got me there, Sergeant Texeira."

"So surely you'd like to fill us in a little, Ms. Selzmann. I'm sure Keoni here understands that you'd like a chance to explain yourself." Lei indicated the defense attorney and his careful comb-over with a contemptuous thrust of her chin.

"No comment." Selzmann picked at her diamond bracelet. Chapman patted her hand patronizingly, and Selzmann flicked him away, in sudden annoyance, straightening up in her chair. "You know what? I've done nothing to Danielle."

Lei cocked her head, and Selzmann went on. "Frankie and I've been having an affair for two years. It's unfortunate, what happened to his wife, but not entirely a surprise to me. She was always flirting with danger."

"You've been flirting with danger a bit yourself, Ms. Selzmann," Bunuelos said. "Tell us about your relationship with Frankie, as you call him."

"It's my nickname for him. We've known each other half our lives, actually. Frank and I renewed our relationship at Maui Country Club through playing tennis. Danielle could never be bothered with such 'time wasters' as she called them."

"Seems like you didn't care much for Danielle," Lei said.

"I was neutral on Danielle herself. It was Frankie's marriage I didn't like," Selzmann said. "I thought he deserved someone who understood him. He married Danielle in an idealistic phase."

"So you said you've known him even longer than you've been having an affair."

"I've known him since college. And after my divorce, we reconnected."

"You realize this gives you motive." Lei smiled, not a friendly expression.

"Barbara, this is why I advised you not to even engage with these people." The lawyer patted Selzmann's arm again.

Selzmann never broke eye contact with Lei as she lifted a slender, toned arm. The diamond tennis bracelet sparkled. "Really? I killed her? I heard she drowned ninety feet deep off Molokini. I've never scuba dived in my life. Ask anyone. And besides, Frankie was leaving her. We were going to get married eventually. There was no need for drama."

Selzmann's eyes reminded Lei of pictures she'd seen of glaciers: opaque and cold as blue topaz. The woman stood and picked up a tiny gold purse. "I've more than cooperated with this ridiculousness. My assistant will provide you with a printout of my schedule the day Danielle died, and you can verify all my activities. As you say, I've got nothing to hide." Her gaze raked Lei contemptuously, from Lei's frazzled, haphazard bun held up by a pencil, to the scuffed athletic shoes on her feet. "Good luck with your investigation. I hope you catch Danielle's killer."

Lei took a few deep breaths, suppressing her urge to rip the blonde's hair out by the roots as Barbara Selzmann swept out with the lawyer in tow. Being judged by the likes of that woman made her want to kick ass, even as her womanly side cringed in embarrassment at her own lack of grooming. She stood, smoothing down her rumpled shirt as Bunuelos turned off the recording equipment.

"Selzmann seems pretty confident she's going to be the next Mrs. Phillips," Bunuelos commented.

Lei nodded. "I wonder if 'Frankie' knew they were getting married," she said. "Bring him in. I'll be back in a few minutes."

Lei went to the women's room. She combed her hair and captured it in a tidy twist with bobby pins, teasing a few curls out around her face. She put on a swipe of lipstick to combat the exhausted-looking pallor left over from another bad night's sleep. Advertising how stressed out she was wouldn't help their case.

Frank Phillips had cleaned up for the interview, too. Freshly shaved, dressed in a long-sleeve cotton shirt and chinos, he smelled of spicy cologne and defensiveness. His lawyer, a leathery-looking woman with ripped arms and a no-nonsense shag haircut, introduced herself, shaking Lei's hand with an overly strong grip.

"Davida Fuller. My client is fully cooperating and eager to see his wife's murderer brought to justice." A chunky turquoise necklace enhanced the woman's eyes.

"How nice." Lei flashed her teeth. They all sat down at the steel table. "Perhaps he could begin that cooperation by telling us more about his relationship with Barbara Selzmann."

Phillips fiddled with the pearl cuff links on his dress shirt. Lei couldn't remember seeing actual cuff links in Hawaii before, except at weddings. "Lani and I were not happily married. But that doesn't mean I didn't love and respect her."

Lei snorted. "Just tell us about Ms. Selzmann and how she fits into that love and respect."

Gerry Bunuelos smiled, getting eye contact with Phillips. "Hey, I get it. You weren't sleeping with Danielle. Barbara, your friend from college, comes back into your life, divorced. One thing leads to another…"

"That's exactly it." Phillips leaned gratefully toward Bunuelos. "Lani and I did nothing but fight. We'd only been married a year when I realized I'd made a mistake. She was really married to that job of hers, not me. Ate, breathed, slept ocean science and conservation. She married me for financial stability. I'm sure she'd deny it, but before we got together, she'd barely been getting by on her UH salary as a first-year professor. Rented a room in a house with some students. Her biological clock was ticking, quite frankly, because she told me she wanted to start a family right away. I was overjoyed at first. I'd always wanted kids. Anyway, we tried and tried." For the first time that Lei had seen, real emotion clouded the man's dark eyes. "We got pregnant four times. The babies never made it past four months."

This echo of Lei's own secret agony set up a throb deep inside her, in that place that had once been filled and now, she feared, would always remain empty. Once again she felt a kinship with Danielle—a mirroring of pain, dedication, and ultimate loss.

She reached down to pinch her own leg, hard, through the fabric of her pants. She was here now. Danielle wasn't. This was a case, nothing more. Danielle was just another body on a slab that deserved justice.

"So it seems like not being able to have a child hit you guys hard," Bunuelos said sympathetically.

"It did. And finally we stopped trying, stopped sleeping together. She got deeper and deeper into her activism, busting people for the DLNR and agitating with the environmental nuts on the island."

"So you turned to other arms for comfort?" Lei said.

Phillips hung his head. "I'm ashamed of it now."

"But why didn't you just divorce?" Bunuelos asked. "That's what I'd do."

Lei suppressed a smile. She happened to know that Gerry was a Catholic with five kids and a wife he adored at home. He'd sooner cut off his own arm than leave them.

"We talked about it often. We just hadn't gotten around to finalizing things."

Davida Fuller spoke up. "Do you have any specific questions for my client?"

"Yes," Lei said. "How did you upload your data and sneak out of your office in the afternoons? I have a tech guy working on it, so we'll know in a day or two. You might as well tell us."

Phillips lifted his head and his dark eyes blazed briefly with rage. Then he clenched his fists and looked down. "I did that to be with Barbara. My secretary is very loyal to both myself and Lani. I didn't want her to know about the affair. So I did the work at other times and then uploaded it remotely on days when I met Barbara."

"So you were with Barbara the day Danielle was killed," Lei stated.

"Yes." His cheek twitched, a tic-like movement.

"So things were in the works for a divorce?" Bunuelos persisted. "If we check with your attorney, she'll verify that?"

"That's protected information," Fuller said quickly. "I'd need a warrant to release that."

Lei inclined her head. "We'll obtain one. We'd also like a copy of both of your wills."

"Those are kept at my estate lawyer's," Phillips said. "And they're of no interest, I can tell you right now. Lani and I inherited from each other."

"Will you save us time and give written permission to review those documents?" Lei pushed a pad and pen over to Phillips.

Fuller turned to Lei, her collagen-enhanced lips pulled tight. "In light of your attitude, I'm advising my client against any further cooperation. You can get warrants for those documents, too." Fuller rose, straightening a narrow tunic top over leggings, an outfit that was all about classy comfort. Lei mentally noted that this was a defense attorney who bore watching, new as Fuller was to the small legal scene on Maui. "Come on, Frank. We're done here."

Bunuelos got up and opened the door for them courteously. "Thanks so much for your time. We'll be in touch."

Lei remained sitting and collected her small tape recorder, pad, and pen slowly. She finally rose and shut off the wall-mounted video recorder. "He's hiding something."

"Not surprising." Gerry joined her as they exited the interview room. "He knows that affair looks bad."

"I don't care what the captain says," Lei said. "I want to see those financials. Let's see if Miller has been picked up, and if not, I'm going over to Ching's office."

She was coming to care, very much, who had killed Danielle Phillips. There were just too many things she had in common with the victim to stay objective.

* * *

Truman Ching was a short, rotund Chinese man with a bald head encircled by a gray tonsure of hair and trifocal glasses that made his shrewd dark eyes sparkle, hinting at secrets and laughter.

"I hear my dear client Lani Phillips is no more." He shook Lei's hand with a soft, dry one. "Make yourselves comfortable. Jenna, bring them some water, please," he directed his assistant.

"Thank you, Mr. Ching," Lei said as Bunuelos shook the little man's hand. He led them into a luxuriously appointed office. A long mango-wood desk gleamed in the light of a green-shaded lamp, and stacks of papers were held down with beautiful chunks of mineral.

"What a nice collection." Lei leaned close to look at a specimen.

"Oh, yes. I once hoped to be a geologist, but not much call for it here on Maui, and I inherited my father's business." Ching gestured to a couch and chairs around a matching coffee table decorated with a big branch of black coral, glass fish artfully poised in its branches.

Lei examined it. "Is this coral from Maui?"

"It is. From the bad old days when there was no regulation of the reefs." Ching picked up a file from his desk. "My father was an avid diver. He got that off Lanai forty years ago."

The coral was a large, glossy, delicately branching fan; the glass fish miniature works of art themselves. "I've never seen an intact piece of coral this big before outside of a museum," Lei said.

"Lani Phillips told me that's where it should be. But I'm sentimental. I plan to donate it on my death, and until then, I enjoy looking at it every day. Now, I understand you want to see the Phillipses' financial portfolio? While I entirely understand the reasons, I must insist on a warrant to release such confidential and sensitive information."

"Of course," Lei said. They'd been busy on the phone for a couple of hours since the morning interviews, getting warrants for the estate lawyer, divorce lawyer, and financial planner faxed in. She handed over the paper, and Ching reviewed it briefly, setting it on his desk.

"Seems to be in order. Here is their file. Why don't you have a seat? It will be easier if I explain what these documents are and what they contain." Jenna, a young woman whose stocky stature and thick glasses indicated a relationship to Ching, brought in two chilled Perriers on a tray. Ching lifted a summary sheet off the top of the file and handed the rest to the young woman. "Please make copies of this file."

Jenna inclined her head and took the file, leaving silently. Lei chugged her Perrier, enjoying the chill tickle of the bubbles at the back of her throat. Ching was a classy guy. She liked his attitude.

"Now. They had life insurance on each other. Danielle's was lower, with five hundred thousand as a death benefit. That sounds like a lot, but actually isn't when you consider how young she was and her future earning potential. If she'd got tenure with UH, she'd have had a solid income. Frank always made considerably more than she did as a CPA, and he carried a million on his life." Ching showed them the figures. "They had retirement accounts, too. Nothing exciting. Frank was mostly contributing to them. Danielle had a little from her UH pay that went into the state system."

Lei took the summary sheet, feeling disappointed. There was no clear financial motive here. Though five hundred thousand seemed like a lot, she knew Ching was right—that figure was actually low for life insurance. "Were there any other assets?"

"Only Lani's land," Ching said. "She inherited a nice big chunk of land from the Hawaiian branch of her family. A rancher leases grazing rights on it to keep the taxes paid, as far as I know. But it was part of their portfolio, and worth quite a lot if it got developed."

Lei's pulse picked up. "Where was it located?"

"Out by Makena, which is a desirable growth area. It wasn't developed because there was no available water. But I heard recently that some developers drilled a new well nearby. There's a nice artesian source under the land that they know about now. Development is possible, so the parcel has likely tripled in value."

Jenna returned and Ching leafed through the file and pulled out a tax map. "Here's the location and the tax number of the parcel."

"Who gets this land now that she's gone?" Lei asked.

Ching shrugged. "That's a matter for their lawyer, Shawn Shimoda."

Lei remembered the frosty Japanese lawyer too well from other cases. She wasn't eager to be in the same room with him again. "I thought he was a defense attorney."

"Everyone has to diversify on Maui," Ching said. "Good luck."

* * *

Shimoda was not nearly as cordial as Ching. After they had a hostile interaction with his receptionist, the tall, well-groomed Japanese lawyer reluctantly allowed them a brief audience in his heavily air-conditioned inner sanctum. He gave no sign that he recognized Lei, though he'd deposed her as a hostile witness for a case a few years before.

"Here's a copy of the will." He'd spent an inordinate amount of time studying the warrant and now reluctantly handed over the multipage document. Lei scanned it, and the meaning was obscured in legalese.

"Can you explain this to us?" She held it up.

"I charge three fifty an hour," Shimoda said. "Would you like to make an appointment?"

"You can charge the court. You are under court order with this subpoena." Lei locked eyes with the attorney.

"I hate dealing with you assholes," Shimoda hissed, his eyes narrowed.

"You won't deal with an asshole? Neither will I." Lei spun on a heel and yanked the door open so hard it banged into the wall, leaving a dent. She made herself head for the door.

"I'll send MPD a bill for damages to my office," Shimoda called after them.

"Yeah, you do that," Lei called back over her shoulder. "And good luck collecting."

"Take a chill pill." Bunuelos pushed the elevator button. "I should have talked to him. You two obviously don't get along."

"What a prick," Lei said, once in the elevator. "I'm losing it. I need lunch." Her stomach growled loudly, confirming this.

"It's about time. I was ready to eat my arm hours ago. It's past two p.m."

They went to Koho's, a restaurant in the Queen Ka'ahumanu Mall notable for dim lighting, high booths, and inexpensive local food. While waiting for a plate of chicken katsu, Lei scanned the document again. "I just really can't understand this thing."

"Let me see if we can get some help. My cousin's an estate lawyer." Bunuelos took out his phone. "I'll see if he wants to join us. He works nearby."

"We'll have to have him sign a confidentiality agreement," Lei warned, and he nodded.

Sal Bautista was as wiry as his cousin, but older. A few threads of silver brightened hair in a style that had gone out in the 1970s, which he wore with a bright purple nylon shirt and a thick gold chain.

"I'm e-mailing you a copy of our confidentiality agreement." Lei worked her phone.

"Of course." Sal removed reading glasses from a pocket and put them on. Lei dug into her chicken dish as he skimmed the document. "Looks pretty straightforward. The husband inherits from the deceased, and if he'd died, she'd have inherited. Except for this land trust."

"What's the deal with that?" Lei's interest sharpened.

"Well, there's an exclusion clause. It looks like Danielle inherited it with a condition. She had to pass it on to any offspring she might have to 'keep it in the family.' It only went to the husband if she died without issue."

Lei went absolutely still as she absorbed this.

If Phillips had known she was pregnant by another man, the land would provide a powerful motive for murder. She and Bunuelos exchanged a look.

"Anything else?" Gerry asked his cousin, who was now slurping a bowl of saimin noisily.

"No. Like I said, straightforward except for that land addendum."

"Is there anything about the value of the land?" Lei asked.

"No. You'll have to talk to a real estate broker." He slurped some more.

Lei threw a twenty down on the table. "Thanks, Sal. Gerry, can you look into that? I want to swing by Ma`alaea Harbor and see if I can get any confirmation on our case." She waggled her brows, not wanting to discuss the case any further in front of Gerry's cousin. "We can meet back at the station if we hear that they brought in Miller, or when I'm done, whichever comes first."

"Sounds good."

She picked up the copy of the will. "Thanks again, Sal. Your saimin's on me."

Chapter 17

Lei was relieved to be heading to the harbor by herself. Much as she liked Gerry, she didn't quite have the comfort level with him that she did with Pono. Work with Pono had an ease and give-and-take rhythm of purpose that came from years of sharing cases. She drove down the straight freeway that bisected the middle of the figure-eight shape of Maui, toward the windiest harbor in the world.

Ma'alaea was quiet with the morning crowd of whale watchers and other boats out to sea. She parked her Tacoma at the utilitarian half-moon of harbor and took out a clipboard and pen, along with a photo of Danielle that she'd laminated at the office.

It was a full-body shot, much as Lei imagined Danielle must have looked as she got in the UH Zodiac and took it out toward Molokini. Danielle wore her long brown hair in a careless knot at the back of her neck, and a bright bikini peeked out from under her tank top. She wore nylon running shorts with it. Her tanned, athletic body was eye-catching and her smile memorable.

A lot of people were likely to know her down here. Lei took a pull of water from the bottle in her cup holder and hopped out of the truck. Gusts of wind tugged at the MPD ball cap she tugged low on her brow. The coconut palms surrounding the harbor swayed gracefully, their fronds rattling.

Canvassing was never boring. Lei talked to a woman at the snack shop who often saw Lani but hadn't that day. She talked to one of the maintenance men from the docks, who expressed tearful regret over her passing but didn't remember seeing her go out the day she died.

She found a witness at last, over at the gas pumps where boats pulled up for fuel.

"Yeah, Lani came by and filled up her gas tank that morning," the grizzled older Portuguese man who ran the fueling station said. "It was early, only six a.m., and I'd just opened. There she was, carrying her can."

"Tell me about her demeanor. How she was acting."

"Nothing special. Said 'Hi, Teddy. Fill 'er up. I'm heading out to Molokini today.'" The man took off his stained cap and scratched the thin greasy hair beneath it. "I didn't know that was the last time I'd see her until I heard on the news."

"So there was nothing different about when you talked to her?"

"She seemed happy." Teddy fiddled with the gas pump mechanism, his mouth turned down with sadness. "I remember noticing that. I even said to her, "You're in a good mood today." She just laughed. Said she had some personal good news, but it was too soon to share."

The pregnancy. Lei's stomach twisted.

"Was there anyone with her?"

"No. But when I looked over at the boat, there was a guy in there, stowing stuff."

Lei's pulse picked up. "Anything you can tell me about him? Height, weight, ethnicity, anything?"

Teddy straightened, looked at the sky. Arched an obviously aching back. "The guy was bent over in the boat, sorting dive gear. Had a ball cap on. Not small, but I couldn't really tell you more. I realize it's important now, but at the time..." His voice trailed off, and his dark brown eyes gazed at her mournfully from pouched lids. "At the time I just remember thinking I was glad she had company, for once."

Lei's chest tightened in sorrow as well. She looked around the area. "Are there any surveillance cameras in the area?"

Teddy perked up. "Yeah, we have one aimed at the harbor's main entrance. Coast Guard uses it to see who's coming and going. It's aimed to get the registration numbers, so I don't know how much of a shot of them it will get, but it's worth a look."

"Thanks so much, Teddy." Lei smiled at him with genuine warmth. "This has been very helpful."

She continued her canvassing, to no avail. No one else there remembered seeing Danielle leave, nor anyone else in her Zodiac. Lei knew that she had to get the footage from the Coast Guard and come back early in the morning, when the boats would be loading and people who might have seen the couple would be there.

A call to the Coast Guard meant contacting Petty Officer Aina Thomas.

She wasn't sure if the uptick in her heart rate was dread or anticipation as she dialed the contact number she'd stored for him. She went to her truck and got in, rolling down the windows before she made the call.

"This is Thomas." The Coast Guard officer's voice was brisk, all business.

"Hi. This is Sergeant Texeira from MPD, calling about the Lani Phillips case," Lei said. "Hope it's okay to call your cell phone."

"Of course. What do you need?" Immediately his voice warmed, and she smiled, too.

"I have a lead I need to follow up on. Can you find me the surveillance footage from Ma'alaea Harbor on the morning Phillips was killed?"

"Sure. I should have thought to offer that," Thomas said. "Got caught up in stuff here and never made that call. When can you pick it up? It's all digital, sorted by day, so I can just make you a copy of that day on a stick drive."

"How soon can you get it ready? I'm at the harbor now."

The Coast Guard building was adjacent to the harbor, so she wasn't surprised when he said, "I'm on duty, so I need to get someone to cover me while I go access the files. Give me a half-hour?"

"Sure." Lei rang off.

Lei took the downtime to call in and update Omura. "This is the first confirmation we've had that she had someone with her," Lei said. "It's unlikely to have been Costa, whom she had a hostile relationship with. Perhaps it was the father of her baby, or Miller...or someone else we don't yet have in the mix." She filled the captain in on the financial motive they'd also uncovered through the will.

"I still think it's the unknown boyfriend or the stalker," Omura said. Lei could hear the captain typing in the background. "This also punches a hole in the theory that it was just one of the poachers she was photographing. If it was a crime of opportunity, where's the man she went down with?"

"Maybe there's another body," Lei said. This was a whole new slant. "And we just haven't found it."

A long pause as they both considered this.

"That's unlikely. There's a lot of scuba and other traffic in that area. Even weighted, a body would probably have been found."

"I don't know, sir. You didn't see all the shark action I did. If they shot the other diver and removed the tanks, then stuck the body under a coral head, it would likely be eaten by ocean predators. Might never be found."

"Who else is missing in the community?"

"I don't know. We haven't been looking at that." Lei pulled a loose ringlet impatiently as she gazed out the truck's dusty window. "Like I said, this is the first confirmation we have that she wasn't alone."

She hung up and called Bunuelos next, updated him with the new information. "Where are you at?"

"Back at the station, sifting through leads. Want I should look for any missing persons in case there's another body?"

"Yeah. Male, between twenty-five and fifty. I'd be willing to bet the father of her baby is somewhere in that age group, too."

"On it." Bunuelos hung up.

Stifling anxiety, Lei called Wayne next. She could hear the busy sounds of the restaurant in the background as her father answered: the clashing of dishes, voices, and a tinny sound of Hawaiian music.

"Sweets!" Her father greeted her cheerfully. "I have my junior sous chef here to say hi." He handed the phone to Kiet. Her son's voice sounded cheerful, too.

"I'm helping Grandpa," Kiet said proudly. "I already chopped three big pieces of kalo."

"It was cooked, I hope." Lei thought of the purple tubers that were a staple of the Hawaiian diet. Cutting hard, dense raw taro root was hazardous even for adults.

"Yeah. They're squishy and easy to cut," Kiet said. "Grandpa is making them into hash browns." Taro hash browns were a specialty of Wayne's Hawaiian Grinds.

"Sounds yummy. How was school?"

"Fine." He shut down at that question.

Lei sighed. "I'll be home by dinnertime today, I hope, son. Put your grandpa on, okay?"

She firmed her return time up with Wayne and hung up, feeling lighter. She checked the time on her phone. The half-hour had passed. She started the truck and drove to the Coast Guard headquarters a few blocks away.

The brass on Thomas's uniform glittered under fluorescent lights, and he smiled a handsome, three-cornered grin, already waiting for her, as Lei pushed the glass door of the Coast Guard building open. She felt her own face light up in an answering smile.

"I admit to being curious. I loaded the footage on a monitor. Want to take a quick look with me?" he asked.

"Sure." Lei followed Thomas up a metal set of stairs to an office area filled with cubicles, officers at work all around them. He rolled a second chair into his cubicle for her and sat down, hitting a button on his computer.

"The day's footage begins at midnight. Let's fast-forward."

"I think we should start watching beginning at around six a.m. The gas guy who told me there was someone with Danielle said he'd just opened the pumps and she talked to him."

They both leaned forward as he scrolled. Lei's shoulder brushed Thomas's. She noticed the contact and shied away, rolling her chair farther back. He glanced at her curiously.

"I think we're almost there." Lei kept her eyes on the monitor.

The surveillance camera was angled so that it caught the bows and sterns of boats as they passed through. Thomas slowed the feed, and images flashed in the yellow glow of the lights at the portal of the harbor. Thomas slowed further, to real time.

Suddenly, there was the Zodiac, low enough in the frame so that they saw Lani's face clearly as she sat in the stern, her hand on the tiller. Seated on the bench in the center of the craft was the distinct shape of a man. He was leaning forward, resting his hands on his knees, his gaze straight ahead. A ball cap was pulled low. All they could see of his face was the angle of a jaw, the hunched shape of his body, giving little away.

"Looks like he was trying to keep a low profile," Lei said.

"Replay that, will you? Let's go frame by frame and see what we can see." Lei couldn't tell height, coloring, much of anything else in the black-and-white feed, other than that the figure was male. It was disappointing. She spotted a flash of something behind the boat.

"Replay that again, Sergeant. What's that?" She pointed.

They both leaned in to look, but even with Thomas blowing up the frames, it was hard to make out. "Could be something tied to the back of the craft," Thomas said.

"Like a kayak?" She looked at Thomas, her eyes narrowed. "If someone was with her when she died, he needed a way to leave the scene."

"That makes sense." They watched the recording again, but other than a blur of something behind the craft, there was no way to tell exactly what was being towed.

"Thanks. This isn't the identification I was hoping for, but it definitely puts another person, male, in the craft with her, with a possible means of departure. And that's something."

Thomas saved the file to a stick drive, ejected it, and gave it to her. "Glad I could help."

"Me too." She stood. "Call me if you guys get anything more. The captain and I are now wondering if this man might also have been a victim and maybe his body just hasn't been found. So for sure, call me if you find any trace, at Molokini or anywhere else."

"Will do."

Lei smiled and gave him a little two-fingered salute as she left. He grinned at her and stayed at his desk, but Lei felt his gaze on her all the way to the stairs.

Yes, she needed to avoid Aina Thomas. He wasn't the only one feeling an attraction. The months of stress she and Michael had been under had definitely left her vulnerable.

Lei slid the stick drive into her pocket and headed for the station.

* * *

Kahului Station was beginning to settle into quiet as the shifts changed. Lei met Bunuelos in her cubicle. Gerry leaned back in Pono's office chair, brushing his fingers through short black hair. "They still haven't picked up Miller, but I dug into his alibi today. So far it's holding up. I talked to several students who saw him in the tutoring center during our window."

"Well, let me show you the footage that shows Lani was with someone the day she died." She plugged in the stick drive and they reviewed the recording together. "Possible escape craft attached to the back of the boat, but no ID available off this. What do you think? Find any John Doe possibilities?"

"I did a quick scroll through missing persons. Nothing in that age bracket of men since the victim's body was found."

"So that's a dead end at the moment, until we find something indicating that's a possibility. And, as far as ID on the man in the boat, I can't see Lani going out with Costa for any reason, especially since the gas guy said she was 'happy' that day." Lei made finger marks to illustrate the man's comments. "She and Costa didn't get along. So that leaves Miller, the father of her baby, whoever that is, Frank Phillips, or some unknown perp."

"Still too many suspects." Bunuelos looked up at the clock.

"My kids have soccer. My wife took them, but there are multiple games. If it's possible for me to get off on time, I need to get home."

"Yeah. I told my boy I'd be home for dinner. He's having some problems since Stevens left." Lei stood, turned off the computer. "Let's call it a day. I'll log this stick drive in, and we'll get back to it tomorrow morning. I still need to interview the divorce lawyer and meet with Kevin about all the trace we collected. And then there's the sample I dropped off at the morgue." Lei told Bunuelos about the hunch she'd had about Lani's friend Mark Nunes, the DLNR agent. "Be interesting if he's the guy."

"And if he isn't, the field is still wide open," Bunuelos said. It was unfortunately true.

Chapter 18

L ei was chasing Stevens. He was looking at her from the back of a pickup truck as they raced across a desert, drawing farther and farther ahead of her, bound and on his knees. Clouds of dust rose behind the vehicle as she pursued on a quad, never gaining, the four-wheel drive vehicle hopelessly outmatched.

And then the truck swerved.

She failed to make the turn and went off an unseen cliff, spinning out into space, the emptiness of a vast, deep gorge swallowing her and the cartwheeling four-wheeler.

Lei woke, heart pounding, just before she hit the rocks at the bottom.

Beside her, undisturbed, Kiet slept on. She leaned over to check on him. He'd turned away from her on his side. His thumb was in his mouth.

She swung her legs out of her side of the bed and stood up. Her knees were wobbly from the adrenaline blast. Her hair was stuck to her neck with sweat. She padded out of the bedroom into the kitchen. Keiki and Conan lifted their heads to watch her, their eyes soft black gems in the dim light.

"It's okay," she whispered. Exactly as if they understood her, both dogs lay their heads down on their paws. But their eyes still tracked her as she went to the sink and ran a glass of water. A draft of cool night air came in through the window, sliding like fingers across her loose breasts, teasing them awake.

It was almost too bad she'd reconnected with Michael on the eve of his departure. She'd have been better with her sensuality shut off, stuffed in that box where it had been before their night together brought it back to life. But it was too late now. They'd made up, physically at least, and now she missed him more than ever.

She was done waiting. She needed to reach out. Maybe the time difference was such that he'd get her call.

Lei unplugged the satellite phone from its charger and went into the office that had been her bedroom for months, closing the door so as not to wake Kiet. She dialed the number he'd programmed into the device. It rang and rang, a tinny buzzing that taunted her, finally ending in a beep. Not even a voice mail message comforted her with a trace of his voice.

"Michael, this is Lei. It's the middle of the night and I had a bad dream. It's silly, I know, but I'm missing you. Worried about you. It's been five days. Surely you can call me by now? I'm living on a text message, and I have to tell you, it's not enough." She pushed a hand through her jumbled hair. "I love you. Please call me."

She punched off. It felt like giving up. Sitting there on the edge of the bed, she shut her eyes and prayed for his safety.

The dream had left her with a sick feeling.

* * *

Kiet woke her in the morning. She'd slept in, and he was almost late for school. She rushed through their morning routine and dropped him off at the turnaround, finally having a moment to check the satellite phone as she pulled out of the school's driveway. She'd slept with it beside her but had turned the ringer off. She'd missed his call.

"Damn it." At least he'd left a message. She didn't bother with the Bluetooth, simply put the phone to her ear as she pulled out of the school's turnaround and onto Hana Highway for Kahului.

"Sweets, I'm so sorry to miss your call." Stevens's voice sounded rough, and he coughed. "I really want to talk to you, too. It's tough here. Long days, very physical. A damp environment, that's all I can say about it." He coughed again. "I'm wondering what the hell I was thinking, coming out here, but it's too late now. No way out but through. I've got some concerns about the op here, too, but don't worry. I'm sure I'll adjust. Let's talk tonight—I'll call in ten hours. Have the phone on, and we'll catch up. I love you, and I miss you and the little man."

She felt tears prickle her eyes as she heard the *click* as the message ended.

"Damn," she muttered, and blew her nose on an old Burger King napkin wedged beside her seat. "I miss you, too."

At least she had a phone call to look forward to.

Gerry Bunuelos had beaten her to the station. "I was about to put out a BOLO on you." He handed Lei a cup of murky station coffee. "You're always the first in."

"Another bad night," she said. "Kiet was almost late to school. Tell me something good."

"Okay. We got a line on Costa. Someone spotted him out around the corner from Ulupalakua. You know that settlement out at Kahikinui? Apparently he's got relatives off the grid out there and is hiding out. Omura has authorized a little home visit with plenty of backup." Bunuelos tossed her a Kevlar vest. "Hammer down your coffee, Sergeant. We're on a manhunt for Pono's shooter."

The action was welcome. The adrenaline blew the last of the nightmare out of her brain as they got on the road in their vehicles, two MPD cruisers bristling with armed officers as backup.

Ulupalakua was the last node of civilization after the town of Kula. Beyond that, the long wild coast all the way to Hana began. Most of the land was owned and operated by the Ulupalakua Ranch as a cattle enterprise. Past the ranch and the last rock formations of Haleakala volcano that caught rain, the stretch of steep, rocky coast was populated by the hardy and desperate, most of them living in "off-the-grid" homemade structures of roofing tin and plywood.

There was a sense of vastness to the sweep of open coastland. Raw lava crags raked the sky, snagging rain clouds on their sharp edges, and the land, bare but for tough grasses, tumbled to a wide-open, cobalt sea. Great swaths of boulder-strewn rugged grassland and steep valleys carved by the occasional heavy rains had given Kahikinui a savage, untamed beauty. Windswept and barren, there was nothing to interrupt the broad sweep of tumbled lava, soil, sea, and sky but a few twisted wiliwili trees.

The team kept siren and radio silence. It was forty-five silent, speeding minutes up the volcano into an area that boasted stunning views of the deep blue ocean in all directions.

Lei kept both hands on the wheel of her Tacoma as she followed Bunuelos in his 4Runner as the GPS *ping*ed the address of Costa's brother. Both of them had extra officers riding shotgun. They turned off the paved, two-lane highway onto a red-dirt track carved out of the wilderness, bordered in dry scrub, giant lava boulders, and the occasional hardy Christmas berry bush.

They pulled into a cleared dirt area surrounded by rough dwellings constructed of plywood and corrugated roofing. A few trees provided spotty shade, but the sun beat down on Lei's head as she leaped out of the truck, taking a cover position behind her vehicle and drawing her weapon. Bunuelos, who'd coordinated the effort, due to her late arrival that morning, lifted a bullhorn to his mouth as the MPD vehicles pulled up and took defensive positions, blocking in a motley assortment of vehicles parked on the dirt in front of the houses.

Loose dogs came boiling out from the structures, barking and complicating things as Bunuelos yelled, "T. J. Costa, this is the Maui Police Department! Come out with your hands on your head!"

A long moment of silence filled with nothing but the hysterical barking of the dogs followed this opening salvo.

Suddenly, a flurry of sound and movement. In one of the sheds, a roar of an engine announced a vehicle. A quad burst out of the lean-to, and someone wearing a helmet headed straight up the nearby mountain. At the same time, another quad burst out from behind the houses, heading in the opposite direction.

Bunuelos threw up his hands in frustration.

They had no means to pursue those vehicles in this rough, boulder-strewn country with no paved roads.

"Move in and scoop up anyone who's left," Lei yelled, waving in the backup officers. Fanning out, they moved in on the houses, finding five family members gathered in the living room of one of the dwellings, everyone kneeling with hands on their heads.

"You're under arrest as an accessory." Lei cuffed the man she identified as Costa's brother from his driver's license photo. He spat perilously close to her leg but didn't resist as she and the other officers restrained him, his wife, and the other three adults.

Once secured, Lei returned to the front door. "Sergeant Texeira." One of the uniforms gestured for her to follow him. "You need to see this."

He led her to a back bedroom, where several filthy children were huddled, crying with fright.

"Hey. Everything's going to be okay." Lei squatted beside the littlest, a tiny boy no more than three, folded in an older sister's arms. Another child, a boy, had his arm around the other two. He glared at her defiantly.

"What you chasing Uncle for?" he said. "He never done nothing."

"We think he did a bad thing," Lei said. "So we have to ask him some questions. He'll be fine. You don't need to worry." She took her phone out, scrolling to the number for Child Welfare Services. *These kids should be in school.* Their unkempt hair and filthy clothes confirmed the need for some outside intervention.

"Uncle T.J., he never going to jail," the boy said. "He said he goin' *make* first."

The Hawaiian word for 'die' sounded like profanity in the child's mouth. His lips quivered with fear and grief, hidden by anger. Lei straightened up, the phone to her ear as it rang through to her favorite social worker, Elizabeth Black. Liz's calm, matter-of-fact manner put kids at ease, and she was a fierce advocate for them with both parents and the system.

"This is tough," Lei told the boy as the phone rang through. "But you have to trust us. There are better places for you than here."

She walked out of the bedroom to talk to Liz. She hoped like hell the foster home the kids ended up in really was better, but looking around this pigsty of a room, she didn't think it was much of a gamble.

The team swept through the buildings, finding evidence of further meth production in one of the back houses. They took the adults in for questioning as Liz arrived in a white county SUV, her long gray braid tidy down her back. She was some degree of Cherokee, and her mannish brows drew together in a frown as she took in the decrepit house.

"Glad you called me," she told Lei. "I've had multiple complaints on this family, but they always had some slick excuse for why the kids weren't in school. Now I can finally get them out of here."

Lei swabbed the kids' hands for traces of methamphetamine and wordlessly held up the chemical-infused wipes, which changed color in the presence of the drug, for Liz to see. The two older kids tested positive for trace, indicating they'd had some role to play in the meth production.

Liz tightened her mouth into a thin line and gave one nod of her head. "Come on, kids. Let's pack your favorite things. I brought new backpacks for you to put your stuff in." The children went with her without protest, subdued by the drama.

Hours later, finally back in air conditioning, Lei splashed her dirty, sweaty face at the sink of the women's room. Disappointment was corrosive in her veins as she did her best to clean up before she had to report to the captain on the failed raid.

Costa was probably dry camping somewhere on a mountain he knew like the back of his hand. It could be months before they caught him.

"But the truth is, I don't think he was Danielle's killer," Lei said a half-hour later in Omura's office, Bunuelos beside her. "Picking him up doesn't answer who was with Danielle in the Zodiac. I'd like to turn the Costa investigation over to Narcotics for follow-up, much as it pains me to let go of Pono's shooter that way."

"I agree," Bunuelos said. "I think we're looking for someone close to her. Or a second victim."

"Which, since we don't have another body, we can't pursue," Omura said. "I see you called Child Welfare on those relatives of Costa's. Was there any evidence of abuse or neglect?"

Omura always kept an eye on Lei's motives, knowing Lei's history as a sexual abuse victim. Lei felt the back of her neck heat with anger. "Those kids were filthy, not in school, and had traces of meth on their hands from helping package product at the family's factory. If that isn't enough, I don't know what is."

Omura held Lei's gaze for a long moment. "I know you have a sore spot for these kinds of cases. Just protecting you and our department. So, next steps." She flipped through the file. "I'm okaying transferring the pursuit of Costa to Narcotics. They will also have the most info on his known associates. As for you two, find Ben Miller. He's the priority now. Dismissed."

Lei and Bunuelos went back to Lei's cubicle. Gerry mopped his brow. "Thank God for air conditioning," he said. "We've had a BOLO out for days now on Miller, and officers went by his known address. What else can we do?"

"Let's call the college again. He was pretty determined to get his PhD. That would be a lot for him to flush down the toilet just to avoid another round of questioning. After all, we don't have anything hard on him. In fact, the baby's DNA ruled him out as father." Lei remembered the sample she'd dropped off at the morgue. "Let me check with Gregory about that sample I asked him to run."

She picked up the phone and dialed Dr. Gregory's line. The ME picked up.

"Maui Memorial Death Department," Dr. Gregory intoned.

Lei was startled into a snort of laughter. "You must have known it was me."

"There's this wonder known as caller ID. What can I do for you, Lei?"

"I'm calling about that DNA paternity sample I dropped off. Any results?"

"Oh, damn, I knew I was forgetting something. I'll get right on it. Takes a couple of hours to run the comparison. I'll call you as soon as I have anything."

"And since I've got you—we're keeping an eye out for a second victim. Found any John Does lately between age twenty and fifty?"

"No, nothing new. Always got a few old ones waiting for someone to claim them, sadly."

"Nah. If this was related to the case, it would be because this man went down at approximately the same time as our vic Danielle Phillips. Well, do call me when you have anything on that DNA sample." She hung up, turned to Bunuelos. "Let's go over to the University of Hawaii campus and rattle some cages, shake Ben Miller loose."

Chapter 19

L ei shook Dr. Farnsworth's hand a second time in her tidy office at the University of Hawaii. "This is my partner, Gerry Bunuelos."

"Pleased to meet you," the dignified head of the Maui campus said. "I wish I were meeting you in happier circumstances. Lani's death has hit us hard, and she'll be difficult to replace."

"We're here because our officers haven't been able to locate Ben Miller," Lei said. "We need him for a second interview, and he's not at his usual address. We wondered if you knew where he might be."

"As a matter of fact, I do." Farnsworth went around to her desk. "We sent him out to wrap up part of Lani's fish-population study. He's out at La Perouse Bay doing fish counts." She picked up a sheaf of papers, along with a couple of detailed topographical maps of the area. "I'll have my assistant make copies of these. I'm not sure exactly where he is. I'd call him for you, but there's no phone reception out there."

"Thanks so much." Lei took the papers. "How does one do a population study, by the way?"

"You grid off an area. Count the fish within that area. Grid another one randomly, count that area. Average and project for an entire area. You use random sampling to extrapolate."

Lei imagined being in scuba gear, floating at just the right height, counting off the fish that wandered into a gridded area. It sounded so peaceful compared to what she did all day. She really wanted to get back in the water. Aina Thomas's invitation to dive the wreck out in Lahaina seemed like a wonderful, tempting break from all of this.

But no. She had a job to do. There was no room in her life for time wasters like recreational diving with a good-looking guy who wasn't her husband.

"Thanks so much for the lead. Can we get those map copies now?" Lei asked.

* * *

La Perouse Bay, almost directly below Ulupalakua but at sea level, was a swath of raw black lava deposited by the island's last active flow four hundred years ago. As Lei drove her Tacoma down the single-lane, potholed road through the lava fields, crystalline waves breaking on the rocks beside them, Lei felt a deep excitement—the familiar and addictive feeling of a hunter closing in on prey.

"Right now I think he's our guy." She navigated a deep puddle in the road's pitted surface. Tall, spindly wild tobacco and bushy native naio plants studded with feathery white blossoms were the only vegetation in the rugged area besides the occasional hardy kiawe tree. They still had a couple of miles of rough road before they'd arrive at a parking area that led into the reserve. "He's out here carrying on her work. I can see Miller justifying her death even as he steps into her shoes."

"Don't know who I like for it," Bunuelos said. "On the one

hand, there are the poachers she caught on the GoPro. We have never identified them. I felt pretty confident it was Costa until we got the footage of a male in the boat with her. Even if that guy didn't kill her, who is he? How did he get back from Molokini? And why hasn't he come forward to help us if he didn't kill her? I'm with you. I don't think she would have taken Costa out on the Zodiac. On the other hand, Costa had a speargun the right size, and his own Zodiac."

"So here's how I think it went down," Lei said. "I think she knew she was pregnant, and that's why she was happy in spite of the husband, in spite of everything. She took Miller out for a research trip to Molokini to count fish or whatever, bringing her GoPro to catch any poachers, as she always did. Maybe she told Miller she was pregnant, or that it was over, something new that pushed him over the edge. When they were down there and spotted the poachers she photographed, he shot her to frame them."

"I thought you liked the husband for this."

"I just don't like the husband, period." Lei smiled at Bunuelos. "The guy's a slimy two-timing prick."

"No argument there. Well, back to Miller, then. I'm still having the same problem putting him at the scene. How did he get back to shore if the UH Zodiac was still tied up on the back side of Molokini? He tried to make it look like she went out alone, which she did plenty of times."

"Yeah. We never found any definitive trace in that boat except the sperm."

"Speaking of that." Bunuelos gave her a quick, apologetic glance. "Kevin Parker told me it matched Ben Miller's DNA."

"So he was probably beating off in the boat that night he said they did it," Lei concluded. "Yuck."

They mulled in silence. Lei's gaze wandered over the great

black plain of frothy, razor-sharp lava in the reserve area, which was getting a total rest for two years due to the wear and tear of both heavy tourist and local use. She knew several heiaus and burial sites added to the area's cultural as well as environmental sensitivity, but all Lei could see was a forbidding expanse of barren, hot black rock in all directions.

They reached the parking area. Lei spotted a white Maui county truck. Mark Nunes was behind the wheel, using binoculars to watch the ocean off the parking area where a diving float bobbed. She parked, and they got into Kevlar and checked weapons. She didn't expect trouble from Miller, but after Pono's shooting, she wasn't going to take any chances.

Nunes came over, holstering the binoculars at his waist. "What's up?"

"We're looking for Ben Miller," Lei said. "Wondering if you know the guy? He was Lani's grad student."

"Sure, I know Ben." Nunes rocked back on his heels, his eyes narrowed. He was wearing the standard navy DLNR enforcement uniform with heavy boots. He hooked his thumbs into the belt at his trim waist. "He in some kind of trouble?"

"No. We just need to talk with him about something and heard he was out there doing some fish counts," Lei said.

"I know the area well, including the areas where Lani was doing her research," Nunes said. "I'll take you there."

It was tempting to have his help, because the maps Farnsworth had given them were hard to understand, just a series of lines of paper with little context. But Lei remembered another case where one of the helpful park rangers had turned out to be involved and decided against it. It was still a possibility that Nunes had more of a relationship with Danielle than they knew.

"Nah, we better do this solo. Though I'd appreciate it if you'd mark the areas where you think he might be." Lei got out the map and handed Nunes a pen. He described the route to a hidden bay some miles in and marked the area for them.

"Thanks." Lei took the pen and map back from the agent, liking the attractive angle of his jaw, the intelligence in his dark eyes. She could see Lani falling for this guy. Her glance flashed to his hand—no wedding ring. "We really appreciate it. Looks like you've got your hands full keeping an eye on those divers. What are they doing, so close to the reserve?"

"Aquarium fishing. It's legal up to the line of the reserve, and a lot of these guys go straight out here off the parking lot. There are more fish near the protected waters, and the fish don't know where the line is."

"That sucks." Lei looked out at the float. "I didn't know that was legal out here at all. So how do they do it, exactly?"

"See how the float is circular? It's attached to a container. They're circling the area with nets and putting the small reef fish they catch in the container. It doesn't look like any other kind of diving, so I can always spot them doing it."

Lei frowned. "There's no regulation of that?"

"They have to have permits, and there are some size and frequency counts for some fish. I'll check everything when they get in. But, yeah, they can mostly keep all they get."

Bunuelos slid his arms into a light backpack. "I've got water and some snacks. We should go." They donned MPD ball caps, waved to Nunes, and set off down a well-worn trail through the lava field.

Lei hit a rapid stride along the trail, the sun hot on her hat but a warm breeze wicking the moisture off her body. A parallel path of rounded, inset stones ran closer to the ocean.

"I bet that's the old Hawaiian trail," Lei said. "They have those on the Big Island, too. The kanaka really took time to make their paths well." Fishing, and their own system of aquaculture, had provided a big part of early Hawaiians' staple diet, and the traces they'd left behind in this area were the carefully constructed paths they'd walked to their fish ponds and fishing grounds.

Bunuelos just nodded. Sweat was already trickling out from under his ball cap as they reached the shade of a stand of kiawe trees lining the old road along the coast, a four-wheel drive mogul field of twists and turns. Lei looked back at her new partner, teasing, as he wiped his forehead on his shirtsleeve and replaced the ball cap. "You need to get out and run with me some time, Gerry."

"When hell freezes over," Bunuelos panted. "I have five kids. You think I have time or energy left over at the end of the day for anything but collapsing with a cold one? I go to work as a homicide detective to get some peace and quiet."

They walked past the small bay containing the well-known La Perouse surf break, today flat and calm, and continued on across the reserve. Lei felt sweat soaking her shirt under the tight casing of the bulletproof vest. She checked their map at the third small inlet, waves splashing up on a beach of tumbled white coral mixed with black volcanic rocks worn smooth by wave action. "We're almost there."

In the next tiny bay, they found a cluster of tents deep in the shade of a stand of kiawe trees up against a bluff of steep, jagged lava, but no one was there. Lei glanced inside the tents and saw a jumble of sleeping bags, water containers, and backpacks. "Looks like Miller has company out here."

"Where is everybody?" Bunuelos wondered aloud. They followed a well-worn path to the ocean and found the campers lying around naked and in various states of getting high, the smell of weed thick in the air. Someone was drumming on a djembe, and someone else, who would have looked better covered up, was dancing trancelike in the sand above the pebbly beach.

Lei frowned, hands on her hips as she looked around. "We should probably cite all these people."

"You want to go to all those court dates?"

"Hell no." She sighed. "Let's see if they know where Miller is."

It didn't take long before the alternative nature lovers had directed them over another crest of stone to a small, bright turquoise bay, almost entirely enclosed by steep walls of lava. A red diving buoy in the water marked Miller's location.

"We might as well take a break while we wait for him." Lei found a spot of shade under one of the slender, gnarled kiawe trees. She and Bunuelos loosened their Kevlar vests, taking time to drink water and eat some granola bars.

Lei loosened the Kevlar all the way, tugging it off over her head, and took out some field glasses, training them on the bubbles that marked Miller's location more truly than the red dive float. "I guess pursuing a suspect could be worse than this," she told Bunuelos. "We could be in LA on the streets or something. Instead, here we are, catching an ocean breeze, waiting for a guy to come up from scuba diving."

"Maybe *you* would be in LA." Bunuelos had a dimple high in his cheek and looked much younger than his fortysomething years as he grinned. "I'll never live anywhere but this island. *Maui no ka oi*."

"Yeah, it's the best." She leaned back against the tree trunk and held the cool bottle against her forehead. "Except when it's this hot. I think I've got a little heatstroke."

Miller eventually rose to the surface, still unaware of them. Lei watched the young man stow some recording gear in his bag and head for the rocks. They met him as he was coming out of the water, peeling the rubber suit down to his chiseled waist.

"Hey." Miller's blue eyes were wide with surprise as he shook water droplets out of his blond hair. "What are you guys doing out here?"

"We've been looking for you, Ben." Lei gave her friendliest smile. "We need you to come down to the station and answer some questions."

For a moment Miller looked terrified. She saw his eyes dart back to the great sweep of open ocean outside the mouth of the secluded bay. She waited, almost sympathetically, as his escape fantasies ran their course and he turned back to face them, firming his jaw. He gave a stiff smile. "Sure. Whatever I can do."

* * *

Miller sat at the interview table at the station. He finger-combed his hair, which had dried in salty tufts.

"We want to revisit the day Danielle died." Lei opened her file on the case. She glanced up at the mirrored observation room, where she knew Omura was watching, but she'd Mirandized Miller and turned on the recording equipment after he refused the reminder about a lawyer. Beside her, Bunuelos smiled at the young man, working his good-cop angle.

"I told you. I was at the tutoring center."

"Yes, you were. But you were not seen by anyone there before ten a.m., and we have a video that puts you in the Zodiac with Lani at six a.m. out of Ma'alaea Harbor." Lei watched him closely.

He paled and reached down to rub his hands up and down his jeans-clad legs. They'd let him change when he got back to the parking lot at La Perouse, but he hadn't showered, and the salt was clearly irritating on his skin. None of them had had time to shower, though there was an employee locker room down by the gym. Lei's own body tingled and itched with dried sweat from the hot hike across the lava on top of the adrenaline bursts from the raid this morning.

"It wasn't me in whatever video you have. I wasn't with her that day. I told you. I went in to the tutoring center at nine, when they open."

"So where were you at six a.m.?" Lei asked.

"In bed. I got up, showered, shaved, like that. I get up at seven, so at six I was sleeping." He frowned. "I'm telling you, it wasn't me in the boat with her. It was probably her boyfriend, that DLNR agent Nunes."

Lei felt the back of her neck prickle as she went on full alert. Nunes and the county truck had been gone when they'd returned to the La Perouse parking lot. She wondered at the nip of intuition that had told her both to turn in his sample and not to have him guide them across the lava.

"What makes you say he was her boyfriend?" Lei asked. "I thought *you* were her boyfriend."

His jaw bunched. "She wouldn't have me."

"So why do you say that now about Nunes? You never told us anything about him in your other interview."

"I've been doing a lot of thinking since she died. Wondering who killed her. Knowing you think it might have been me. And I saw them together." He bunched his fist, looked down. Lei almost felt sorry for him.

"Saw them together? What does that mean?"

"I saw them. Kissing." Saying the words obviously pained him.

"But I thought you just had to prove your love." Lei couldn't resist poking him a bit, to see what came out.

"And I would have. I mean I was. She just needed time to see that I was sincere, that I was right for her."

"But maybe you got tired of trying to do that. Especially once you found out she was pregnant."

The young man's eyes flew wide, staring at her in disbelief as he paled further under his tan. It wasn't acting. He hadn't known.

"I would never hurt her, no matter what," Miller whispered. "If she was pregnant, I'd just want to take care of her. If she'd ever leave that bastard she was married to."

"But what if the baby wasn't her husband's?"

"Doesn't matter. I loved her."

"I find that hard to believe. I think you ran out of patience and killed her."

"No. Never. And maybe I do need a lawyer."

Lei probed more, but Miller just stubbornly repeated everything he'd already said and asked for an attorney.

Lei gestured to Bunuelos. "Let's cut him loose. Thanks for your help, Ben."

"Check on Nunes. That guy was making a move," Miller said as he got up. They ushered him to the door. Lei turned off the recording equipment.

"I don't like Miller for it after this," Lei said thoughtfully. "I'd bet money he didn't know she was pregnant. And even though he'd seen her with Nunes, it didn't seem to penetrate his deluded bubble about Danielle. Most of all, it would be a stretch to get out to Molokini, go down ninety feet, kill her, find some way back to the harbor, and be at the UH tutoring lab by nine o'clock, which we can verify by his time card even if no students saw him."

"So that leaves us with two unidentified poachers with a hard-bottom Zodiac, Costa, Phillips, and whoever fathered her baby," Bunuelos said.

"And I'm really starting to wonder if that might be Nunes." Lei told Bunuelos about the sample Dr. Gregory was supposed to run as she shut the door of the interview room and she and Bunuelos headed down the hall toward their cubicle. "I have to make a call down there and see if he's done the paternity test. Can you bring the captain up to speed?"

"You got it, partner."

She hurried to the cubicle alone and picked up the phone to Dr. Gregory, hoping like hell he'd had time to run that DNA sample.

"Twice in one day!" Dr. Gregory's ever-cheerful voice grated on Lei's nerves as the ME picked up the phone. "You're in luck. I ran the paternity DNA, and it's a match for the sample you dropped off."

Lei felt a surge of adrenaline.

"Can you e-mail me the results? I need them right away." Lei sprang up from the squeaky old office chair. "I've got to pick up the suspect." She banged down the phone.

Chapter 20

L ei and Bunuelos took his vehicle this time. They kept the siren off but put up the cop light on the dash of the SUV as they headed for Mark Nunes's last known address. Lei shook her head as they sped down the road.

"I don't want it to be him, Gerry. I like the guy." Lei pushed a plush baby toy out from under her butt into the back seat, where two booster seats competed for space with a bag of soccer equipment.

"It might not be him. We just have to see. You always tell me not to jump to conclusions."

They turned into a tidy subdivision in Wailuku Heights. It wasn't far from the Phillips's house, and Lei felt her heart sink a little as they turned into a driveway with a plastic kid's wagon parked next to Nunes's county truck and a Subaru SUV.

"Looks like he has a family," Lei said. Bunuelos's mouth tightened, but he refrained from comment. They approached the house and Lei rang the bell.

A slender young woman in shorts and a spaghetti-strap tee answered the door with a friendly smile. Her long black hair brushed her hips, where she held a toddler wearing nothing but a diaper and a pacifier. She looked as fresh-faced and young as a high school student, and Lei felt her already-upset stomach curdle further. "Is Mark Nunes home?"

"Sure." She turned and hollered into the interior of the house. "Uncle! Some cops stay heah fo' talk to you!"

The wave of relief Lei felt made her almost giddy. She knew she was getting way too emotionally involved with this case, but she couldn't seem to help it.

Nunes came to the door. He'd changed out of his DLNR outfit into a plain black tee and nylon athletic shorts. His dark brows knit with concern. "Sergeant Texeira! What's going on?"

"We need to talk with you. Down at the station." Lei kept her face expressionless, even as her heart broke a little bit. She really, really didn't want this man to have been Danielle's killer.

He stared at them through the screen door, a long cool look, and then he turned back to the girl hovering in the background. "Don't worry, Kalei. I'll be back soon."

* * *

Nunes sat stone-faced through being Mirandized, and Lei tapped a pad of paper before her with a pen. "So we'd like to know the exact nature of your relationship with Danielle Phillips."

"I told you. We were colleagues. Friendly colleagues." Nunes gazed back at Lei levelly.

"Is that all you've got to say on the subject? Did things ever get personal?" Bunuelos asked. "I mean, I'd get it if it did. She was a beautiful woman in a shitty marriage. You're single. One thing led to another…"

"It wasn't like that." Nunes looked down, moved restlessly in his chair. "Okay, I liked Lani. More than liked her. She was brave. Dedicated. She…" His throat seemed to close, and he cleared it. "She cared about the ocean like no one I've known before or since. It was something we had in common."

"Did you ever sleep with her?" Lei asked bluntly.

He looked up at her, his eyes widening, then narrowing in anger as his mouth tightened. "None of your business."

She opened the file, flipping to a picture of Danielle's discolored, naked body on the autopsy table. "This woman was murdered. No one gets to have any privacy as it relates to her. So I ask you again, did you ever sleep with her?"

A long moment passed. Nunes's shoulders sagged. His hands came up to cover his face. "Yes," he whispered.

"Say that louder. For the record," Lei rapped out, feeling the heat of righteous anger on her neck. If this prick killed Danielle, Lei was going to nail him and enjoy doing it.

"Yes, I slept with her. Yes, I loved her!" Nunes exclaimed, smacking his hand down on the steel table, startling Lei and Bunuelos. "Yes, I wanted her to leave that bastard she was married to and be with me! Is that what you wanted to hear?"

"In fact it is," Lei said. "How long have you known she was pregnant with your baby?"

Nunes blinked. "What?"

"She was pregnant. With your baby."

"Oh God." Nunes collapsed against the table. Lei felt the hair on the back of her neck rise as he groaned, a terrible and haunting sound of mortal pain. He slammed his head down on the table.

This reaction was so extreme and unexpected that Lei froze. Bunuelos jumped up and ran around the table as Nunes slammed his head down again. Bunuelos grabbed him, pulling him backward, and cuffed his hands behind his bolted-down chair. Nunes continued to moan in an extremity of grief as blood and tears trickled down his face.

"So I guess you didn't know," Lei said weakly.

"Frank! That greedy asshole found a way to kill her," Nunes snarled now. "Let me go. I'll take care of him like I should have a long time ago."

"Why do you say that?" Lei leaned forward, composing herself. "Did you know about Miller? Ben Miller? He was in love with her, too."

"That puppy was nothing to her." Nunes looked up. The congested blood was leaving his face, rendering his dark skin sallow but patched with red. A bruise was forming, distending his forehead, and the skin had split with the blows. Blood trickled down from the contusion, running beside his nose and catching on his lips. "She was going to leave Phillips. But she hadn't told him yet. She said she had to get some things lined up with her lawyer. Meg Slaughter. You should talk to her."

"We will." Lei jotted that down, remembering it as a to-do she hadn't gotten to yet. "Why did you think Frank killed her?"

"He didn't want to let her go. She had something he wanted."

"Maybe she had something *you* wanted. And you killed her when she wouldn't leave him," Lei said.

Nunes shook his head so hard that blood flew from the wound on his face, spattering the table. Bunuelos patted his shoulder. "Hey, man, take it easy."

"I only wanted her," Nunes said. "She was who I'd been waiting my whole life for. I could have gotten married a dozen times, but Lani—she was the woman for me."

"So who's that young woman at your house?"

"My niece. In case you didn't hear her call me 'Uncle.'" Nunes aimed a bloodshot glare at Lei. "Her parents kicked her out when she got pregnant, so I gave her and the kid a place to stay. Let me go, damn it."

"Maybe. When you tell us what you were doing the morning

Lani died. I don't believe we ever got an alibi from you."

Nunes tried to straighten in the chair, clearly uncomfortable as the strain of his arms cuffed behind him and his other injuries began to be felt.

"I had work. Began my shift at seven a.m. I monitor that area you found me in, Kihei to La Perouse Bay. I start the day in the harbors, looking to see who's going out. That morning I was at the boat launch near Kamaole Three Beach. I stay back, get a bead on who's going out early in the morning, check boat registrations, things like that." Nunes looked miserable, physical pain setting in along with the reality of the news Lei had given him. She watched his emotion play out, a movie of heartbreak, as he sagged against his bonds. "I cited a couple of guys for expired registrations. That's on record. You can check."

"We will. And in the meantime, we can hold you for twenty-four hours. I think you need to cool off. I don't want you to go off half-crazy and hurt yourself or—someone else." Lei stood up, gathered her papers and file. "Bunuelos, book him into holding. Give him his own cell and follow suicide watch protocols."

"Let me go. I wouldn't do anything, I swear," Nunes said, but the ooze of blood on the man's face told a different story.

Lei reached for the door handle. "I'm sorry, Mark. It's for your own good. I'm going to update the captain," she told Bunuelos. "See that he gets some first aid, too."

"You got it, Sergeant." Bunuelos gave her a two-fingered salute as she left.

Out in the hall, Lei took a couple of deep breaths and opened the door into the observation room. Captain Omura sat in the dim light in front of the mirrored window and a bank of monitors.

"I don't think he killed Danielle," Lei said.

"You're too emotional about this one." Omura was scrolling

on a tablet with her finger. The surface glowed faintly, an oracle in the cavelike space. "This case is not about opinions. It isn't going to be solved through emotion. Follow the evidence. Check and double-check alibis. This murder was done by someone who had the means, motive, and opportunity to do that crime. A crime scene in scuba gear ninety feet down does its own job eliminating suspects."

"Yes, sir." Lei felt a twist to the guts watching Nunes being led from the room to holding, his proud shoulders slumped, every line of his body eloquent with grief and pain. She knew her boss was right. "But so far everyone's alibis are holding up. Who was the man in the boat with Lani?"

Her stomach growled loudly.

Omura looked up with her cool gaze. "Get home and eat some dinner. Spend some time with that kid of yours. You did enough today, and I'm not paying overtime."

Lei swung by her cubicle on her way home and made a list of next steps to kick off tomorrow morning, beginning with a visit to Meg Slaughter, Esq. and trips to both boat harbors.

She put her Bluetooth in and waited for Stevens's call, setting the satellite phone on the seat beside her as she got on the road for home.

It had been ten hours, and she couldn't wait to hear his voice.

Lei drove all the way home and pulled up at the gate. She punched in the gate code and drove up to the house, feeling exhausted and hollowed out. Too much adrenaline in one day had taken a toll, and the phone still hadn't rung.

Kiet ran down the steps with the dogs to greet her, and other than putting Stevens's phone in her pocket and leaving the Bluetooth in her ear in case he called, she gave the last dregs of her energy to greeting the little boy with an upbeat hug and throwing a ball for the dogs until they were all ready to go in.

Through a brief visit with her father and the dinner he'd brought home from the restaurant, then reading Kiet a story and finally tucking him into the big bed, she kept the phone on and nearby. But Stevens never called.

The little boy finally down for the night, she left the bedroom door cracked and went into the office. It was time to find out a whole lot more about her husband's deployment. She couldn't shake the sense that something was wrong.

He'd taken his laptop with him, but she knew his e-mail password and went into his account on their shared desktop. Lei scrolled until she found the correspondence between Stevens and a recruiter from Security Solutions.

She'd been tempted to do this before, but finding out that Kathy Fraser had known more than Lei did had quenched her desire to find out more—she was afraid she wouldn't like what she found out. She'd also been trying to hope for the best, that it would all work out smoothly—but the broken communication was not reassuring.

Lei then looked up Security Solutions's website, scrolling through the slick-looking pages advertising the company's services, which included everything from home security systems to bodyguards. They had headquarters in Virginia, Malaysia, Hong Kong, and a satellite office in Honolulu. They even offered crack mercenary teams "dedicated to achieving whatever your goal is, from dealing with kidnappers privately to keeping your home secure."

From what Lei had understood, Stevens's role was in providing investigation training to US military police at an overseas training camp. She searched and searched, but couldn't find anything on their website that advertised that service.

Lei went back to the e-mail and clicked through the progress of Stevens's recruitment. First an e-mail reached out to him, dated a year ago, asking if he was interested in passing on his "unique and important skill set" in a "first-time-ever private-contract situation" and naming a ridiculous amount of money.

"Holy crap," Lei muttered under her breath. "No wonder he wanted to go."

The correspondence went on, a series of questions from Stevens's side: How long? How would he be paid? What was the risk level? Was extra life insurance provided?

"Damn it," Lei muttered, reading the response. *Yes, Lt. Stevens, we insure all of our operators for an additional three million in life insurance for the duration of their time with us.*

Michael had been so depressed and so tormented by PTSD symptoms. Could this be some elaborate suicide attempt on his part, disguised as a job opportunity? Her stomach churned at the thought.

"No. He wouldn't," she muttered. She copied and pasted the address of the recruiter, the only real contact she could find, into a terse e-mail, squelching the worry that her husband would find out and be angry.

Too bad. He should have called if he didn't want her getting in his business.

My name is Sergeant Leilani Texeira, and I'm writing to you after breaking into my husband's e-mail correspondence. He has been incommunicado for an unacceptable amount of time after leaving five days ago for a deployment with your company. Please send a copy of his contract, job description, location, and a schedule of communication/visitation to me at this address or I will be reporting you to the Justice Department for mismanagement of government fee-for-service contracts.

I suggest you get back to me immediately regarding my husband's health and well-being or you'll be hearing from outside agencies. This is the satellite phone number he left with me. I will wait for your call or a response to this e-mail.

She punched Enter so hard her finger hurt.

"Damn him. Damn them," she muttered, shutting down the computer, filled with impotent, worried anger as she stalked down the hall. She needed a shower. Had needed one since that morning. Maybe then she could relax enough to get to sleep.

Under the warm fall of water in the oversized stall, Lei gave in to the tears that had been threatening all day, having a good cry into her washcloth. She missed Stevens. Badly. And she was afraid.

Her gut was telling her something was wrong. She'd learned to trust it, even when she didn't like what it was saying.

Chapter 21

Meg Slaughter was a short, apple-shaped woman wearing a flowing, ankle-length flax-colored dress, and her iron-gray hair in braids. Birkenstocks provided a solid foundation for a woman who would have looked at home as a garden gnome. She smiled with good humor at Lei, gesturing to a seating arrangement of beanbags in her office.

"Make yourself comfortable."

"I'll stand, thanks." Lei wasn't sure she'd want to get up once she sat on one of the plush, velvet-covered beanbags. "My partner, Detective Bunuelos, and I have come to talk with you about one of your clients, now deceased. Danielle Phillips."

"Yes. I've been expecting you." Slaughter went behind her desk, pulled open a drawer, and extracted a folder. "I had my girl make a copy in advance of your visit." She brought the folder out and handed it to Lei. "I'm so very sorry Lani is gone. She was a beautiful soul."

"Yeah, we've been hearing that." Lei took the folder. "Is there anything you can tell us about what was going on with her? We've heard rumors there was a divorce in the works."

"Oh, yes." Slaughter sat on a beanbag, crossing her legs

under the shapeless dress like a plump female Buddha. "We had several meetings. I was waiting on her signature to finalize the paperwork and file for her divorce."

Lei and Bunuelos looked at the beanbags, each other, and finally sat. Lei sank into hers and was surprised by how supportive and comfortable it was. She gave an experimental wiggle and then opened the file Slaughter had provided. Inside were a series of worksheets, filled in with hieroglyphics.

"I can't read your writing," she said.

Slaughter laughed. "It's shorthand. I'm dating myself. And it has the additional benefit of protecting my clients' confidentiality further."

Lei looked up, realizing that Meg Slaughter's smiling brown eyes, sunk in wrinkle fans of good humor, were coldly intelligent. She shut the file and leaned toward the other woman, deciding disclosure was in order.

"Meg. May I call you Meg?"

A nod.

"Meg, I know protecting your clients is deeply ingrained. I get it. But Danielle is dead. Brutally murdered. Her last moments were a horror show of being shot with a spear and then having someone yank her regulator out of her mouth so that she drowned. And she was pregnant. So anything you can tell us about who she loved, hated, feared, what she was dreaming of, what she hoped to get out of being divorced—anything at all might help us."

Meg Slaughter blinked owlishly three times and then gave a slight head nod and a sigh.

"She was over Frank. She knew he was having an affair with Barbara Selzmann. She was in love with someone, but she didn't tell me who. And she was afraid of a couple of people—Ben Miller and T. J. Costa."

"She wasn't afraid of Frank?" Lei thought of the Beretta she'd retrieved from Danielle's nightstand.

"No, but she probably should have been." Slaughter proceeded to confirm much of what Lei and Bunuelos already knew. "She didn't tell me she was pregnant, but I had seen her will and I knew about the clause reverting her Hawaiian family's land back to her child if she had one. My money's on Frank. He's calculating, that one, and smarter than people give him credit for."

"Why was she afraid of Miller and Costa?"

"Ben Miller was obsessed with her. She wasn't sure how he was going to react to her divorce and her relationship with another man. She wouldn't tell me who that was, though—said it was too early to share. But she was worried Miller would do 'something crazy.'" Slaughter made air quotes. "As for Costa, she was onto his fish-poaching operation and suspected he was involved with the drug scene. She called him paranoid and violent, and she feared running into him alone."

"Thank you." Lei unwound herself from the beanbag. "We really appreciate your cooperation, and it confirms some theories we've had."

Bunuelos, who'd been silent until now, got up and shook Slaughter's hand. "I can tell you cared about her."

Slaughter stood, much more gracefully than Lei had. "I cared about her greatly. And I want you to find her killer. You can count on my testimony when and if you bring in a suspect."

They got on the road back to the station in Lei's truck. She was thoughtful. "Well, nothing really new there, but that Danielle was more afraid of Miller than I realized. He bears watching."

"But there's his alibi," Bunuelos said.

"And therein lies the rub." Lei used a favorite saying of

Stevens's. He'd minored in English lit and liked the occasional poetic or Shakespearean reference. The memory gave her a pang. She slid the cell phone out of her pocket to check it. Still no call.

Back at the station, Lei's desk unit rang with a call from Dr. Wilson. "Lei! Your captain asked me to do a post-incident debrief with you. Do you have time to talk? I'm in your area."

Lei sighed, ran a hand though her disordered hair. "Yes, Dr. Wilson, I'm available. When can we meet?"

"Within the hour, if you can make it."

Lei held a hand over her phone and addressed Bunuelos. "Are you able to go out to the harbors and check on Nunes's and Miller's alibis? We need to go down now, in the morning, when the boats and crews are still there getting ready to go out for the day."

"Sure." Bunuelos stood, grabbed a light jacket off the hook by the door. "I'll take Abe. Get the big guy out of his chair." He took off, clearly eager to see his old partner.

* * *

The petite blond psychologist had reserved an empty conference room on the third floor for them to meet, where the bureaucratic machinery behind the Maui Police Department took place. Lei couldn't help glancing at the closed door with LT M. STEVENS on it. A new plaque had been added above his name, emblazoned with SGT. K. FRASER. Lei's gut churned at the sight. Maybe she'd pay the brunette woman a visit on her way back downstairs.

Maybe Fraser has heard from Stevens.

Lei wanted to vomit at the thought. Instead, she took a few calming breaths outside of the conference room, plastered on a smile, and went in.

Dr. Wilson hadn't changed much in the nine years since Lei had first met her. The petite psychologist was dressed in a pretty floral wrap dress, her feet in low-heeled slingbacks, shoulder-length hair all the colors blond could be from cream to bronze. "Lei. So good to see you." She pulled back from the hug when Lei finally let go. "What's wrong, my dear?"

"I don't know," Lei said. "Maybe nothing. Maybe something. It's Michael. He's overseas somewhere and is out of contact. I have a bad feeling." She sat down at the long conference table and filled Dr. Wilson in on recent events.

"Oh my. Well. Let's take a break from that subject and come back to it," Dr. Wilson said. "Why don't you tell me about your case?"

Lei went through the whole thing, spending some time on the second visit to T. J. Costa's house, which had gone so badly wrong, the shooting they were primarily assigned to discuss. "Pono's supposed to come back to work in the next day or two."

"Yes, I spoke with him at his home. He's doing well. Misses you and the office, though." Crinkles bracketed Dr. Wilson's bright blue eyes. "I think the inactivity bothers him."

"I know. Neither of us is good at that." Lei felt better, having unloaded all her concerns in the last twenty minutes. Now they needed to sort through them. "I met Michael's partner on the training task force. And I didn't know he had a partner."

"Oh?" Dr. Wilson's eyebrows climbed.

"Sergeant Kathy Fraser. Pretty, blue-eyed brunette. Single, or at least not wearing a ring. He never mentioned her. And she's in his office and had the cojones to tell me that she told him, quote, 'months ago,' unquote, not to go overseas. She knew his departure date, and he didn't tell it to me until the day before."

"Oh." Dr. Wilson sighed, in an entirely different tone. "But surely you don't think…"

"No, I don't. But things hadn't been good with us for a while. A year at least, more like two if I'm honest. And a goodbye screw in the shower doesn't cancel all that," Lei said. "Sorry for the crudeness."

"Well, there's a lot going on here." Dr. Wilson frowned. "I've been concerned about Michael's state of mind for some time. I'm sure that's not a surprise. As we discussed before, he has symptoms of post-traumatic stress disorder."

"And a drinking problem," Lei said baldly. There were no secrets between her and Dr. Wilson, and that was a relief. "But he wouldn't ask for help. Wouldn't talk about any of it. And this thing overseas—my biggest worry is that it's some sort of one-way mission." She stood up, rubbed her hands up and down her pants, and paced back and forth beside the table. "He did it for the money, at least in part. I broke into his e-mails. He made sure he had extra life insurance."

"Those are sensible things to make sure are in place when going overseas to a dangerous area," Dr. Wilson said. "Doesn't mean he was suicidal."

Lei sat abruptly. "You're right. I'm just going nuts because he didn't call me back last night when we had a plan." She described their phone date and how she'd written Security Solutions a threatening letter.

"There could be a dozen reasons he hasn't called. You just have to wait until you have more information."

"And that's hard to do." Lei rubbed her gritty eyes. "Anyway, I really appreciate having a chance to hash through everything. So you don't think I should worry about Kathy Fraser? What she is to him?"

"You're a cop." Dr. Wilson gave a rueful chuckle.

"Everyone's motives are going to be suspect, especially with this case and all its layers of infidelity staring you in the face. You want my thoughts, honestly?"

"Yes." Lei braced herself.

"I think the fact that he had a female partner and confided in her is symptomatic of your marriage being at risk, yes. But I'd be willing to bet my psychologist's license he's never been unfaithful to you."

Lei couldn't help thinking of Anchara, Michael's first wife, and the conflicted loyalties of that relationship that had died with her. Their love for each other had doomed that marriage to failure before it began. Could something like that happen again? For her or for Stevens?

She was afraid to think about it. She already knew the answer.

"I guess I better get back to it." Lei stood. "Thanks." She hugged the psychologist and left. She walked rapidly past the closed door behind which Sergeant Kathy Fraser, with her blue eyes, tight uniform, and shiny brass, worked at her husband's desk.

She didn't have the courage to ask Fraser if she'd heard from Michael.

Bunuelos was waiting for Lei in their cubicle a floor below. "Nunes's alibi checked out. And no one has positively identified either Frank Phillips or Ben Miller at the harbor the morning of the murder."

"Damn it. I was really hoping something would break there." Lei's phone rang and she yanked it up, annoyance in her voice. "Sergeant Texeira."

"Sergeant?" A weepy female voice. "This is Barbara Selzmann. I have to come in and speak to you. I have some important information to share."

Chapter 22

Barbara Selzmann didn't look polished and put together this time as she walked into the interview room, preceded by her lawyer. They Mirandized her and turned on the recording equipment.

"I want to make a statement." Selzmann's eyes were red-rimmed, her highlighted hair a tangled mass on her shoulders. "I suspect Frank of killing Danielle."

Lei kept her face and voice neutral. "This is quite a turnaround from your previous statements. What has changed since you were here last?"

"I found out he's being unfaithful to me." Selzmann groped around until Chapman, her lawyer, handed her a tissue from his pocket. Clearly the waterworks had been on for a while. "Frank came over to my house several days before Danielle died. He was enraged. He'd found out she was pregnant from a discarded pregnancy test box in their bathroom. He knew he wasn't the father; they hadn't slept together in six months according to him. Not since he started seeing me." She blew her nose. "I know this sounds bad, but I said, 'Who cares? You don't love her; she doesn't love you. Now we can be together publicly.' And then he told me about her land." She waved the tissue. "He had plans for that land. He had it surveyed already. Was beginning grading and infrastructure. He was planning to tell her his plans and present it as a nice fifty-fifty split for them at the divorce. Only he wouldn't get anything if she had a child."

Lei leaned forward, frowning. "So why didn't you tell us this the first time we interviewed you?"

"I really didn't think he did it. I mean, I saw him the day she died. It was just like we both told you earlier. He went in to work, did some stuff with the receptionist, and then went out the back and uploaded remote entries on a timer. It's what he always did when he was meeting me. But he wasn't with me until after lunch."

Lei made a note, glancing at Bunuelos. He'd have had time to go out on the boat with Danielle and come into his office at his usual ten a.m., then leave again to meet Selzmann.

"I spotted pictures of him with another woman on his phone. And sexy texts. He's seeing someone else. I don't owe him shit." Selzmann held out her hand toward her lawyer and he put another tissue in it. She honked her nose. "I think he killed Danielle to get that land. And I won't stand by and let him get away with it."

"At least, not now that you know he's not going to be raking in the profits with you at his side," Lei said dryly. Selzmann looked away with an eye roll as if such things were beneath her. "So who was this other woman? Any other information?"

"Angie. That's all I know. Her name is Angie. She has dark hair and she's ethnic-looking. Not that pretty."

That seemed to have outraged Selzmann as much as anything.

"Ethnic-looking. In what way?" Lei kept her voice neutral.

"You know. Local." Selzmann shrugged. "I know better than to try to guess what blend. Everyone's so mixed around here."

The woman's carelessly expressed racism made Lei's eyes narrow.

"Well, you seem to think you're breaking this case wide open for us, but so far you haven't told us anything that makes him the murderer. We were aware of Danielle's land, but it seems pretty thin as a motive, considering the challenge of killing her in ninety feet of water," Lei said. "Has he said anything to you about her death? Is there any evidence you're aware of?"

Selzmann chewed her lower lip. Lipstick adhered to her bleached teeth. "No. I just know he talked a lot about her land, his plans for it. 'Even if I give her half the value when we sell it, we'll both walk away with a couple of million,' he told me."

"When you saw him later in the day, was there anything unusual about his behavior?"

"He was tired. And agitated. But he just said he and Danielle had had another argument before she left that morning. We had sex. It wasn't very good." Selzmann fiddled with the diamond tennis bracelet. "I remember thinking he was starting to take me for granted, because he barely got done and then fell asleep. I hadn't got mine, if you know what I mean."

Lei kept her face expressionless. Scuba diving and murder could have a taxing effect on a body. The fact that he could do it at all was remarkable if he'd been the man with Danielle in the Zodiac. Still, Selzmann's comments, while incriminating, were far from putting Phillips at the scene. "Well, thanks for coming in and telling us this. We may well need to talk with you further. Please stay available."

Selzmann stood. "I just want to do my part to get Danielle some justice."

Lei bit her tongue on the snarky retort she wanted to make and showed Selzmann and her lawyer to the door.

It was time to squeeze Frank Phillips hard and see what came out.

* * *

Lei and Bunuelos rolled up on Frank Phillips's handsome little office in Wailuku with their lights and sirens off. Lei led the way in, and as before, the receptionist looked up, drawing her brows together in annoyance. "Mr. Phillips is in a meeting."

"Mr. Phillips is under arrest," Lei said. "His mistress turned him in."

"His what?" The woman's mouth fell open. "You're kidding, right?"

"I'm afraid not." And Lei brushed past the woman's desk to push open the door. Phillips was talking with a man in business-casual across a pile of folders on his desk. His expression was identical to that of his assistant as Lei came around and pulled him up by the arm, clapping cuffs on him with satisfaction. "Frank Phillips, you're under arrest for the murder of Danielle Phillips." She recited the Miranda catechism as she pushed him toward the door.

"Call my attorney, please," Phillips told his assistant, and the astonished young woman nodded as they walked out to the cruiser they'd driven over for the occasion.

"I didn't kill her," Phillips said. "I don't know who did."

"Save your breath. We'll be taking a statement down at the station." Lei got in the driver's seat as Bunuelos patted Phillips down and put him in the back of the car.

Phillips's attorney, Davida Fuller, well-groomed with gleaming, toned arms, didn't take long to join him in the interview room. Lei, Omura, and Bunuelos watched them confer through the observation window.

"I am still having a little trouble with this." Omura seemed to put into words the nagging unease Lei felt with the conclusion of the case, in spite of how good it had felt to arrest Frank Phillips. "Phillips has means, motive, and opportunity for this crime, but we still don't have anything hard. Nothing tying him to the body, the Zodiac, the scene, not even a positive ID from the recording. I've called the DA; he's going to be here to observe the interview and we'll all confer afterward."

"I suspect his lawyer won't let him tell us anything," Lei said. "She's a sharp one, from what I saw before."

Once in the interview room, recording equipment on, Davida Fuller shook her glossy hair at Lei. "I've advised my client not to say anything regarding the date in question."

Phillips complied with Fuller's directions at first. "No comment," he said to every question, stone-faced. Finally, Bunuelos slapped the tablet down on the table in rare temper.

"We'll get you on this, you cold-blooded son of a bitch."

"I'd like to see you try." Phillips's contempt for the smaller man curled his lip. "You've got nothing."

"Nine times out of ten, when a woman dies violently, the murderer is her husband," Lei said. "The other times, it's her boyfriend. We have a witness, your mistress, rolling on you and destroying your alibi. We know about Angie. And we have your phone." She held the phone up. She'd taken it from him at the office but hadn't had a chance to look through it.

"Steady, Frank." Fuller patted his hand. "None of that is anything but circumstantial." She addressed her comments to Lei. "You will have to prove, beyond a reasonable doubt, that Frank went out to Molokini with his wife, shot her ninety feet down with a speargun, swam back to the boat, somehow made it to work on time, where he put in a few hours, then met with his mistress, had sex with her, and went on with his day. That's going to be a tall order."

"Couple of things we think will tie you to this, Frank." It sounded unlikely when put like that, but Lei gave no outward sign. Instead, she opened her folder, ignoring Fuller, her eyes on Phillips's pale, angry face. "The kayak. You have one in your garage. We caught you, and that kayak, on a video recording leaving the harbor the morning of the murder at around six a.m., which is plenty of time to go out there to Molokini, do the deed, paddle back, and go into work like nothing happened. The kayak even has a small motor on it."

"No, that's not how it went!" Phillips exclaimed, ignoring Fuller's restraining tug on his sleeve. He yanked his arm away. "I was trying to work things out with Danielle!"

"So our witness, who tells us you found out Danielle was pregnant, was lying?"

"Damn it!" Phillips fisted his big hands and tugged at his short hair.

"Don't worry, Frank. Stay strong. Don't say anything. They have to prove this, and they've got nothing," Fuller persisted, but Lei knew she had Phillips when he looked up at her, righteous anger bringing his dark brows together as he bunched his muscular arms.

"Okay, I knew she was pregnant! I had divorce papers all ready. The night before she died, I told her I wanted a divorce. She was happy about it, said she was ready, too, and had her own papers ready to sign from Meg Slaughter. She was going out to Molokini the next morning for one of her fish counts, and she invited me to come along. For old times' sake. She seemed to want to end on a friendly note, and I did, too. I decided to appease her. I thought if I could get her to sign the papers before she remembered about the clause about her land, I could still go ahead with the sale. I'd already put a lot of money into prepping the property for subdivision. So we went out, and it was all good. But when we got there, I made a mistake. I told her I was really excited about the progress the engineers were making on the land. Said we were both going to make a bundle off it, so it was okay we were breaking up. And she was pissed."

"Frank, stop!" Fuller commanded, but he clearly wanted to unburden himself.

"We argued. She said no way was she selling that land. That it was her child's inheritance. And I said, 'Good luck with that. What makes you think you'll keep this baby when you lost all of ours?'" Phillips was panting with anger, and a deep grief shone in his dark eyes. Lei felt a stab to her own guts, registering that. This man was opportunistic and greedy, with the sexual morals of an alley cat, but some part of him had loved Danielle. Their losses and various problems had eroded the marriage.

Just as losses and problems had eroded her own marriage.

"Please. What happened next?" Lei prompted sympathetically, with a "go on" hand gesture.

"We had words. Ugly words. And I said, 'This is a waste of time. I'm out of here. I'm going to someone who appreciates me.' She laughed. 'Good luck with that, you cheating asshole,' she said." Phillips hung his head. "I took my dive stuff on the kayak and left."

Lei felt her stomach hollow out. This had the ring of truth to it, as did the conviction in Frank Phillips's squared, tight jaw and direct gaze as he looked at Lei. "I was a jerk. I get that. And a cheater. But I didn't kill her."

Davida Fuller leaned forward. "Tell them the good part, Frank, since you've been telling them everything anyway."

"Someone saw me come in at Kamaole Three Beach. One of

the lifeguards. He gave me a ticket because I motored in and pulled up on the beach. We're not allowed to launch off that beach. So I have the citation. It's in my office drawer. I hadn't gotten around to paying it, but it has the date and time on it."

"And you'll see by that ticket, only an hour after their departure from Ma`alaea, that Frank would not have had time to dive with Danielle, kill her, return to the craft, and paddle all the way to that beach park," Fuller said.

Lei ignored this. "Who picked you up at the park?"

"Angie. My other girlfriend." Phillips held Lei's gaze defiantly. "I called her from the park. She has a truck. Took me and the kayak home."

"We'll need her contact information," Lei said.

"She's not going to be happy with me. She didn't know about Barbara," Phillips said, looking uncomfortable for the first time. "I don't know if she's going to be cooperative."

"Don't you worry about that." Lei bared her teeth in the smile she reserved for perpetrators she despised. "You just worry about how you're going to get through the weekend in jail. Your arraignment is Monday."

She and Bunuelos left Phillips arguing with his lawyer, unable to believe he wasn't able to just leave.

"You might as well let him go," the district attorney, a short, dapper Japanese man named Hiromo, told her in the observation room. "Even if his story doesn't check out, I'm going to have a hell of a time proving he was the guy."

"I want to hold him while we check his statement," Lei said. "I want him behind bars for the weekend. Captain?" She turned to Omura in appeal. "Let's sweat this scumbag, at least."

Omura's sharp brown eyes sparkled. "We're on the same page, Texeira," she said. "Even if he didn't do it, he deserves a few days in jail. Just for being a disgusting human being."

Hiromo stood, buttoned his jacket. "Okay, then. I'll brace for all the motions Fuller files." He left.

Lei scrolled through the photos on Phillips's phone. The file was empty. So were his texts. Phillips had cleared out evidence of his double infidelity after Barbara caught onto it, but apparently "Angie" was still unaware. Lei couldn't help remembering how well Fraser filled out her uniform and the sight of her name on a plaque above Stevens's. Almost reflexively, she checked his phone again. Still nothing.

She refocused her attention on her team. "Damn. Phillips erased everything. I wanted to get eyes on this Angie woman."

Omura tapped the Formica counter. "Husband down. Boyfriend down. Stalker down. Who does that leave? Who could have physically been at that dive site and shot Danielle?"

"The fishermen in the hard-bottomed boat that Danielle caught on the GoPro footage," Lei said. "And we don't know who or where they are."

"We need T. J. Costa," Bunuelos said. "He knows the poaching scene. And I think I have a lead on him."

Chapter 23

L ei and Bunuelos, with backup units, headed down the
highway. Bunuelos was behind the wheel of his SUV,
sirens off but lights on and radio silenced. Lei checked her
weapons in the front seat as he drove, releasing the magazine of
her Glock and refilling it from a box of ammunition before
ramming it home. She filled a second magazine and slid it into a
pocket on her vest. She checked and filled her small backup
ankle rig as well as they headed out Waiehu Beach Road, a
frontage alongside Kahului Harbor in an industrial, run-down
area of the island.

She used the moments of calm to mentally tick through the
case. Had she covered everything? As much as possible, yes, and
she didn't regret Phillips's arrest one bit. Even if ultimately he
wasn't guilty of Danielle's murder, he deserved a measure of
suffering and she was happy to make sure he got it.

Onshore wind blew constantly off the ocean, peeling the paint
of decrepit rentals hunched along a rocky beach. They turned
into a graveled drive surrounded by patchy, salt-burned grass,
blocking in several vehicles parked around the entrance of a
battered-looking bungalow.

Lei tightened her Kevlar vest and got out of the vehicle,

taking up a defensive position and holding back with Bunuelos behind their vehicle. Lei felt the ocean breeze wicking the nervous sweat from her brow, teasing the curls escaping from under her MPD ball cap, as the SWAT unit approached the house. They surrounded the exits before identifying themselves and knocking in the door with a cannon.

Of course Costa wasn't going to come easy, she thought, as gunfire erupted inside the battered house. She and Bunuelos glanced at each other, waiting for the signal to go in.

Suddenly, the front window burst outward in a shower of glass and welter of exploding screen. T. J. Costa, tatted-up, meth-producing fish poacher, hurtled through the opening to land in a rolling flurry of glass in the threadbare yard.

Lei surged up and dashed around the car, weapon ready. Costa was up, staggering a bit but already moving. He shook his shaved head, tossing shards of glass off, and bolted. He must have been hopped up on meth, giving him imperviousness to pain and extra strength.

Lei barreled into the man from the side with all she had, and far from going down, he stumbled a bit but kept moving as she bounced off his rocklike body. She latched on to his back, grabbing him, yelling, "Stop! Police!"

Costa didn't go down until Bunuelos tackled him, too. It took their combined weight to bring him to the ground, and then they'd had to sit on his back to subdue the man. It was with distinct pleasure that Lei said, "T. J. Costa, you're under arrest." She was only able to get the cuffs on him with Bunuelos's help.

The SWAT unit was able to secure the premises, and two more suspects were taken into custody. Lei and Bunuelos hauled Costa, spitting curses, out to the SWAT van.

"Bring all the suspects down to the station for us," Lei directed. "We need to interview them."

Following the black SWAT SUV containing the surly dealer and his compatriots, Lei glanced at Bunuelos. "How'd you know he was at that house?"

"Had a call to the tip line. Pono's got fans who don't want to see his shooter go free."

"Speaking of, I better call him." Lei found her partner's number and dialed it. "Hey, Pono. Gerry and I are bringing in Costa. Scooped him up with a few other lowlifes."

"I'd love to be there. I should be off medical tomorrow." Pono's voice sounded upbeat.

"How's the arm?"

"Not bad. Gonna have a fun scar. Tiare thinks it's hot."

Lei smiled. "Whatever works to keep the flame alive. Anyway, I just thought you'd want to know. And it looks like we might be on the homestretch on this one." She updated him on the case so far. "Hoping Costa says something that puts him at that scene. We're having trouble finding anything that sticks to the husband," Lei concluded.

"Well, I'll be in tomorrow to shake things up. Tell Gerry not to get too comfortable in my chair."

* * *

Costa immediately asked for representation, but he didn't have a lawyer. This meant rousting the public defender, who wasn't happy to be roped in this late in the day on a Friday. While they waited, Lei called home and got Jared.

"Yeah, took the little man surfing at Ho'okipa after school." Stevens's brother's voice activated a visceral longing for her husband. "He's tuckered out now. We're watching some cartoons and having Popsicles."

"Good. No more than one, though. He has trouble sleeping if

he gets too much sugar, and he's already had trouble going to sleep ever since Michael left."

A short, charged silence. "I could kill my brother," Jared said.

Lei forced a laugh. "Don't wish for that. I can't get ahold of him. I'm starting to get really worried. Security Solutions hasn't responded to my bitchy e-mail asking for updates, either. I'm not sure what to do."

"Let's talk about it when you get home. Any idea when that will be?"

"Don't know. Got a pretty heavy interview ahead. I'll text you when I'm on my way home."

"Okay. I'm making enchiladas for dinner tonight—my favorite dinner for the guys when it's my cooking night at the fire station."

"Tell me why you're single again?" Lei asked.

"I'm too pigheaded. Can't find anyone who will put up with me," her brother-in-law said.

"I don't believe it. It's you who's too picky. I'll see you soon. Not too much later, I hope." Lei hung up and went to join Bunuelos in the interview room with Costa.

Costa was seated at the table with the public defender beside him. His shaved-bald head gleamed greasily, and his arms, revealed by a sleeveless shirt, were covered in tattoos of intricately coiled snakes with the faces of people as heads. He looked up at them from under bushy black brows.

"I'm Kent Haywood," the PD said. "My client would like to make a statement."

"Terrific." Lei pushed a pen and pad over to the man, trying not to look too closely at the strange tattoos. "Perhaps he'd like to confess to killing Danielle Phillips, as well as shooting my partner?"

"I didn't kill her." Costa had a voice like driving a stretch of bad road. "But I know who did."

"Yes," Haywood piped up. "He has some information to trade for a reduced sentence."

Lei looked at Bunuelos, who snorted. "You serious, man? You shot a cop and we have you cold on meth production and distribution. You're getting hard time."

"I know who did it," Costa said. "I can give him to you."

"We need a moment to confer with our commanding officer." Lei tugged Bunuelos's sleeve. Her temporary partner had sunk his teeth into the bad-cop role, though, and exchanged another long stink-eye stare with Costa.

Finally she got Bunuelos out into the hall. "The captain's going to want to check with the DA on this. What's got your panties in a bunch? Costa shot my partner, not yours."

"Costa's a scumbag. You know those kids we took in from the house in Ulupalakua? They've talked to the social worker, and Liz Black let me know today that, from what they're telling the foster family they're with, he was the uncle whose visits they hated the most."

Lei felt her stomach lurch. Revulsion rose up to choke her. "You're kidding."

"Nope. Guy likes little kids."

"I was better off not knowing that." Old pain twisted Lei's gut as she flashed to her own rape by her mother's boyfriend at age nine. "So do you think we should bother trying to help him get a deal?"

"Let's screw him over as best we can." Bunuelos had an unfamiliar dark light in his brown eyes. "He shot Pono, cooks meth, and plays doctor with his niece and nephews. He deserves a lot more than he's got coming to him."

"Let's sweat 'em a few more minutes, then. Meet you back

here in five." Lei headed for the break room, where she got a cold glass of water, sipping and breathing, her fingers touching the bone hook pendant around her throat. She was doing all she could for those kids by busting their uncle. Unfortunately, she couldn't take them home, too.

She checked Stevens's satellite phone. Still nothing. Frustrated, she pulled up her e-mail on her smartphone and at last saw a message from the recruiter at Security Solutions.

Dear Ms. Texeira,

Attached you will find a copy of your husband's contract with our firm. As you will see, the terms and conditions are more than generous. Unfortunately, due to ongoing security concerns, we cannot disclose the area in which he is working, but we can confirm that it is in South America.

There is no regular communication schedule we can apprise you of. Many factors may interfere with communications, everything from weather to equipment malfunction. Our personnel are closely monitored in the field, so if there is some legitimate problem, you will receive prompt notification from our Oahu-based management team or armed-forces liaison.

Sincerely,

Clayborne Rumsfeld, VP of Field Operations, Security Solutions.

"What a crock of shit," Lei muttered. Rage at Security Solutions coupled with anger at Costa powered her back into the interview room. She took a moment to check the recording feeds as Bunuelos rejoined her.

"We have an agreement," Bunuelos lied carefully to Costa and the PD. Lei knew he was aware of being recorded and was making vague statements that sounded good. "Your testimony is an important part of this case, and we appreciate your cooperation."

"It would be so great to be able to give you credit for helping solve the murder." Lei tried some feminine charm as she divided a bright smile between the public defender and the surly fish poacher. "We know you were just defending yourself when you took that potshot at your residence." She fluttered her eyelashes, sure she was laying it on too thick and feeling sick at schmoozing this pedophile—but when she looked up, Costa had settled back in his chair in a satisfied way. Haywood, preoccupied with a handheld tape recorder, had neglected to ask for the agreement in writing.

She and Bunuelos resumed their seats and Gerry led off. "So. What can you tell us about who killed Danielle Phillips?"

"I didn't go out that day. To Molokini." Costa jingled the handcuffs attached to the table in a way that let them know he didn't like the restraints. "I loaned my boat to some— colleagues."

"Colleagues," Lei repeated.

"Yeah. The guys who actually catch and ship the fish off-island." Costa went on to disclose the names of the other two men they'd picked up, currently in holding. "They came back in from diving that day, really agitated. Said they had to 'shut down' some woman who was taking pictures. I didn't ask any questions."

"So it didn't occur to you that 'shut down' meant murder?" Bunuelos asked.

"I know when to ask questions and when to keep my mouth shut," Costa snapped. "If you reduce my charges, I can tell you who said it."

"We'll have to check on that," Bunuelos said. Again, the public defender failed to ask for proof of any of their agreements. The heads on the snakes on Costa's right arm were those of his niece and nephews, the children she'd had taken to foster care. Lei stifled an inward shudder of horror and regret. Costa leaned forward, giving some sincere eye contact.

"The guys have a shipment going out tonight," Costa said. "The fish you confiscated? They just went out and got more. They've already dropped them at the airport." He gave them the airline and flight times. "They put the barrels, with bubblers and whatever the fish need, in crates. Then they air-ship the crates. These are going to LA. Lot of aquariums there."

"Thanks," Lei said. "You said you'd share the name of your friend who told you about 'shutting down' Danielle Phillips?"

He told them. Lei noted it on her tablet.

"And what is your alibi for the time of the murder?"

"I don't have one." Costa spread his fingers. "I was tired from the other time I went out with the guys, so I passed on that run out to Molokini, like I said. I was at the house. Doing that other thing I do." He smiled for the first time, and Lei winced at the state of his teeth.

"Well, we've got some actionable information here," Bunuelos said. "And we'll see you again at your arraignment."

They left the public defender explaining the process. Lei flagged down a uniformed officer. "Can you book Costa into the jail? We have to do some more interviewing."

Lei took a moment to call Mark Nunes as another officer fetched the man Costa had named. "We've got a lead on some poachers shipping fish out," Lei said. "Can you intercept the shipment at the airport and take possession of the fish?"

"Of course." Nunes's voice was short and clipped. Lei remembered that the last time she'd seen him, she had him escorted to a cell on suicide watch. "Where and when?"

She told him and asked, "You okay, Mark?"

A pause. Finally, "I will be. Someday."

"I'm sorry I had you spend the night in jail."

"I'm glad you did. I don't think it would have been a good idea for me to be driving by myself after hearing that news. I'm better now. Talking to the pastor at my church, and that's helping. It feels good to do the work Lani loved so much."

"I'm glad." Lei said goodbye, feeling a little better about how Nunes was coping.

* * *

Emilio Rodriguez was a short, barrel-chested man with a crew cut. He hung his head as the officer clipped his handcuffs to the interview table. He'd been cooperative and unarmed when Lei and the team had captured him at the house.

"So tell us about Costa." Lei hoped to point the man toward thinking the police were mostly interested in Costa. "What can you tell us about him?"

"Not ratting on my friend." Rodriguez fisted his hands in the handcuffs.

Lei let a beat go by. "Funny. He had no such loyalty to you."

Rodriguez looked up. Beads of sweat gleamed in his broad brown forehead. "What you say?"

"I mean that the reason we're talking to you is that he told us to."

Rodriguez's jaw bunched. "I nevah believe you."

Bunuelos narrowed his eyes and leaned in. "You had to shut someone down. Ring a bell?"

Rodriguez's eyes flared wide. "Costa don't know nothin' about that!"

"Oh, yeah? Why don't you tell us what he might have meant?" Lei said.

"I need a lawyer."

"Probably. But not to tell us more about Costa," Lei deflected smoothly. "How'd you get in with him, anyway?" She opened a folder that contained rap sheets for the men who'd been scooped up with Costa. "Says here you did a little time in juvie, had a burglary rap. But nothing serious like what we got on Costa—meth production and shooting a police officer. If he's a friend, who needs enemies?" She gazed at Rodriguez sympathetically, head cocked to the side.

"T.J. always had an angle," Rodriguez said. "Me and my cuz, we went to him when we needed a little work. He always had ideas."

"Was it his idea to shut down this lady photographer out at Molokini?"

"No. It was my cuz." Rodriguez, clearly not that bright, clapped a hand over his mouth. "I never said nothin'. I want my lawyer now."

"Okay. If you want to play it like that, we'll be here all evening," Lei said. "When we could just clear up this misunderstanding and have you on your way."

Rodriguez seemed to think this over. "I think I better get a lawyer no matter what."

Lei and Bunuelos picked up their recording equipment and went into the hall. The young PD was just coming out of the other interview room.

"Got another customer for you." Lei pushed the young man into the room.

She went into the observation booth and called Captain Omura on the phone from the dim, cool space. "Captain, I think we might have Danielle's murderer."

Chapter 24

The interview with Rodriguez resumed a half-hour later, with a more formal feel to it. The public defender kept clearing his throat, and Lei suspected he'd heard things he wasn't entirely sure how to handle. She started off gentle, with a kind smile, sensing Rodriguez was a man who responded to a soft female approach.

"I'm sorry for the hassles Mr. Costa's comments about you have caused," Lei said. "Can I get either of you a glass of water? A snack?"

Rodriguez began to nod, but the lawyer shook his head. "No, thanks. We need to get going. I've advised my client it's in his best interest not to comment further."

"All right. Mr. Rodriguez, are you a friend of T. J. Costa?"

"Not anymore," Rodriguez growled.

"I don't blame you a bit," Lei said. "So, according to your statements before, you went to Costa when you needed work. That's how you met Costa, who is a known meth producer and fish poacher."

Rodriguez nodded. The lawyer elbowed him, and he said, "No comment."

"So you deny that T. J. Costa is a meth producer? Or a fish poacher?"

Rodriguez looked confused. "He's both."

"So it's your testimony that you helped and assisted him in these illegal endeavors, including murder to cover it up?"

"No! I never did nothing! It was Keone!" Rodriguez burst out.

Lei kept a straight face. "Keone Perreira? Who we picked up at the same time as you?"

"Yeah. Keone, he shot the woman. But he my cuz, so I told him I would never say notting." Rodriguez seemed to realize he'd just implicated his cousin and hung his head. "No comment."

"It's too late for that," Lei said gently. "I'm so happy to hear you weren't the one to murder a woman." The delicate inflection implied anyone who did was less than a man. "You should tell your story. For the record. Just so no one gets the wrong idea, like that you were the one who did it."

"Rodriguez, keep quiet!" the lawyer snapped, but Rodriguez was nodding like an automaton.

"She my cousin, too. Angie."

"Angie is also a cousin?" An idea bloomed across Lei's awareness. She dove into it like a hawk on a mouse. "Did Angie tell you to kill Danielle Phillips?"

"Not me. She told Keone. Keone more smart. But she said there would be a big payday for all of us if it was done."

Lei addressed the lawyer now. "I know you want to keep him from talking at all, but we aren't after him if he wasn't the one to pull the trigger. We want the people whose idea this was in the first place."

"Okay." The young man's Adam's apple bobbed. "I expect concessions for Mr. Rodriguez."

"Of course," Bunuelos said. "We'll give him the same kinds of concessions Mr. Costa is getting."

Lei smiled grimly. "Exactly." Costa wasn't getting anything but maximum charges.

"Mr. Rodriguez, tell them what you know about the murder," the lawyer instructed.

"Yes, Mr. Rodriguez," Lei said. "I thought the woman was shot because she was taking pictures of you."

"Yeah. And because my cuz said she needed fo' go *make*." The Hawaiian word for "die" sounded harsh in the man's mouth. "Angie told my other cuz that other girl was going be out there, and make sure she never came back. And if we did, was going to be one good payday for us all."

"So then what happened?"

"We went out like usual. Was early on Molokini. No tourists out there yet, so we was catching some fish. And sure enough, the girl, she come. My cuz, he saw her taking pictures. He chased her. He shot her." Rodriguez hung his head. "You not going tell him I told you notting, right?"

"Of course. I won't say a word." Lei was all sweetness.

"So then we get back." Rodriguez picked at a thread on his sleeve. "Keone, he call Angie and he say, 'It's done. She's gone.' We take the fish to Costa. I tell Costa we had to shut someone down, but Keone, he slap my head outside fo' tell."

"Not another word, Mr. Rodriguez," Haywood said. The man hung his head.

"Thank you, Mr. Rodriguez." Lei stood. They needed to find this mysterious Angie. "Your lawyer will advise you of the process. You're going to jail to await your arraignment."

She and Bunuelos left Rodriguez agitated and arguing with Haywood. Lei felt almost sorry for the young public defender.

"One more to go." Lei gestured the SWAT officer to bring their last suspect.

Lei and Bunuelos sat with truculent Keone Perreira, a younger, meaner-looking version of Rodriguez. The man picked at his filthy nails and wouldn't make eye contact.

"No comment," he responded to all of their questions. "I want a lawyer."

Lei rolled her eyes and got up to call. She and Bunuelos grabbed a quick bite of drive-through fast food and returned while they waited for another public defender to arrive. This one turned out to be blond and young, with too short a skirt.

"Leslie Fogarty." The blonde handed them a card, embossed like a real estate agent's with her name and a smiling photo of her face. "Where's my client?"

They directed Fogarty to the interview room. Behind the observation mirror, the two of them ate their Burger King meals while watching.

"I really need to learn to read lips." Lei sucked a long draft of root beer.

"I already can." Bunuelos stirred a fry into a dab of ketchup on his burger wrapper. "'Oh, my, what dirty nails and big tattoos you have,'" he said in a falsetto voice, imitating Fogarty. "'You must be guilty of murder. Tell the nice detectives everything.'"

"We wish," Lei said. "But if Costa and Rodriguez are right, we are looking at the murderer."

A few minutes later, Fogarty walked to the door with her knees close together, tugging at her skirt, and called out into the hall, "Detectives?"

They bundled up their trash and Bunuelos handed his to Lei. "Captain will kill us if we leave any food stuff in here. I'll get the recording set up."

"I'll run this to the break room." Lei moved quickly down the hall, dropping off the trash and washing her hands. After all the intensity of hunting the killer, it appeared he might be sitting right there in the room—but somehow she couldn't find the anger she'd used for fuel.

She'd wanted the killer to be Frank Phillips, and now he was going to move on with his life, a rich man. Deflated by the pettiness of Danielle's murder, the pointless waste of it, Lei felt exhaustion tug at her.

Back in the interview room, Bunuelos had turned on the video. Lei reminded Perreira of his rights.

"Would you like to begin by telling us what happened on the dive the other day?"

"Which one was that?" The whites of Perreira's eyes were yellowish, indicating liver trouble.

"The day you and Rodriguez had to 'shut that lady down.'" Lei pretended to consult her notes. "Your cousin. He was telling us all about how you did the deed."

"Oh, really?" Perreira lunged toward Lei, an abrupt movement brought up short by cuffs clipped to the table. Fogarty jerked farther away with a little cry. "That numbnuts. I goin' kill him."

"Don't say anything, Mr. Perreira," Fogarty warned. Her voice wobbled. She was afraid of her client, and Lei didn't blame her.

"Yeah, he was happy to rat you out for a reduction in charges." Lei fiddled with the file, a satisfied smile tugging at her mouth. "Not the brightest bulb in the box, Mr. Rodriguez."

"It wasn't my idea," Perreira said. "It was my cousin's!"

"Oh?" Lei's brows climbed. "He didn't exactly strike me as a criminal mastermind."

"No, my other cuz! Angie!"

"Negotiate." Fogarty put a tentative hand on Perreira's arm.

"Yeah, I like one deal!" Perreira said. "Angie! She the one!"

"Oh, really? Your cousin Angie, she went diving out at Molokini using Costa's boat. She dove down with tanks and caught illegal aquarium fish. She saw a woman shooting pictures, swam over, and nailed her with a speargun. Then, because that just wasn't sure enough, Angie pulled Danielle Phillips's regulator out of her mouth, watched her drown, and then stuffed her under a coral head for the sharks to snack on? Angie did all that?" Lei's voice had risen to a shout. She'd found her anger again, and it felt damn good.

"Angie! She called me that morning and told me to do something about the woman that was going to come out diving. She said there would be one big payday for us when she married that CPA. And when the girl came, taking pictures, I had to. She caught me with the illegal fish!" Perreira shouted back. His tanned face had drained of color, and so had Leslie Fogarty's. Lei wasn't terribly surprised when Fogarty stood up. Perreira turned toward Fogarty and opened his cuffed hands in mute appeal toward her. "It wasn't my fault. Angie. She told me to. I had to."

Just then the radio on Lei's belt went off. It was Dispatch. "Got a nine-one-one call from a residence in Wailuku Heights, claiming a home invasion and asking for you by name."

"You two, stay here," Lei said to Fogarty. "Who's the vic?" Lei turned away from Perreira and his lawyer, pushing out the door of the interview room with Bunuelos right behind her.

"Barbara Selzmann. One forty-nine Valley View Lane, Wailuku."

"We're on it." Lei and Bunuelos broke into a run as they headed down the hall.

Chapter 25

Dark had fallen as Lei and Bunuelos streaked toward Wailuku Heights. Lei tried to get more information from Dispatch as Bunuelos, driving, sped with emergency lights toward the address.

"Dispatch. What was the situation?"

"The caller said someone had broken into her house. That she was in the bedroom and afraid for her life."

"Any other details?"

"No, Sergeant. She hung up before telling us more."

"Roger that." Lei clicked off the radio. "Damn. Dispatch has some units on the way to back us up, but I want to get there first."

Barbara Selzmann's house was in one of the exclusive planned communities off the main highway, a commanding architectural design of angles and views atop a plateau. Bunuelos's SUV roared up the turnaround driveway to park behind a nondescript blue Honda CRV.

Somehow Lei didn't think that was Barbara's car.

"I'll go around the back," Lei whispered. "You take the front. Make some noise."

Bunuelos nodded, and Lei drew her weapon as she trotted

around the side of the house, bending to stay below the sight lines of the windows.

"Open up! This is the Maui Police Department!" Lei heard Bunuelos boom from the front of the house. Off in the distance, she could hear sirens, which went abruptly silent. She navigated some decorative shrubs in the dark, still trying to stay close to the house and out of range of a shooter. She heard a disturbance coming from the bedroom window above her.

"You won't get away with this. The cops are here," Barbara Selzmann's haughty voice said. Lei heard the distinct sound of something hard hitting flesh, a kind of muffled smack, and the woman gave a cry.

Lei glanced at the window above her. Light spilled out into the darkened yard. The windowsill was too high for her to pull up into and she hadn't yet reached the back door, which was likely locked anyway.

Bunuelos continued to yell and pound on the front door, creating a distraction. Lei looked frantically around. If she could get up higher, she might be able to cover the home invader until backup arrived.

A door in the lattice led under the house. Lei pushed the hinged section in, wrinkling her nose at a damp mushroomy smell. There was light enough to see a garden bench and a wheelbarrow.

Lei pushed the barrow out and over to the window. Standing in it elevated her the necessary three feet or so to look into the bedroom. She eased up, blinking as the light of the bedroom shone into her eyes.

Selzmann was lying on a bed directly in front of Lei. Her hands were bound. Lei could see blood on the side of her face and hair. Soft sobs shook her. There was a dark figure at the door, but even as Lei tried to get a look at it, the bedroom light went out.

Lei ducked down into the wheelbarrow, considering her options. She'd turned her radio off so that the perp didn't hear any calls, but that also meant she didn't know how far away backup was. She could hear Bunuelos still making noise at the front of the house.

"Come out with your hands on your head, and we won't shoot!"

Suddenly the screen above Lei burst out with a clatter and a rending sound and landed on top of Lei. She hunched smaller in the wheelbarrow, hoping the dark and the fallen screen would hide her.

"You have to die, bitch," she heard a voice say above her, guttural with rage. And before she could stand or react, she heard the loud report of a weapon inside the room. Selzmann screamed and kept on screaming.

Screaming meant Selzmann was alive, and that was something.

Lei stood up, knocking the screen aside, turning toward the jamb with her weapon out, just as the dark figure jumped out of the window. The falling perpetrator crashed into Lei, tipping over the wheelbarrow and crushing her to the ground in a bone-jarring collision that knocked the wind out of her.

Tiny white explosions filled Lei's vision as she struggled to draw breath and drag some air into her lungs. The metal edge of the wheelbarrow stabbed her in the hip. She felt the weight of her assailant smothering her, then lift away. Lei rolled over and hauled herself to her knees, finally breathing again.

She could see the assailant running away across the yard.

"Stop! Police!" Lei yelled, with all the volume she could muster.

The dark figure kept running, gaining ground across the lawn lit here and there with spotlights on clusters of palms and shrubbery. Lei scrambled to her feet and ran after the fleeing figure, grabbing her radio off her belt.

"On foot in pursuit of the suspect, moving out of property boundaries."

"Roger that," Bunuelos said. "Backup units arriving."

"Need medical assistance at the house," Lei panted, pouring on as much speed as she could. "Selzmann is down."

She stowed the radio and focused, gaining on the fleeing figure as the perp dodged bushes and lawn furniture, finally reaching the road.

Lei wasn't far behind. Running was one of the things she did best. Reaching the asphalt road, she poured on effort, digging deep to tap the place where her own demons lived. They provided bloodthirsty fuel for a burst of speed that brought her up to the straining runner, tackling the suspect around the waist and knocking him to the ground.

But Lei could tell right away that the perp, flattened beneath her weight on the asphalt of the road, was definitely a woman by the soft feel of her body. Lei sat up, retrieving her cuffs from a back pocket. She pulled the woman's arms behind her back, snapping the metal bracelets on. Lei could hear the wail of an approaching siren as one of the backup units came down the road. She stood and waved her arms, one foot pinning the suspect down.

The unit stopped. The siren shut off, but the headlights still blazed over them in a harsh spotlight. Lei rolled the woman over with her foot and got a good look at her face.

A. Vargas, Receptionist, spat a chip of bloody tooth at Lei.

Chapter 26

"So let's sort this out," Captain Omura said the next morning. The whole team was gathered at the conference table, including Dr. Gregory; Kevin Parker; Jessup Murioka; Pono, back on duty; Lei; Bunuelos; and District Attorney Hiromo.

Lei, her head bandaged from a cut she didn't remember getting the night before, stood up with her Styrofoam cup of black station coffee in hand. Her mouth tasted bitter from two Tylenol she'd just swallowed. She hadn't made it home at all last night and was grateful that Jared had spent the night with Kiet and taken care of the dogs. She felt stiff, grubby, and older than her years. She took a sip of coffee and picked up an erasable pen.

"Yes, sir. Let me talk us through the case, make sure we have all the holes filled in." She turned to the board, where their timeline and suspects were already mapped out. "First, some setting events. Danielle was pregnant from her affair with Mark Nunes of the DLNR and was very active in helping catch poachers. Meanwhile, Frank was sleeping with two women: his receptionist, Angela "Angie" Vargas, and Barbara Selzmann. Danielle owned valuable land that Frank wanted to develop, which was attached to any offspring she might have." Lei looked around to see if everyone was on board and saw nodding heads.

"At approximately six a.m. on the morning of the murder, Danielle and her husband, Frank, went out for a dive at Molokini atoll, leaving from Ma'alaea Harbor, towing their kayak behind and using the University of Hawaii's Zodiac. According to Frank, he and Danielle argued, not surprisingly, about the disposition of her land in their upcoming divorce and parted ways at Molokini. Frank went in on his kayak, got ticketed, and called Angie for a ride from Kamaole Three Park. He then went in to work after a shower with Angie and later on sneaked out of the office, as he often did, for his affair with Barbara."

"Po' ting. He must have been so tired. No wonder he wasn't up to making sure Selzmann got hers," Pono said, to general snickering. Her partner had spent time reviewing the interview tapes at home to stay up to speed on the case. Omura's mouth quirked at the comment, but she made a "go on" gesture.

"Angie, Frank Phillips's enterprising receptionist, had her eye on marrying Frank after the divorce." Lei paused. "Angie has a good lawyer. She denies having anything to do with Danielle's death. After her initial statement, Angie and her lawyer blew me and Gerry off all night. Wouldn't say a thing or answer any questions. She did submit a written statement. According to her statement…" Lei retrieved the statement the receptionist had made with her attorney present and held it up to read aloud. "She suffered temporary insanity, leading her to think that the only way forward with Frank was to eliminate her competition, Barbara Selzmann."

Lei set the document down. "Fortunately for her, Selzmann appears to be recovering from her gunshot wound." She took a sip of coffee and went on. "This is what we currently believe and can cobble together from Angie's actions and statement. She knew about Danielle's DLNR activities and was related to

Perreira and Rodriguez, the poachers. She told her cousins to take Danielle out so she could share the land profits and life insurance benefits with Frank—and her family, too, eventually. Meanwhile, Frank Phillips adamantly denies knowing anything about Angie's plot, let alone any plans to marry her. 'She's a crazy bitch,' Frank said, in the interview we just did with him. 'I've known she was psycho jealous for a while, but I didn't know how to get rid of her.'"

"Yeah. We got statements backing up the accusation against Angie from Keone Perreira and his dimwit cousin, Emilio Rodriguez," Bunuelos said. "Perreira, the actual murderer, is trying to pin it all on Angie Vargas. But they say she was in her right mind and cool as a cucumber about marrying Frank next. Talked to them like it was a done deal."

"Phillips did admit that he texted Angie the morning of the murder, told her that he was trying to finalize the divorce with Danielle and that they were going out to Molokini. He then texted her again that they'd fought and he was leaving and would need a ride from the nearest beach, which was Kam Three, where he was ticketed. But he denies that he had any involvement with Angie's plan to kill Danielle," Lei said.

Omura snorted disbelievingly, and Lei nodded in agreement.

"I'm not going to go for Angie as the main perp." District Attorney Hiromo had a way of speaking as if his words were too precious to waste, his lips barely moving as he eked them out. He smoothed a slippery-looking blue tie. "No one held a gun to Perreira's head and forced him to shoot the victim with his speargun, then pull her regulator from her mouth so that she drowned. I'm going for first degree on him, second degree for Vargas, and conspiracy to commit for Rodriguez. I don't feel I have enough on Phillips to charge him."

"Sounds good to me," Omura said. "Go on, Texeira."

"Well, Perreira did the deed out at Molokini and tucked Danielle's body under a coral head to delay discovery. They took their fish catch and reported in to Vargas, who thought she'd done her lover boss a favor. Rodriguez let slip to Costa what had happened when they delivered the fish, so he knew about it but didn't ask any questions. Then Angie Vargas lost it when she found out that Phillips was two-timing her. It's a good thing for Frank he was in custody when the attack on Selzmann went down, or we might have been looking at him as being behind it. But he has been in jail all weekend. Couldn't have put Vargas up to it."

"I'm afraid we're going to have to release Phillips," Hiromo said. "And sadly, he will likely get his wife's land and life insurance, unless we can show that he was behind the plot somehow."

"We got nothing tying him to the murder at this point," Bunuelos said. "Though I'm with you, Lei. I want to see that slimy bastard pay. Instead it looks like he's going to walk away a rich man."

"I think we can contact Danielle's remaining relatives and get a civil suit going against him for possession of her land," Omura said. "Kind of like the O. J. Simpson case—he might get away with murder, but he won't get rich, too. The burden of proof is lighter in a civil case. Still, those phone calls can't come from this office."

"I'll figure out a way to get that to happen." Lei's phone beeped with a text. "Excuse me." Without waiting for permission, Lei darted into the hall, reaching into her pocket for the satellite phone.

But it wasn't her husband's phone. The chime had come from her regular cell, with a text from Marcella: *Baby Kamuela is on the way! We're headed for the hospital. Get here ASAP!*

A wave of mixed feelings rose up in Lei, everything from excitement to worry—and, deep down, grief over the child she and Stevens had never had. She texted back.

On my way as soon as I can get out on a plane. Don't have that baby until I get there!

Chapter 27

I t was early afternoon by the time Lei left the meeting, made an anonymous phone call to Danielle's Hawaiian family to get the civil suit against Frank Phillips started, went home, packed up Kiet, and got the next plane to Oahu. Due to hospital regulations forbidding visits from children under twelve, Lei dropped her son off with her grandfather, Soga Matsumoto, at his immaculate little bungalow near Punchbowl. She borrowed his car to get to the Queen's Medical Center in downtown Honolulu and found her way to the maternity floor, where she asked for Marcella.

She was led to a private room, where Marcella, propped up in bed, turned a shiny, beaming face to grin at her. Her friend was holding a wrapped bundle, and the blue color of the blanket told Lei that Baby Kamuela was a boy.

Lei hurried over to hug her friend and gaze at the child's crumpled, sweet face. The baby had lovely caramel-colored skin, and his eyes were shut tight, the tiny plump mouth working as if he were sucking in his sleep.

"What a cutie. He sure has a lot of hair!" Lei touched the thick black shock peeking out of the blanket. "You didn't wait for me." She put her hands on her hips, eyeing Marcella accusingly.

"Holy crap, seestah, Jonas Egidio Kamuela was waiting for no one!" Marcella exclaimed, snuggling the dark-haired bundle close. "I barely got my feet up before he came shooting out!"

"Where's Marcus?" Lei looked around for Marcella's big Hawaiian detective husband.

"He was wiped out after all the screaming and the mess," Marcella said. "I mean, I've done some scary shit as an agent, even been shot, but having a baby natural is the most intense thing I've ever been through, hands down. He was great, with me every step of the way, but now that it's all over, he went down to the cafeteria for a snack and to call all his relatives. You came at the perfect time, actually. We just got settled in this room, and you're our first visitor. Though I warn you. My parents are on their way, and they're pretty hysterical. You know, Italian first-time grandparents."

That was all the warning Lei had before Anna Scatalina, Marcella's mother, elbowed Lei out of the way with all the fierce excitement of a pro football player moving in for a tackle. The small bright figure in a shapely muumuu exclaimed rapturously as she reached for the baby.

"'Cella! My grandson! He is here!" Anna lowered her excited shriek to a whisper as the baby twitched in reaction to the volume. Tears gleamed in her eyes and she held out her arms. "May I hold him?"

"Of course, Mama." Marcella handed off the baby to her ecstatic mother, who turned to face her husband. Egidio Scatalina was unabashedly crying, mopping at his face with a handkerchief.

"Oh, 'Cella! We never thought to see this day!" He waved his hands, exclaiming in a wave of delighted Italian over the bundle in Anna's arms.

The new grandparents sat down with the baby on the visiting

chairs, so Lei hoisted herself up to sit on the edge of Marcella's bed.

"The most intense thing ever, huh?" Lei asked.

On closer inspection, Marcella did look exhausted. Her lustrous brown hair was a tangled mess around her shoulders. She smelled strongly of something yeasty and dark. One of her eyes had a broken blood vessel. But Marcella's smile was victorious and suffused with a joy Lei longed to experience.

"I feel so gross. I really need a shower," Marcella said. "Can you help me? I'm still a little wobbly. It was like running a marathon and then shitting a watermelon."

"Marcella!" scolded Anna Scatalina, covering the baby's ears with a hand. "Language!"

Lei helped her friend to the bathroom and came back out. By then Marcus had returned, and she hugged the man she thought of as a brother-in-law.

"I hear you were the hero of the hour," Lei said.

Marcus shook his head. He shared the musky smell Marcella had, and Lei realized it was the smell of birth, of physical extremity, and of new life. "No one can prepare you for something like that. Terrifying. And amazing." He pointed his chin over at the baby, clearly the center of his grandparents' devotion. "I can't wait to get Marcella and the little guy home and have them all to myself. Taking some family leave from HPD."

"So when are you getting out of here?" Lei gestured to the room.

"Tomorrow, if the baby's tests and Marcella's checkup go well. Brace yourself for more relatives—my parents are on the way from Maui. The Scatalinas are going to have some baby-holding competition."

"I could use some help getting dressed," Marcella called from the bathroom. Lei moved toward the door, but Marcus's eyes lit up.

"I'm next in the shower. I'll help you, honey." He slipped inside the little room just as baby Jonas began crying, a thin mew like a kitten. His grandparents stood up in agitation, and Lei saw her chance.

"Let me hold him a minute, until Marcella gets back." Anna Scatalina handed the infant over reluctantly. Lei put him against her shoulder, humming and rocking, one hand stabilizing his neck, the other under the baby's plump bottom. Jonas went quiet, though still snuffling around, and clearly hungry. His plump weight felt delicious, the smell of his tender neck intoxicating.

A moment later Marcella came out of the bathroom, dressed and looking for the baby. "I thought I heard him cry."

"Your friend, she knows how to hold a baby," Anna said approvingly.

"Yeah, I remember this from when Kiet was tiny," Lei said. "But I can tell he's hungry." As if on cue, Jonas emitted a fierce squawk that made them all jump and laugh. Marcella got back into the bed.

"Hand him over, Lei. We're still getting the hang of this breastfeeding thing, but I'm ready for more practice, and he obviously is, too."

Lei handed the baby over while Anna helped Marcella get situated with a pillow and blanket over her shoulder. Soon they were settled, the baby feeding contentedly. Lei watched the tableau of the Scatalinas enjoying their grandbaby as Marcella fed him. Loneliness and not belonging felt like a bubble around Lei, separating her from everyone in the room. She blinked gritty eyes, not sure why she wanted to cry.

"I'll just go—make some phone calls," she said to no one in particular, and went out into the hall.

Lei walked down the antiseptic-smelling hallway. All around her, people were bustling with purpose—nurses on errands, doctors with that important air they always had, and other visitors headed toward rooms with bouquets of flowers. Lei felt unmoored. Her feet were too far away, her vision telescoping in and out as she wandered, and she realized it had been more than twenty-four hours since she'd slept. She found herself in front of the floor's nursery window.

Clear plastic bassinets filled with precious cargo wrapped in pink and blue blankets dotted the room. Nurses moved among them, checking on the babies, adjusting blankets, changing diapers. In the back of the large space, Lei could see the neonatal unit with a tiny, wizened preemie inside, and beside that, a few incubators.

Lei stood there, staring. The sight of the babies was utterly absorbing and yet brought tears welling up from that deep, empty place inside her. She leaned her forehead on the cool glass and let the tears slide down her cheeks.

In her pocket, the phone rang, vibrating against her leg. Her heart jumped. She wiped an arm across her face hastily, scrubbing the tears away, and reached down into the cargo pocket where she kept the satellite phone.

At last, a call. An unknown number showed in the little window. Her heart beat with heavy thumps, drumming in her ears. "This is Sergeant Lei Texeira."

"Sergeant Texeira? This is Lieutenant Commander Chad Westbrook. I'm working with Security Solutions as a liaison between the company and the United States Armed Forces. I have some news of your husband. I'm on Oahu at the Pearl Harbor naval base, and I'd like to speak to you in person, if I may."

Lei's lips felt numb as she told him her grandfather's address and arranged a time to meet in a few hours.

There was a terrible roaring in her ears as she hung up the phone and slid it back into its special pocket. She clicked the snap shut, took one last look at the babies, and turned away to face whatever came next.

Chapter 28

Lei didn't remember leaving the hospital. Didn't remember driving back out to Punchbowl through the crowded, colorful streets. Didn't remember getting to her grandfather's modest ranch house. Didn't know how she ended up with her grandfather and her son in his tidy greenhouse out back. It felt like a fast-forward film that finally slowed to normal only when she held Kiet in her arms.

"Grandfather, an officer from Pearl Harbor is coming over to talk to me in a couple of hours. He has news about Michael."

"What is it?" Soga, who had been showing Kiet how he trimmed his bonsai trees, widened dark eyes in the fans of wrinkles that bracketed them.

"I don't know. He wouldn't say. I have to get some sleep first, before he comes. I can't function right now. Can you...?" She nodded down at the boy, who'd latched on to Lei with both arms and legs. "Maybe something fun, like the zoo?"

"Zoo?" Kiet leaned back, looked at his great-grandfather. "I want to go!" The Honolulu Zoo was a big treat they'd been looking forward to. Lei had planned on taking Kiet herself, but she needed privacy for whatever this news was.

"Of course. Why don't we pack a snack, little man?" Soga

ruffled the boy's hair. "I can show you how to make musubi. I have all the ingredients."

Kiet gave Lei a smacking kiss on the cheek. "Get a nap, Mama. Your eyes look all tired."

"I am all tired." Lei forced a smile.

Her grandfather walked the child back into the kitchen. Lei heard the light tone of her son's voice, the deeper rumble of Soga's in the background. She forced her legs to move, walking into the guest room, where she set an alarm on her phone. She fell facedown on the bed.

The next thing Lei heard was the beeping of the phone alarm. Disoriented, Lei felt a surge of panic. *Something bad is coming.* She looked around wildly.

The room was dim. Late-afternoon light fell gently through windows curtained in translucent muslin. A tiny breeze stirred her hair as she sat up. Her grandfather must have shut the door, and Kiet's colorful backpack was missing.

Lei checked her phone. She had twenty minutes before the lieutenant commander showed up, and she needed every one of them. She showered and squished Curl Tamer into her hair so it would dry into ringlets. She dressed in a favorite shirt, a scoop-necked tee in a deep olive green that Stevens had said made her look like a woods elf. She'd loved those little comments he'd make. They showed her how differently he saw her than she did herself.

She wouldn't let her mind go to the worst-case scenario. This meeting was simply the update she'd asked for. She'd even thrown her weight around to get this information. Now the military was responding in person. It could be good news. His contract was canceled, or he was being shipped home with some minor injury.

She could hope.

Her face in the mirror was colorless, her eyes huge and haunted. Lei put on mascara and a swipe of deep rose lipstick. She tried some of the lipstick on her cheeks as blusher—a mistake ending up in clown-like circles. Lei was scrubbing the lipstick off her face when the doorbell rang.

She jumped like she'd been stung, clutched the bathroom sink, did a couple of relaxation breaths, and headed for the front door.

Lieutenant Commander Westbrook was dapper in a uniform trimmed with braid and colorful medals. A plain black sedan was parked at the curb behind him.

"Lieutenant Commander. Welcome. Please come in." Lei opened the door and stood aside. Her movements were stiff, her voice wooden, because every physical movement was something she had to tell her body to do.

"Call me Chad." Westbrook took her hand in his, holding it longer than necessary. Longer than a handshake. Long enough for Lei to know it was bad news.

Black spots filled her vision as it closed down to a dot. *Keep breathing.* Westbrook gave her hand a tug.

"We should sit down."

They sat on her grandfather's hard futon couch. Westbrook took off a snowy-white hat trimmed in gold braid and set it on the low lacquered table.

"I'm very sorry to tell you that your husband has been captured."

"Captured." Lei's breath blew out on the word. "Not dead?"

"Not dead. No. In fact, we have proof of life."

Lei swallowed the bile that boiled up her throat as Westbrook opened a briefcase she hadn't even noticed he was carrying. The clasps clicked open. Inside were several files and a small brown-wrapped package.

"Our lab has gone over this packaging thoroughly. There was no usable trace," Westbrook said. He was talking to her like a cop, like she'd be interested in the details, and that kept Lei from vomiting all over his lap as the officer took a box out of the packaging and opened it.

Lei had been prepared for a severed finger, an ear, even a lock of Michael's brown hair—so the sight of the bone hook pendant she'd given her husband the night before he left felt almost anticlimactic.

"They also left a photo of him holding that day's paper," Westbrook said.

Lei took the pendant out of the box and stroked the ivory-colored bone, touching the slightly rough, handmade coconut-husk cording that banded the top of the hook and formed a necklace.

It had been a little stiff and new when she'd put it on Stevens. Now the cording was darker and softer with skin oils. It had been cut off his neck. She could tell because it was missing the bone eyepiece used to attach the necklace to a loop on the other side. The hook itself had deepened from bright white to a soft ivory.

"What happened?" Lei felt the bone warming under her fingers as she stroked the symbol of Maui and of fishermen providers.

"We aren't totally sure. His encampment was attacked. There were casualties, and several captives were taken."

"Where was he stationed?"

A long pause. Lei looked up into Westbrook's cool blue eyes. She felt her own grief and anger blazing in the intense stare she gave the officer, and he finally looked away, his shoulders sagging. "I can't tell you. It's classified. But it was in South America. A jungle area."

"What's being done to get him back?"

"We've sent troops over. Investigators. We're waiting for a ransom demand."

"So how did you get the bone hook?"

"It was left at the camp, along with other proof-of-life items from the other captives. The photos were on a stick drive. No ransom demand yet, but as I said, we're expecting that anytime now. All the contractors carry kidnapping insurance. Unfortunately, this isn't the first time this situation has occurred."

A surge of adrenaline swept through her, powering Lei to her feet. "I have to go over there. I can track him."

"Absolutely not. Sadly, we've dealt with this situation before. We have experts working on this."

"Experts like my husband? Good law enforcement people you've sucked out of their jobs or retirement with promises of easy money?" Lei snarled.

Westbrook stood. The officer didn't back away, though now he was too close, looming in an intimidating way. His voice was measured and slow. "Your husband understood the risks he was taking. He's a patriot, and you should be proud of that. He would not want you to come after him and endanger yourself. You're in shock and grieving. That's to be expected."

"I'm also pissed as hell." Lei's fists were balled. She wanted, very badly, to hit him.

He nodded with dignity. "Also to be expected."

Finally Lei whirled, pacing back and forth in the small living room, quickly covering the length of the sparely furnished space. "What's next?"

"As I said before, we're waiting on ransom demands for the lieutenant as well as the other prisoners. We'll keep you informed, every step of the way, via the phone you were provided. Try to relax. He's going to be fine. Now, if you'll excuse me. You aren't the only family I have to inform."

Lei followed the officer to the door and shut it behind Westbrook, unable to think of anything to say that felt adequate to express the chaos of emotion she was stifling. Turning away from the door, she realized she still held the pendant.

The bone hook felt warm, almost alive, the organic material holding the heat of her skin. Lei tied the hook around her throat with the broken cord and touched it where it rested against the battered white gold pendant she always wore.

"This isn't coming off until I can give it back to him," Lei said aloud.

The words were a vow and a promise.

Aloha, dear reader family!

I'm so sorry to do this to you. A cliffhanger, ack! I've had subplots I didn't resolve before, but this is a new thing even for me, and I'm as tortured as you are, wondering what's happening to poor Stevens. I hope you will bear with me. I'm writing as fast as I can to get the sequel, *Red Rain*, out to you and resolve the suspense of what's going on with him. The good news is, it's going fast and it's a barn burner of a book so far! Read on past this letter for a sneak peek.

Bone Hook was a very special book to write. From the beginning, when a fan, writer Ron Logan (now working on a Lei Crime Kindle World novella starring Dr. Phil Gregory!) suggested doing a mystery involving a murder related to illegal fishing and reef conservation, I was caught up in the story and it had a special, crackling energy and *"mana."*

I asked for a consultant to help with the technical aspects of reef conservation from my wonderful Facebook friends and followers and got the name of a lovely young marine biologist, Danielle Kornfiend.

From the moment I met Danielle, we both remarked on her resemblance to the victim in the story—but I'd written the first chapters before I met her. She asked if I'd name the victim after her, and to thank her I did. Danielle, in real life, is a former DLNR agent and a passionate advocate for the ocean and conservation as well as sensible, sustainable fishing practices that support the economy of Maui. Thanks so much, Danielle, for your great help and support and for our research field trip out to La Perouse Bay. If you're interested in finding out more, check out my blog on that research here: http://tobyneal.net/2015/08/19/reef-conservation-research-for-bone-hook-lei-crime-series-10/.

Another important encounter happened around the amazing cover photo and design. Stacia Pang, who works at our favorite gallery, Native Intelligence, loaned me her deceased husband's incredibly beautiful hand-carved bone hooks to shoot for the cover in his memory.

Mahalo nui loa to Winston Healani Koon Kau Pang, born October 17, 1955, on Oahu, of Hawaiian and Chinese heritage. He and Stacia were married in Honolulu and moved to Maui in 1980, where he worked as a heavy-equipment operator with Hawaiian Dredging and Construction until his sudden death in August of 2009. Winston was a hard worker, loving family man, and beloved by all who knew him. He carved the hooks out of cattle bones he found while hunting in Kahikinui, a colorful area I was excited to include in the book. Read the full cover story here: http://tobyneal.net/2015/09/07/a-bone-hook-infused-with-mana-and-story/.

As always, thanks to my precious beta readers, retired Captain David Spicer, who keeps Lei's police work honest; Noelle Pierce, who caught a lot of dangling clues in this one, and most of all, Holly Robinson, whose challenging red scrawls on my manuscript push me to the next level. And as always, your reviews matter SO MUCH! I read them all, the good, the bad, the indifferent. Please leave one and let me know your thoughts!

I'm blessed to be living my dream, writing stories about Hawaii and its unique people that both educate and entertain. Hold on to your hats, folks, as we take off into *Red Rain*!

Until next time, I'll be writing! Much aloha,

Toby Neal

P.S. Sign up for my e-mail list at http://tobyneal.net/ and receive a free full-length, award-winning novel! Read on for Chapter 1 of *Red Rain.*

Sample

RED RAIN

A LEI CRIME NOVEL

BY TOBY NEAL

Red rain, in Hawaiian culture, is an omen associated with royalty. An incident of "blood rain" or red rain, such as a primarily red rainbow, a shower at sea colored red by sunset, or an unusual red mist of cloud—all of these things heralded the birth, death, or transition of a chief.

—Summarized from The Fornander Collection
of Hawaiian Antiquities and Folklore

Chapter 1

I woke with that jerk that happens in a falling dream, my whole body ajangle with alarm and a sense of impending disaster. But nothing bad was happening.

The military transport C-130, open and echoing, was still roaring along on its journey to whatever the godforsaken mission destination was. I was still strapped into the over-hard upright seat against one wall, alongside the military police troops I was supposed to be training when we got there, along with a couple other civilian contractors.

At least I'd finally slept. That was something. I rolled my sore neck, using the occasion to gaze around the interior of the aircraft. Several heavy-duty Jeeps were strapped down the length of the plane, along with a huge pile of supplies held down with a webbed net. I unstrapped from the five-point harness and stood, stretching my sore muscles. I took a walk up and down the length of the plane, getting circulation back into my legs.

I felt shitty. Throbbing headache, dry mouth, a twitchy sense of frayed nerves. Perhaps left over from the dream, but more likely that other thing. I dug in my olive-drab backpack, stuffed with all the personal possessions I'd have for the next six months. I took out my shave kit and went to the head.

It was a bare-bones closet with a metal toilet and sink and a steel mirror above it. I did my business and opened the shave kit.

I had a flask in there, a flask filled with booze disguised as a shave cream can. It had been a simple enough thing to buy online. This ration was all I going to get, and it was strictly for medicinal purposes, so I could stave off the DTs as I dried out.

Because that's what this crazy-ass trip was all about. Kicking the booze, and the other shit, too. I swigged a gulp of the alcohol, looking at my hollow-eyed reflection in the steel mirror with contempt.

The foul stuff seared my throat and made my eyes water, burned my esophagus and went off like a bomb in my empty belly. It tasted horrible. I wanted to retch, but instead I felt immediately better, as flu-like symptoms of withdrawal receded.

Just one more hit.

It still tasted horrible, but now it felt good, and that second drink activated a fierce longing to finish the rest. But I was in trouble if I did. This had to last, and then I was done. I screwed the "shaving cream" top back on, and feeling steadier, actually shaved with a sliver of soap.

Working the razor around that stubborn square edge of my jaw, I caught sight of the hook pendant Lei had given me. The white bone seemed to glow in the dim silver of the mirror, filling the shadow at the base of my throat, almost hidden in the olive drabness of my uniform shirt.

I still remembered her small hands pressed together over the pendant and her curly brown head bent before me as she murmured a prayer of blessing over it. I remembered the way she'd risen up on her knees in the bed before me and fastened the slightly scratchy coconut-husk necklace with the simple bone-and-loop closure behind my neck.

My face had been so close to her breasts: small, round, and

perfect in the tank top she wore. I'd looked my fill at them and breathed in the smell of her, shut my eyes, and felt the love in the gift wash over me. I'd soaked it in, reveled in it—as I had in her body.

I didn't deserve it. I'd almost destroyed us. But I'd make up for it now, by dealing with my shit and making some money. The company I was working for, Security Solutions, paid very well. This six-month stint would be a good start for our son Kiet's college fund, if nothing else.

I finished shaving. Splashed my face. Buttoned up that last button so that the bone hook I told her I'd wear until I returned was hidden. Zipped up my kit. Returned to my seat.

When I shut my eyes, for a moment I could still smell her. Close. So close.

I slept again.

* * *

I woke again, this time with a full-body spasm.

The plane had crashed in this dream, and I'd been on fire at the end. Crawling. Dragging my dog, burning and desperate.

Like that time the house was on fire.

But the plane hadn't crashed, really. Must have been another dream. Or a memory. Maybe it had crashed. Who the hell knew?

I was never sure about anything, since we were captured.

I shook, the bone-jarring, full-body shudders of hypothermia. My jaw ached with tension from trying to keep my teeth from clattering together. I shivered so hard the water around me made tiny waves.

Tiny waves that splashed against the mud walls of the deep pit I was in.

"Lieutenant. Move back here." Someone was pulling me up.

A man hauled me under the armpits out of the puddle I'd fallen over into, propping me against the slimy mud wall. The rain from above continued to pelt down on us through a bamboo frame covered with palm fronds above us. I couldn't stop shivering: My teeth chattered, and my body quaked. I couldn't even form words, I was so racked with shudders.

"I think he's sick," the man who'd helped me said to someone else. I tried to remember his name. I knew this man, this fellow prisoner, filthy in his mud-crusted clothing. His eyes were dark and shiny as he looked into my face, briefly touching my head. "He's got a fever."

I realized he was talking to someone on the other side of me.

"You think they give a shit?" The other guy's voice was scratchy and hard.

"But we should tell them. He's no good to them if he dies," my helper said. He sat down in the mud beside me and threw an arm over me. "Relax, L.T. We got you. Carrigan, get over here. Lean against him on that side. Let's warm him up."

I felt the reluctance in Carrigan, but he shuffled over and pressed against me. Sandwiched between the two men, I eventually began to thaw a little as our shared warmth loosened my locked muscles. "Thanks," I whispered through cracked lips.

I rested my forehead on my knees.

A dim memory came to me. Carrigan was another of the civilian contractors. We'd all gotten to camp together—and the plane hadn't crashed. Definitely hadn't. I remembered his cold blue eyes. We hadn't hit it off—I thought he was an entitled asshole. He wouldn't change out of his polo shirt and bermudas into the uniforms they issued us.

"I'm in charge of tech. I don't need to wear this hot, shitty uniform," he'd said.

I didn't tell Carrigan and the man who'd helped me—what

was his name? Kerry? Kelly? Ken? —that I didn't just have the shakes from sleeping in a puddle.

My demons were still my own, even in this particular ring of hell.

* * *

"Shut the door, Texeira," Captain Omura said. She looked away from her monitor, the bell of her immaculate bob swinging as Lei shut the door. "You said you wanted a private meeting."

"Yes, sir." Lei sat down in one of the hard plastic supplicant chairs in front of the desk. "While I was on Oahu this weekend, I had a visit from an army representative of the company Michael went to work for overseas. Security Solutions." Lei pushed her hair behind her ears, groping for words, forcing them past the lump in her throat. "He informed me that Michael was captured."

"Captured? What does that mean?" Omura's carefully groomed brows snapped together and she leaned forward. "What the hell kind of lame-ass operation was this?"

"A training camp for military police somewhere in South America. They wouldn't tell me where. But supposedly he went there to train armed forces personnel on investigation techniques, and he and several others were taken captive. The army officer who informed me said that they expected a ransom demand anytime now and that they'd handle it. The men were insured."

"So they expect that kind of thing?" Omura's tilted dark eyes widened. "This is our tax dollars at work?"

"I don't know about that. I don't know much of anything." Lei threw up her hands, stood. Paced back and forth in front of her captain's desk. "I'd like permission to take some personal leave."

"Denied," Omura said immediately. "I can't spare you."

"Come on, Captain! He's your man, too!" Lieutenant Michael Stevens was one of Omura's steadiest officers, in charge of training new detectives and always working a full roster of lieutenant duties. "Don't you want to know what happened to him?"

"So this leave is for you to hop on a plane to God-knows-where, trying to find your husband 'somewhere in South America?'" Omura made air quotes with her fingers. "First of all, I don't like hearing this news any more than you do. But seriously, Lei—I can't spare you! I'm shorthanded, as you know, and Michael taking that military leave really put me in a jam, as I wasn't shy to tell him. So any personal feelings aside, I couldn't let you go even if I wanted to—which I don't. You're a mother. Or have you forgotten you have a son who needs you, more than ever now that his father's missing?"

Lei rubbed her hands up and down on her black jeans, wicking away nervous sweat. "I haven't forgotten. But I have family who've been helping with Kiet already…"

"No. Just no. And if this officer told you to wait, you need to do that." Omura stood, came around her desk, and did an unprecedented thing—she held open her arms. "Hug."

"Captain?" Lei cocked her head. But she smiled as she leaned carefully into the other woman's space and shut her eyes for just a moment. The Steel Butterfly was hugging her. It was an awkward and stilted embrace, like two triangles leaning against each other—but the emotion clouding the captain's eyes was genuine as Omura pulled away.

"I'll do all I can to support you during this time. Flex time for your pickups with the kid, short days, swapping shifts, whatever. But I can't grant any leave, especially if I think it might end up like that other trip."

That other trip.

Lei's belly tightened at the memory. She'd taken off for the Big Island to deal with an enemy, a move that had worked in some ways and cost way too much in others.

"Shit," Lei said. Her shoulders sagged. "Okay."

"Good." Omura tip-tapped on her pointy-toed heels back around her desk and sat down. "I have a new case for you. Something a little different, in addition to your regular cases with Pono. I'd like you to handle it as a side project."

She reached down into the secure cabinet beside her desk and took out a plastic bag, stapled shut and neatly labeled. Inside was a skull, and by the size of it, it belonged to a child. A cobwebbed hole where the forehead would have been testified to possible cause of death.

"Where'd this come from?" Lei picked up the bag tentatively. The bone of the skull was stained by soil, but it was clean.

"It was brought in this morning. Apparently it washed up on the beach near one of the Hana rivers. This woman found it in some driftwood. She put it in the bag and brought it in. Didn't realize she should have left it there and called us."

"Oh, great," Lei murmured. "Have you had anyone look at it? To date it, or anything?"

"No. That's for you to figure out, and if there's anything that can be found out about this poor kid." Omura pinned Lei with her dark gaze. "I plan to keep you so busy you don't have time to worry about getting that man back. Now go find me a cold-case child killer."

Look for these Toby Neal Titles

Contemporary Fiction/Romance

Somewhere on Maui: (a Somewhere Series Romance)
Somewhere on St. Thomas (a Somewhere Series Romance)
Somewhere in the City (a Somewhere Series Romance)
Somewhere in California (a Somewhere Series Romance)
coming soon

Mystery

Nightbird: a Jet World Novella

Lei Crime Series:

Blood Orchids (book 1)
Torch Ginger (book 2)
Black Jasmine (book 3)
Broken Ferns (book 4)
Twisted Vine (book 5)
Shattered Palms (book 6)
Dark Lava (book 7)
Fire Beach (book 8)
Rip Tides (book 9)
Bone Hook (book 10)
Red Rain (book 11)

Lei Crime Companion Series:

Assorted novellas by other authors expanding the world of Lei Crime. Everything from stories from Keiki's perspective to Pono as main character, Marcella crime solving, and much more!

Stolen in Paradise:
a Lei Crime Companion Novel (Marcella Scott)
Unsound: A Novel (Dr. Caprice Wilson)
Wired In: (Sophie Ang) Coming 2015–16

Middle Grade/Young Adult

Island Fire
Wallflower Diaries: Case of the Missing Girl

Nonfiction

Under an Open Sky: A Memoir with Photos on Traveling and the National Parks
Children of Paradise: a Memoir of Growing Up in Hawaii

For more information, visit:

TobyNeal.net

About the Author

Toby Neal was raised on Kaua`i in Hawaii. She wrote and illustrated her first story at age five and credits her background as a mental health therapist with adding depth to her characters—from the villains to the heroes. She says, "I'm endlessly fascinated with people's stories."

Toby began her writing with mysteries, and has a well-established reputation in that genre. She decided to try contemporary fiction when she discovered that she couldn't write a book without including romance. "I'm a hopeless romantic and I want everyone to know what it's like to be deeply loved."

Toby lives with her family and dogs in Hawaii. Find her online at: http://www.tobyneal.net/

CPSIA information can be obtained at www.ICGtesting.com
Printed in the USA
BVOW08s0752301115

428788BV00009B/132/P